JETSTREAM

The captain held out both hands, palm toward Greco, toward the gun. *'Don't shoot! You need me!'* His peripheral vision told him that one of the stewardesses was coming rapidly down the aisle. Greco remained frozen as he stood – the gun steady, pointed at the captain, his eyes darting nervously. Pete took a chance and motioned to Terry to stay where she was. Fortunately she did.

Pete's mind churned, grasping for anything that would give them time. He looked straight at Greco, his voice firm but subservient. 'There is no need for any more shooting. We'll do whatever you want. You're the boss.' He motioned to the gun. He could hear a whistling sound as air escaped through the hole in the lavatory wall. There was a pungent smell – something mixed with the acrid scent of gunpowder. Pete recognized it as Skydrol, the fluid used in the aircraft's hydraulic system.

Austin Ferguson

JETSTREAM

ARROW BOOKS

ARROW BOOKS LTD
3 Fitzroy Square, London W1

An imprint of the Hutchinson Publishing Group

London Melbourne Sydney Auckland
Wellington Johannesburg and agencies
throughout the world

First published in Great Britain by
Hutchinson & Co (Publishers) Ltd 1975
Arrow edition 1976
© Austin Ferguson 1973

Made and printed in Great Britain
by The Anchor Press Ltd
Tiptree, Essex

ISBN 0 09 912270 7

There are three prerequisites for safe flight:

Altitude, Airspeed, and *Brains*

A pilot can never run out of two at once and stay alive

This book is dedicated to

Walt Burd
Harold Burson
Bentz Elagemann

– for they are the altitude, airspeed, and brains of *Jet Stream*

JET STREAM

> "*Jet Stream, 1. strong, generally westerly winds concentrated in a relatively narrow and shallow stream in the upper troposphere.*"
> The Random House Dictionary of the English Language

1

"Gear down, final checklist!"

Stan turned and looked at the captain across the cockpit, an inquisitive expression on his face. He hesitated with his hand on the gear lever.

"Gear down, dammit!"

The copilot pulled out and pushed down on the wheel-shaped handle which sent hydraulic fluid at three thousand pounds' pressure through the steel veins of the 727. Three massive doors opened, and the wheels fell into place with a solid clunk as the airplane put one wing toward the sky and gracefully turned onto a long final approach to runway 28-left at San Francisco. Stan turned to Mike Fuller in the flight engineer's seat with a shrug and nodded. Mike answered the shrug with raised eyebrows and started to read the litany of the final checklist from the card in his hand. They had each recited it a thousand times.

"Antiskid?"

Stan looked up and to his left. "Switches on, release light on."

"Flight and nav instruments?"

Sixteen hundred miles to the east, a weather clerk stood by a teletype machine in Chicago. He waited for the machine to stop printing, tore off the paper, read it, then took it across the room to Lars Gunter, Chief Dispatcher for Transcon Airlines. The balding man at the desk read the message and frowned.

SEVERE WEATHER BULLETIN #6—BULLETIN #5 CANCELED—DEEPENING LOW PRESSURE AREA NOW OVER NRTHRN ALBERTA—SASKATCHEWAN BORDER MOVING SE 25–30 MPH. ANTICIPATE HIGH WIND, HEAVY SNOW, LOWERING CEILINGS & VISIBILITY PRECEDING STORM. CANADIAN BORDER AT MIDNIGHT LOCAL TIME—CENTRAL S. DAKOTA AT 0700.

The storm was a freak, even for mid-December. They had been watching it for two days. It had begun as a small low-pressure system over Alaska. It had picked up moisture from the Pacific, been given its initial spin by the northern jet stream, that tunnel of air in the upper atmosphere that roars along in winter at two hundred and fifty miles an hour, and developed into a vast storm center —a whirlpool of snow and wind covering thousands of square miles. Gunter looked at the clock on the wall above him. It was 7:00 P.M. He would wait another two hours before making preparations for a major storm, just to make sure that this one was as bad as advertised. "I'll flip you for coffee," he said to the weather clerk. The clerk grinned, reached into his pocket and brought out a coin. Lars lost.

He got up from his chair and walked past the map with a tight pattern of concentric rings over Canada. He picked up the coffeepot and poured two cups.

The warden of Point-of-the-Mountain Prison near Salt Lake City was just finishing his coffee when a guard brought Donald Greco into his office. He motioned for the prisoner to sit down as he sifted through some papers on his desk. The guard stationed himself silently behind Greco and folded his arms across his chest. They stared at each other across the big metal desk.

"You wanted to see me, Warden?" Greco broke the silence.

"Yes, I've finally gotten instructions on what to do with you. It seems that we won't have the pleasure of your company after tomorrow." Greco said nothing. "A federal marshal is in Salt Lake now, and will take you back to Chicago in the morning." There was a long silence. "Any comments?"

Greco sat playing with a button on his prison shirt. "No." It was more a grunt than a word.

The warden couldn't resist getting in one last dig at this unwelcome guest. "After your escape from Cook County Jail, you'll be lucky if you *ever* see the outside again." He motioned for the guard to take Greco out. As the two men went through the door, the warden smiled and called after them, "Have a nice trip!"

The door closed. He picked up the papers on Greco and thought, There goes a real weirdo if there ever was one. So silent, so inward and uncommunicative. The papers he held in his hand told the story in brief legal terms. Greco had been convicted for a murder which had occurred during a bank robbery in Elgin, Illinois. He had been in Cook County Jail, being held for trial, when he escaped—seriously wounding a guard in the process.

The FBI had recaptured him a week ago in Ogden, Utah, when they received a tip from an unknown informer.

Well, thought the warden, I'm glad he's out of my hair. Two fights in as many days. Point-of-the-Mountain had been quiet for some time now, and the warden didn't want any prisoners there that would turn it into another Attica. He put the papers aside and picked up the phone to call his wife.

"Eighty knots!" Stan called out as the airplane slowed on the runway. Pete Douglass eased the three engines out of reverse thrust and gently braked to a speed slow enough to turn off the runway. There was little conversation in the cockpit as they taxied to the terminal, each man preoccupied with positioning switches, turning off radios, and transferring electrical power, making final preparations to leave the airplane. In the cabin, the stewardesses began to hand out coats and hats to the passengers as they were taxiing.

It had been a long day for all of them—leaving New York at 9:00 A.M. and flying to San Francisco with stops at St. Louis, Denver, and Reno. The last passenger had deplaned. The crew collected their bags and walked through the long jetway to the terminal. As they reached the brightly lit corridor Mike said, "Are we all going out to dinner tonight?"

When there was no response, Terry turned and smiled at him with her best stewardess smile—it was dazzling. "Let's see when we get to the hotel, OK, Mike?"

He laughed. "Always the diplomat, aren't you, Terry?"

The three pilots and three stewardesses walked into the Transcon Operations office, and while Mike and Terry signed the crew in for tomorrow's trip back to New York, Pete and Stan took a quick look at the weather maps.

Standing beside the captain, Stan pointed to the storm over northwestern Canada. "Looks like it might be a little tense going home tomorrow." Stan said it lightly.

"I haven't seen a low-pressure system like that for a couple of years."

Pete stared at him—almost as if he hadn't heard what his copilot had said. He waited for a long moment, then snarled, "You don't know *how* tense!" The captain spun around and strode toward the door. Stan stared after him as he walked off, shaking his head in wonder.

Mike and Terry returned from the crew scheduler's desk. As they started to leave, Stan grabbed Mike's arm and held him back a few paces. "Christ! What's with Pete today? Every time I look at him he chews my ass out."

Mike shrugged. He had a rather erotic sense of humor, as most bachelors do. "I don't know," he said. "Maybe his wife cut him off or something. I noticed him jumping all over you on approach a few minutes ago."

"No, it's not his wife, I know her, but it sure as hell is something!"

Mike slapped him on the back. "C'mon . . . we can't solve it here, and beautiful San Francisco awaits us." He made an overexaggerated bow as Stan went out the door.

They caught up with Pete and the girls as they reached the main section of the Transcon terminal. They walked past lines of people checking luggage, buying tickets, and waiting to say good-bye or hello. Stan was lost in his own little reverie, thinking about what emotional places airports are. People always crying, embracing, always a sense of motion. His thoughts jerked to a stop when he saw her. She was in a line at the Transcon ticket counter about ten yards away. Her chestnut-red hair was longer than he remembered, curling gently over the collar of her soft yellow suit. She was alone. There was a small overnight bag next to her.

"Wait just a second, will you?" He left Mike and started toward her. He had covered about half the distance when she turned and saw him approaching.

He saw her give that funny little puzzled frown of hers,

followed immediately by a brilliant smile. "Stan? Stan Burkhart—is it really you?"

"Yes, Susan, it's really me." Stan turned to Mike, who was standing with the girls—they all looked amused. "You all go ahead. I'll meet you at the hotel later." He turned back to Susan before there was a reply. A thousand memories flooded his brain. He looked into her green eyes. "Hello there," he said softly.

She held out her hand and Stan covered it with both of his. Was there a little tremor, or was he imagining? After a moment she said, "This certainly is quite a little jolt— especially today." Stan made no reply and reluctantly dropped her hand. She was gently shaking her head. "I see you made it."

For a second he didn't understand; then he saw her looking at the gleaming silver and gold wings on his left breast. Another assault on his brain by memories, some clouded with bitterness. "Yes . . . yes, I made it. It took more than a year after"—he faltered—"after I last saw you in New York. I've been working for Transcon for seven years." He became aware of the people in the line watching them. "Listen, are you in a rush?"

"Well, no, I have to buy this ticket, but I've got over two hours."

"Have some coffee with me." His confidence was returning. He noticed now that there was no ring on her hand.

"But my ticket."

Stan laughed. "You forget that I have a certain amount of influence at this establishment. Besides, I know of a very romantic coffee shop right over there."

Susan suppressed a giggle. "All right, coffee would be fun."

He picked up her suitcase and they walked to the coffee shop. The terminal was becoming crowded now, bustling with commuters returning to Los Angeles after a day's work in San Francisco. She was pushed against him by the hurrying flow of people. Stan felt emotion that had been dormant for a long, long time.

They took a table by the window. "Still the gentleman," she said as he held her chair. He wondered if she was being sarcastic, but shelved the thought as she gave her own version of a giggle when he sat down.

"What are . . . ?" They both started to speak, then laughed, and relaxed a bit more.

"What are you doing in San Fran?" he said, finally. "And what are you doing at the airport? And a million other things."

"Buying a ticket, of course." The answer gave her time to think.

Susan started to go on, but he was staring out the window at a giant Pan Am 747 just gaining the air—shaking the earth as if it was glad to leave. She studied him then, in that moment of reprieve from conversation. The eyes were the same—grayish-blue and alert. There were little creases at the corners. A little thinner jaw, some gray hair in the light brown. Better looking than eight years ago, she decided. She looked again at the wings on his uniform, the three gold stripes on his sleeve. Yes, she thought, he did make it. He had said he would, even if he lost me in the process. Some of the anger started to well up inside of her—anger long forgotten. He turned and smiled. The anger subsided.

"I'm sorry," he said, "that was rude."

She thought, He wouldn't have apologized eight years ago. "That's all right—I understand, I think." She really didn't.

"Now . . . where are you buying this ticket to?"

"New York."

Stan hesitated. "Is that where . . . ?"

"No. Jack and I were divorced a year ago." The tone told him that her defenses were coming up. "I've been working at St. Francis Hospital for a while, but I miss

New York, and I can get a nursing supervisor's job there. I have some contacts at Flower and Montefiore."

"I'm sorry to hear that."

She looked at him sharply. "What? That I'm going to New York or that I've divorced Jack?"

"Come on, Susan." Stan chuckled. "That's like asking me if I've stopped beating my dog. I meant the divorce. It must have been painful, and I'm sorry for your pain."

The waitress arrived to take their order. He looked at Susan. "Still no coffee after noon?" She was flattered and amazed at his ability to remember details. She nodded and smiled—trying to hide her surprise.

Stan turned to the waitress. "Hot tea with lemon for the lady, and black coffee for me."

The waitress left. They sat quietly for a time, watching the scene below. A Trans-World 707 was moving smoothly into the gate area. It stopped with that gentle up-and-down motion that big jets have when the brakes are applied sharply. Two jetways moved toward the plane like rigid caterpillars about to take a bite out of the fuselage. Baggage carts, loaders, food and fuel trucks swarmed to the airplane in what seemed to be mass confusion. It reminded Susan of the movies she had seen where all the men in brightly colored suits would swarm over the deck of a carrier when they were going to launch aircraft. She had always hoped that one green-suited man would end up among all of the red-suited men, but they never did. She decided that she had a warped sense of humor because now, looking at the seeming disorder below her, she was hoping that one of the baggage carts would run into a food truck. It didn't.

She looked at Stan. He was staring across the ramp at the 707. He looked so calm, so in control of everything around him. That's ridiculous, she thought. How could anyone look in control in an airport coffee shop? Yet, somehow, he did. She looked out the window again. One of Transcon's big jets was pushed back from the terminal finger. A man in white coveralls under the nose had unplugged his headset and was walking away from the plane. He turned, saluted the cockpit, and pointed with both arms to the airport beyond. The captain returned the salute and the DC-10 turned slowly toward the taxiway. The red sun flashed for an instant on the green and gold lettering along the side. She turned to Stan.

"Now it's *my* turn to apologize!" She laughed—he had been watching her.

"You looked like you were in another world," he said. "What were you thinking?"

"Oh . . . nothing really. It seems like such a busy world down there." She nodded at the activity below. "Do you like it, Stan?"

"I love it. Oh, there are days when it's a little rough, like today." She raised her eyebrows. "Pete Douglass—he's the captain I'm flying with this month—he's been in a rotten mood all day. Maybe I'm a little sensitive but . . ." He didn't finish the sentence. "Something's bothering him. There's a big snowstorm moving south from Canada, and we have to fly through it tomorrow, but that shouldn't bother him. I was working with Pete in Richmond when hurricane Agnes hit and it was no sweat. It's something bigger than that." He shook his head. "But the job? Susan, it's the greatest job in the world. I wouldn't trade it for anything." He paused to light a cigarette. "Enough about the sensitive Stan Burkhart! Tell me more about you. If I'm not prying, what happened with you and Jack?" Susan fumbled in her purse for her own cigarettes. Stan noticed her hand was trembling. No imagination this time. He lit her cigarette and leaned back.

The waitress arrived with their order. The interruption gave her time to think. "Stan, it's a long story. You're not really prying but . . . let's save it for another time, OK?" Her female instinct told her not to get too deep into the area they were heading toward.

She looked up from her tea. "Stan . . . are you, well, did you ever . . . ?"

He looked into her eyes. "No, I'm not married—never did." Stan wondered how much he should tell her, then decided that the time for mental games had long past. He tried unsuccessfully to read her expression. "I am, engaged, though. Her name is Ellen Kasvakis. She's a stew for Transcon. We've been engaged for a year—no, longer than that." He thought of Ellen as she would be now, in his apartment near Gramercy Park. "She's a lovely girl—long dark hair, nice figure. She's bright, intelligent, witty. She's an excellent cook. Ellen flies international trips, so we don't see each other for a week or two sometimes. Her folks live near Philadelphia—her dad's an architect, a real nice guy. She'll make a terrific wife!"

He had said it all too fast.

Susan laughed out loud. "Stan, that's the most *tepid* description of a woman I've ever heard!" She was shaking her head as she laughed.

He looked at the ashtray. How does she know me so well after eight years? It's incredible! She reads me better than she reads a chart on a patient's bed.

"When are you getting married?" She still looked amused.

"Well, we haven't really set a date yet. I want to be closer to a captain vacancy so that Ellen can quit if she wants to."

"I thought stewardesses had to be single." It was more of a statement than a question.

"No," he said, "as a matter of fact, the head stewardess on our trip today and tomorrow, Terry Dunlap, is married to one of Transcon's copilots."

"Just like Stan and Ellen—how romantic!" She had said it as if she were reading for Marilyn Monroe's part in the movie *Bus Stop*. There was mischief in the green eyes.

"Oh, come on, Susan, be serious!"

"But Ah ayem.'" The green eyes fluttered at him. They both laughed—an amusement shared from long ago.

Stan wanted desperately to get off the subject of his engagement. His eyes lit up. "I have a wild idea!" He said it before he fully realized the implicatons. He pointed out the window. An airplane with the green and gold Transcon paint scheme was just arriving at a gate to Susan's left.

"That's the kind of airplane that I fly. It's a Boeing 727, used for short and medium-range trips. We're going back to New York tomorrow morning. Why don't you come back on my trip?" Once his thoughts got started, they picked up momentum. "I can get a room at the Sheraton Palace, where we stay, and you can ride to the airport in the morning with the crew. It's flight 602—we make stops in Salt Lake City, Chicago, and St. Louis, so it'll take longer than a nonstop, but it would be fun." He stopped abruptly. "Am I going too fast?"

His meaning wasn't lost on Susan. "I . . . I don't know." She said it softly.

He got up. "Well, think about it—please. I have to go to the men's room."

"Good old ten-minute-bladder Stan," she said, giggling.

He turned from the table toward the rear of the restaurant. *So she remembers, too.* He noticed some high clouds drifting in from the north as he passed the big windows, but their import was lost—Stan could see only green eyes.

Susan looked at the clouds over San Francisco Bay. What the hell, she thought, it won't make any difference if I get to New York tonight or tomorrow night. It wasn't as if there was a reception in her honor awaiting her. It might even be fun. She watched a waitress clear off a table nearby. Damn, she thought, why do all the people connected with the airlines have to be so attractive? She had noticed it before. The men and women behind the ticket counters, the car rental agents, even the waitresses looked as if they could pose for toothpaste ads. What's the matter, Susan? Jealous? No, just defensive, she thought. You couldn't go through what she had been through with Jack and not be defensive. She was startled out of her trance by Stan's return.

"Well? How about spending one more night in San Francisco?" He was sitting now, looking at her with an amused expression.

She stared back, almost defiantly. "Sure, why not . . . after all, we are pretty good friends." She emphasized the word *friends*.

"Good," he said, "the Sheraton is holding a room for you. I called while I was taking care of my bladder problem."

You bastard, she thought, always so sure, so . . .

He read her thoughts. "I wasn't all that sure, Susan, I just wanted to be certain there would be a room if you decided to leave tomorrow." He turned and signaled the waitress for the check.

They walked across the terminal to the side of the Transcon ticket counter, away from the lines of people. Stan waved, and called the supervisor over.

"Hi, Marilyn, how are you?"

"Fine, Stan, how've you been?" The woman smiled.

"Marilyn, this is Susan . . . ?" He turned to Susan.

"MacKenzie," she said quickly.

"Susan, Marilyn Chester." They nodded to each other and smiled. Susan looked at Marilyn, a lovely woman in her early forties. Blond, well-proportioned. Another twinge of . . . jealousy?

"Marilyn," Stan was saying, " could you write out a ticket for Susan from San Fran to New York for me? She's going back on 602 with us tomorrow." Marilyn gave Stan a funny look. "We're old friends," he said.

"Sure, Stan, it'll only take a second." She walked to an unused agent's station and began punching the keyboard that was tied to Transcon's central computer.

Marilyn brought the ticket back to them. "You're con-

firmed all the way to New York, Susan—here's the ticket."
She ran Susan's American Express card through the machine. When the paperwork was finished she said, "Nice to meet you, Susan. Stan—stay out of trouble. 'Bye." She dashed off to another part of the ticket counter.

Stan had decided to rent a car, so they walked over to the Avis counter next to the baggage-claim area. As they were standing there, four Transcon stewardesses passed in their smartly tailored uniforms—soft green jumper with green and gold jacket and matching gold scarf. One of the girls spotted Stan and waved.

"Hi, Peggy!" Stan waved back.

Susan looked up at him. "Do you know every pretty girl that works for Transcon Airlines?"

"No"—he laughed at her—"only half of them, but I'm still trying." He saw then that she was upset. "What's the matter, Susan?"

She lifted her shoulders. The copper hair rearranged itself. "I don't know, I guess I feel like . . . well, like you're on the inside of a big circle with a lot of people, and I'm on the outside of the circle."

Stan looked at her. "Funny, . . . that's how I used to feel whenever I'd pick you up at the hospital."

"Mr. Burkhart?" Stan turned to the girl behind the Avis counter. "I'm sorry, sir, the car you requested is being washed right now, and it's the only one in the garage. Would you like a Plymouth?" When Stan hesitated she said, "If you'd rather wait, it should only take a few minutes—they said that they're almost through."

"Fine. We'll come back in ten minutes." He turned to Susan. "Come with me. I'll show you a part of the glamorous airline industry that nobody sees." He took her arm and they walked out the terminal finger to a door marked:

TRANSCON AIRLINES OPERATIONS

Beneath it, a smaller sign read:

AUTHORIZED PERSONNEL ONLY

Stan opened the door.

Susan hesitated. "Am I an authorized personnel?"

"Go on in." He laughed. "They put those signs on the doors so that everyone going in and out can feel important. Must keep up the mystery about the airlines, you know."

They walked down a short corridor lined on both sides with racks holding hundreds of suitcases and flight kits. At the end of the hall, they walked into a brightly lit large room.

Susan was amazed at the amount of activity. The room was at least seventy feet long, extending off to their left. Across from where they stood a waist-high counter ran the full length of the room. At regular intervals above the counter signs hung from the ceiling with cryptic words: CHI-EAST, or WEST CST-LCL. There was one that Susan could understand: INTERNATIONAL FLTS. These were the sector dispatch stations, and each trip was assigned a sector depending on its destination. Stan took her over to the counter. There were large windows to the rear, and the space between was filled with rows of desks, roughly lined up to correspond with the signs overhead. Most of the desks were filled with an impressive array of electronic equipment; a computer-type television screen with an associated keyboard, a call-director telephone, and several small boxlike speakers. From this equipment trailed a bundle of cables which had been laced together. The bundle disappeared into a hole in the floor. It looked to Susan as if all the desks were attached to the floor by giant umbilical cords.

Stan was enjoying her look of amazement. He said, "These are the dispatchers and clerks." He gestured to the thirty men behind the counter, most of them seated at desks. "All airline flights are planned by agreement between the dispatcher and the captain of the flight. If they should disagree about any portion of the plan—fuel load, for instance—then FAA regulations require that the more conservative plan be adopted. In the case of fuel load, that would be the plan calling for the highest amount of fuel." He took Susan back to the opposite wall, near the door they had come in. There was a slanted shelf extending off to the left about forty feet. Above the shelf were three television monitors giving gate location, equipment number, and tentative fuel load for every Transcon flight arriving or departing in the next three hours. The slanted shelf was covered with dozens of spring clips attached to the formica surface, each holding several sheets of paper. The center of the shelf was dominated by a large map of the United States and Canada. It was covered with groups of figures and curving lines.

Stan pointed to the series of tight circles in the upper left of the map. "That's the storm I mentioned in the coffee shop. The rest of this paper"—he gestured along the shelf—"can tell us the weather in any part of the country, winds aloft, freezing levels, and a bunch of stuff that's . . . I'm boring you."

"Oh no, Stan, it's just that it's a bit confusing."

He opened his mouth to reply, but a voice from behind interrupted. The voice was wearing the dark green uniform of a Transcon pilot. "Hi, Stan," the voice said.

Stan turned around. "Oh, Harry—glad to see you here. I tried to call before we left New York, but there was no answer." He introduced Susan. She tried to see if there was any surprise in Harry's eyes. There wasn't.

"Stan? Can I see you for a moment?" He turned to the girl. "Excuse me, Susan, this will just take a minute."

She smiled at the tall captain and nodded. They walked over to the dispatch counter where Harry Jensen had been filling out the flight papers for his return trip to New York an hour from now. They were standing so that Stan's back was to Susan. Harry was looking at her over Stan's shoulder, taking in the trim figure, the lovely green eyes. "Who's the girl?"

"She's an old friend from years back."

Harry raised his eyebrows. "Is she a stew?"

"No."

The dispatcher came over to the counter, breaking their conversation. Harry turned to him and said, "I'd like to add Pittsburgh as an alternate for New York. Can we add fuel without hurting the payload?"

The dispatcher did some rapid figuring on the flight plan worksheet. "Sure, I'll add twelve thousand pounds of fuel, that OK?"

"Fine—that'll be great." He turned back to Stan, glancing at the girl. "She's pretty. Do you and Ellen still want to go to the theater Wednesday night?"

"Sure, we're both off on Thursday, so we can stay out late—make it a big evening, maybe dinner at The Leopard afterward."

"Sounds good. Who are you flying with?"

Stan shook his head. "Pete Douglass."

"Oh? I talked to Bob Quinlan on the phone this morning. He said Pete's wife was in the hospital."

Stan looked up at Harry. "That explains some things."

"What do you mean?"

"Oh, nothing . . . Pete's just been a little uptight today, that's all." He looked back at Susan. "I've got to run, Harry. I'll call you when I get back tomorrow night."

"OK, Stan, see you." Harry turned back to the dispatcher.

Susan was sitting down. There were several conference-type tables in the center of the room. About half the tables had two or three pilots sitting at them working amid piles of large books, littered ashtrays, and half-empty coffee cups. She had picked the nearest chair at one of the empty tables to sit and wait for Stan.

She looked around slowly. The first impression she had was one of sound—continual sound. Teletype machines running at high-speed print, air-conditioning fans adding background noise, and snatches of coversation.

"Central weather briefing on line twenty-four!" demanded a speaker somewhere in the ceiling.

"I want at least an hour's holding fuel when we arrive over Kansas City, Chuck. Let's ask them for another five thousand pounds of kerosene." The copilot at the table next to her got up and walked to the counter.

It occurred to Susan that this was a lot like the hospitals she had worked in. So much goes on behind the scenes that the general public doesn't know about. She watched Stan coming toward her. He stopped once to speak to one of three stewardesses who had come in. He touched her arm, said something, and they both laughed. He continued across the room.

"Sorry," he said as he reached her, "Harry's based in New York. He's the first captain I flew with as a copilot —we've become pretty good friends."

"Why did he pull you away like that?" She put on a mock pout.

Stan laughed. "He just wasn't sure who you were, and he's getting theater tickets for me and Ellen for next Wednesday."

"Do you all stick up for each other that way?"

He laughed again but didn't answer her question. "Come on, let's go get the car." They walked to the door past the weather board. "Just one second." He had stopped, and was reading the top sheet on a stack of papers. The clip that was holding the stack and the area around it were painted bright red. The top of the clip was labeled: SEVERE WEATHER.

SEVERE WEATHER BULLETIN #7—BULLETIN #6 CANCELED—MAJOR SNOW SYSTEM OVER CENTR. AND SOUTH. SASKATCHEWAN MOVING SSE 30 MPH—WILL CROSS CANAD. BRDR AT 0330 PST. BAROM 28.82 AT CENTER—WINDS 45 MPH GUSTS TO 65 DRIFTING SNOW TO 8 FT—WILL INTENSIFY THRU NIGHT. PROJ CENTER AT PIERRE S. DAK AT 1000 LOCAL   USWEATHBUR

They were driving north on the Bayshore Freeway, past the United Air Lines Maintenance Base, past Candlestick Park, and up the curving, gentle hills toward the city. They drove in silence. Susan was watching the lights of Oakland across the bay as it grew darker, the soft San Francisco dusk giving way to night. When the rising hills cut off her view she turned to look at Stan. He had rented a Shelby GT which was, she thought, just like him. Good old Stan—always first class. She watched him negotiate the traffic and winding curves with ease—all fluid motion, not a move wasted. He did all things that way. She remembered when he had taken her on her first sailboat race. He had been the foredeck captain on a fifty-foot sloop and had talked the owner into letting her go on one of the shorter races as cook. She was amazed when he and one other crewman had set a giant spinnaker without seeming to work at all. The weather had been rough—gusty winds and a short, nasty chop in the waters of Long Island Sound. She had made a game of it, played with herself. All day she had watched to see if he ever took an extra step or unnecessarily lifted a line. He never had.

His face was relaxed. He drove with one hand on the wheel, the other on the shift knob at his knee. No wonder he loves flying, she thought, he's at home in anything that moves—the machine is just an extension of him, nothing more. He reached into his shirt pocket and offered her a cigarette. He lit his own, and then handed her the flickering lighter, his eyes not leaving the road.

"You're quiet," he said.

She sighed a half-sigh. "The city is so lovely—I guess I'm going to miss it."

They left the freeway and drove to the hotel through the city streets, arriving just after seven. Stan took care of checking her in while Susan looked around the lobby. The Sheraton Palace is an older hotel that has been tastefully modernized. The original beauty has not been lost— the soaring columns, the real marble, a dining room with mirrored walls and a glass ceiling high overhead. Like the

William Penn in Pittsburgh, the Brown Palace in Denver, The Palmer House, even the Plaza, this was one of the last great hotels of its kind—a remnant of a more civilized time in the world. Susan was an incurable romantic, and it saddened her to see these beautiful buildings disappear one at a time.

He startled her out of her mood. "Would you like to change?"

"Yes, I think so."

"Well, I have to. I can't very well go to dinner in this uniform. How long do you need?"

Susan thought for a minute. "I'd really like to take a shower and try to make myself beautiful. Is a half hour too long?"

"No, that's fine, and I really don't think you'll have to try too hard."

She wrinkled her forehead, not understanding.

"To make yourself beautiful." He grinned and picked up her suitcase. They walked to the elevators. Stan saw Susan to her room on the fourth floor, then returned to the elevators and went to his own on the sixth. It was like a thousand rooms he'd been in. Hotels save their smallest rooms for the airline crews that are staying there, and this was no exception. There was a double bed in one corner, a chair by the window, with a combination table and lamp beside it, a slightly battered television set, and a slightly battered dresser with a mirror. A small closet completed the picture. But the room was light, and clean, and the view of San Francisco through the single window was magnificent.

Stan sat down on the bed and loosened his tie. Too many things had happened this day, and he needed a minute to sort them out. Susan appearing out of nowhere —Pete in such a foul mood (yes, Stan, you *are* sensitive)— and, fluttering around the edge of his conscious thought, the trip home tomorrow. And then Harry reminding him of Ellen.

When he was a boy in Cleveland, his father had taught him to deal with problems by taking a sheet of paper and drawing a line down the middle. Then you put down on the left side of the line all the advantages of whatever it was you were trying to decide, and on the right side of the line all the disadvantages. It gave you a running picture, visually, of whatever the problem was. The trouble was that his father's system didn't work so well if you were dealing with emotion. You could easily fill both sides of the page if you were trying to buy a car, or take a new job, but what side of the page did her green eyes go on? On what side of the page would he have put her wry sense of humor? And where was Ellen in all of this? Would she go in the middle of the page? He rubbed his face with both hands.

She still excited him—he knew that. But what would tonight bring them to? The hell with it, he decided. Dinner takes a long time, a lot can come out. Play it by ear. He walked across the tiny room to his suitcase.

Susan let the steaming water play over her body. It was as if she were trying to draw strength from the stinging stream of hot water coming from the shower head. It had been quite an emotional day. First the continuing strain of the decision to leave San Francisco, reached only after weeks of trying to find a solution to her restlessness. Seeing Stan was a jolt—and now she was forcing herself, through a possibly reckless and defiant decision, to spend an evening reliving old hurts, revealing old scars. This when the new ones were just barely healed. She stepped from the glass-walled shower and toweled herself dry with a vigor that reddened her skin.

There was a full-length mirror on the bathroom door. She took off her shower cap and let the towel fall to the floor. Then she did something that she hadn't done since she was a girl—she turned to the mirror and looked at her nude body. OK, Susan, she thought, let's see what kind of a woman you really are. She looked at the girl in the mirror, trying to be objective. She turned to the left and looked at her breasts in profile. Pretty, she thought, small, pert, and pretty—she didn't need a bra to shape or change any curves. Her gaze traveled down the mirror —tummy flat, her waist a shade thicker than she would have liked, but still shapely. Thighs still firm and curved. Her legs long for her five-foot-three frame. She nodded to the girl in the mirror—not too bad for an old lady of twenty-seven.

This was the first time she had thought of herself as a woman in almost a year, and it startled her. She had let herself retreat into a shell since the divorce from Jack. She had ignored the attractive young doctors in the hospital who would try to approach her. They had thought her quite a snob, but she didn't care. She rarely went out, and when she did, it was always with one of the older nurses so she wouldn't have to put up with the boring scene at Paoli's or The Cannery, or any of the other singles bars. What had happened in the last two hours to change her thinking?

She forced the question from her mind, and taking one more swift glance in the mirror (sexy from the rear, she thought), walked over to the bed where she had left her suitcase. She had sent most of her clothes ahead to the Barbizon Hotel for Women in New York, so her choice of what to wear was between a pants suit, softly cut in the MacKenzie tartan, and a gaily printed shirtwaist dress that she know would compliment the curves she had been looking at in the mirror. She chose the blue and orange dress.

As she was putting on her underwear, a flash of mischief ran through her mind, and she left the bra lying on the bed. She put on the dress, smoothed it, and went to the mirror over the dresser. She ran a comb through her copper hair and quickly put on a light touch of lipstick. She hadn't worn makeup in years. She didn't need it. She looked at herself in the mirror and the impish grin returned. She cocked her head to one side and said to the mirror, "Eat your heart out, Stan Burkhart!" She unbuttoned the second and third buttons at the top of her dress.

Susan wondered why she had always delighted in teasing him so, and why that hadn't changed in eight years. But why was she even thinking about it? She certainly didn't want to get involved in anything now—especially with Stan. The old feelings welled up inside her. All the men in the world could disappear tonight for all she cared. She'd done pretty well without them for the past year—longer if she considered the last several months with Jack. So dinner with Stan would be just that—a nice farewell to San Francisco, with a nice secure old friend. She picked up the blue angora sweater, retrieved her purse from the bed, and walked to the door.

Stan was anything but calm as he finished tying his tie. He was angry with himself for not packing better clothes for his layover. All he had in his suitcase were a pair of gray slacks and a navy blue blazer. But then, he rationalized, he hadn't known that he'd be doing anything other than have dinner with the rest of the crew. He reached into his bag and took out a pack of Rolaids, putting two in his mouth and chewing rapidly. His stomach had been churning since he sat down in the coffee shop. He had straightened up the room after his shower, smoothing the bed and putting his bag on the luggage rack. What for, Stan? he had thought. Susan's been friendly and warm, but she's in a shell, that's obvious. And there was Ellen.

He had made the obligatory phone call as soon as he got to his room. The conversation had been sterile . . . and brief. "Everything all right?" he had asked.

"Fine, Stan, how's the trip going?" She sounded as if she really didn't care if it was going well or not.

"Routine." He decided not to say anything about Pete.

"Well, let's not support the phone company by ourselves." She said it as if she was ending a paragraph. "Say hi to Pete and Mike for me. Love you, 'bye."

"Mmmm, good-bye, Ellen." He hung up the phone. Why hadn't he answered her? He sat by the phone for a long time, picturing Ellen in the apartment. She had probably been sitting in the living room by the fire, watching a late movie. The phone would be pulled out into the middle of the floor, its long cord trailing into the bedroom. The too-large terry cloth robe that she wore constantly would have been open to the waist as she raised her arms fixing those ridiculous rollers. Stan felt no surge of excitement at the thought. He went to the shower quickly to try and wash away the emptiness that he felt. It only half-worked.

Now, as he put on his blazer, he still felt . . . well, he wondered, what *did* he feel? Perhaps he was just nervous about being with Susan. That's ridiculous, he thought; all of the hurt is long past. She's still dazzling, he had to admit that. But he and Ellen had been together for a long time, and that was comfortable. Susan and I are friends, he decided, and tonight we're going to have dinner, and laugh, and catch up on the years behind us, and . . . and what? The question left the room with him. Before he closed the door he checked his pockets for the room key and extra cigarettes.

He had been waiting in the lobby for less than five minutes when she arrived. "Hi there, stranger." He tried to be casual, but it sounded manufactured.

Susan smiled. "I hope this is all right to wear." She turned around slowly like a model. "Almost all of my things are already in New York." She watched his eyes and was perversely happy when she saw him look at her. The effect of the unbuttoned dress wasn't lost.

"You look fine." His eyes said more than that.

"Where are we eating? I know a few places——"

"Sausalito," he interrupted her. "I have a special place there."

Susan looked at him and wondered why he seemed a little defensive. And how had he known that Sausalito was her haven from the world? She hadn't mentioned it, she was certain. She was glad that Stan had taken charge of the evening. Jack had been so . . .

"We can't eat standing here." He took her hand and led her to the car outside.

It was dark now, the air clear. Stan looked up as he always did. High cirrus clouds obscured the stars—the moon was just a shadow of light in an otherwise black sky.

The clouds were the scout troops of the storm whirling about in the night, flinging its fury for a thousand miles in every direction.

"On layovers of more than twelve hours free from duty, the company will provide suitable accommodations for its flight crews at a hotel near or in the city being served by the airport of landing, and will provide prompt transportation to and from such hotel."

Sec. D, Para. 6(a), Contract between Transcon Airlines and its pilots, as represented by the Air Line Pilots Association

2

Pete Douglass had been quiet during the ride from San Francisco International to the hotel. The crew rode in one of those strange long cars with four doors on each side that Transcon leased to provide transportation for the crews staying overnight. Pete had taken the seat at the extreme rear of the car, shut the door, and stared out the window for the entire trip into San Francisco. Mike sat next to Cathy Armello in the seat directly in front of Pete. They had known each other for a long time and Cathy was telling Mike about one of the passengers on the trip today. Terry was sitting in the front with Cindy Weston, just behind the driver. This was Cindy's first trip to the West Coast, and Terry was telling her about what to see and do in the city. Cindy looked confused and excited—the little girl from Wisconsin was obviously not ready for the sparkling jewels of the city ahead of them.

Terry had sensed her confusion and taken pity on the new girl. "Tell you what, Cindy—the stores are open late tonight and I was going to do some shopping. Why don't you come with me? You should see Gump's, and Magnin's, and we can stop for a drink at the Hungry i . . ."

Cindy's eyes lit up with anticipation as Terry went on to describe the excitement of the magic city by the bay.

Halfway through the drive, as they passed the exit to the Cow Palace, Cathy had turned to Pete. "Captain"—she used the title in mock seriousness—"are you going to have dinner with us tonight?"

Pete continued his vigil at the window, seeming not to have heard.

She tried again. "Pete? Dinner?"

He looked at her for a long second, then quietly said, "No thanks, Cathy. Not tonight." He turned and continued to stare out the window.

Cathy started to say something else to him, but Mike caught her eye and signaled with a shake of his head to leave it alone.

They continued to ride in silence for the remainder of the drive. Only Cindy with her undisguised excitement would break the quiet with an occasional question about the passing scenery.

The crew arrived at the Sheraton Palace just before six. They went directly from the front door to a small window to the right of the registration desk. The hotel kept this special window for the large number of airline crews that stayed there on a regular basis. The rooms were reserved nightly on a contract with the airlines. On the desk were several loose-leaf notebooks that served as registers. They were indexed according to inbound flight numbers. Pete took the book marked *Transcon* and wrote his name next to the room number and added the time for a wake-up call. Then, without saying a word to the rest of the crew, he picked up his suitcase and walked to the elevators.

Cathy Armello turned to Mike. "What's with *El Capitan* tonight?"

Mike shrugged. "I don't really know. Let's talk about it at dinner—that is, if you don't have to wash your hair." It was an old joke between them. Washing hair is the oldest excuse in the airline industry for avoiding an evening out. Mike had once bought several bottles of shampoo and carried them around in his suitcase for months. When one of the stewardesses begged out of an evening by saying that she had to wash her hair, Mike would immediately open his bag and go into a pitchman routine, trying to sell his shampoo.

Cathy laughed, remembering him doing that to her in the cavernous lobby of the Palmer House. By the time he had finished his pitch for the shampoo, a crowd of about twenty people had gathered around them, watching. When one man had seriously asked to buy a bottle for his wife, Cathy and Mike had broken up, doubling over with laughter.

Cathy was smiling with the memory of the scene. "No," she said, "I don't have to wash my hair, and yes, I'd like to have dinner with you—that is, if you're picking up the tab."

"Sure, we'll find the closest hot-dog stand." He grinned, his bushy moustache sagging at the ends. He turned to Terry and Cindy. "Are you two lovely ladies going to eat with us tonight?"

"No thanks, Mike," the older girl said, "I'm going to give Cindy her first taste of San Francisco tonight. We'll pick up a bite to eat at the Wharf."

Mike looked at Cindy—her eyes were bright with anticipation. They got on the elevator. The girls' rooms were on the fifth floor. As they got off Mike said, mostly for Cindy, "Y'all be careful now, y'heah?" He said it with a thick Georgia accent. "Cathy—meet you in the lobby at six-thirty."

"Fine, Mike—see you then." The doors closed and he went up to the sixth floor.

Pete had entered his room and gone directly to the telephone. He looked at his watch, which he always kept on New York time. Nine o'clock. He hoped he wouldn't wake Kitty. He picked up the phone. "Operator, I'd like to place a person-to-person call to Mrs. Katharine Douglass. She's in room four twenty-three at the Harkness Pavilion, Columbia Presbyterian Hospital in New York City." While the operator was getting the number, Pete took off his jacket and loosened his tie.

After a moment the operator returned. "I have your party now. Go ahead."

Pete sat down on the bed. "Hello, Pudge . . . I hope I didn't wake you." He had called her that for twenty-five years—she still weighed around a hundred and five pounds.

"No, I hoped that you would call, so I stayed awake. How's the trip, darling?" Kitty's voice sounded tiny through the telephone.

That's just like her, thought Pete, not a sign that anything is wrong. "Has the doctor said anything more?"

"Nothing more than Jonas told us when we saw him on Wednesday. Dr. Sangford stopped in about five this afternoon to see if everything was all right. He's a kind man. I feel comfortable knowing that he'll be in the O.R. tomorrow."

"The O.R.? You're beginning to sound like a medical type yourself."

Kitty laughed at him—a clear, shiny rush of laughter through the receiver. "One tends to become very slangy when one is surrounded with such efficiency—I never knew about ETAs or ILSs either, until I married a big strong airline pilot."

Pete could picture the teasing in her eyes. There was a

long moment of silence on the phone. They were sharing their fears—something they had developed over twenty-six years of marriage—sort of an ESP that neither of them understood, but both were glad to have. Pete finally said quietly, "Are you all right, Pudge?"

"I'm fine—a little scared, but fine. I just worry that you . . ."

Pete didn't let her finish. "I love you, Kitty . . . I have for a long, long time, and that's not going to change, regardless. We've been over all of this. I just wish I were there."

"I know, Pete, but I'm a woman and I can't help worrying. . . . I wish you were here, too. At least now. But it's easier to get through this way. If you were with me I'd feel worse, because you'd be right here next to the bed, wringing your hands and grinding your teeth."

He knew that she was right. "What time will they operate?"

"Seven-thirty. It seems awfully early, but Dr. Sangford has a long surgery schedule tomorrow."

Pete said, "What time will you . . . will you be awake?"

"The doctor said a little after twelve."

Pete did some quick time calculations. "I'll call you from Chicago tomorrow. We should be there around two."

"Darling, you'll be home by five or so, why not . . ."

"No, I'll call."

"OK, Pete, don't worry about me. I'll be fine." She was ending the conversation.

"I love you, Pudge . . . more than you know."

"And I love *you*, Peter Douglass, even more than cotton candy." An incident long ago, at a county fair, had given the phrase its beginning. Kitty used it whenever she was trying to soothe feelings—one of those secret signals that people who have loved each other for a long time send. "Sleep well, Pete, I'm OK."

"I'll call you from Chicago." Pete hung up the phone. He sat on the edge of the bed for a long time. The lights of San Francisco sparkled out the window, but he didn't see them. He was thinking of Kitty in a hospital bed three thousand miles away.

They had found out about the lump on her breast only yesterday. Well, it was the day before that, really. Kitty had gone to Dr. Kardos in Flemington for her regular checkup. He had frowned as he was palpating her breast, and asked to take more X-rays. That afternoon, he had phoned Kitty and asked her to return to his office the following morning with Pete. They had driven the four miles from their farm to Dr. Kardos' office in silence—both deep in their own fears.

When they had arrived at his office at nine, he was talking on the phone. "Yes, Dr. Sangford, we'll be there by three tomorrow afternoon." He motioned for Pete and Kitty to take a seat. "Fine, the sooner the better. I can't thank you enough for rearranging your schedule for this thing—they're very special friends of mine. Yes. Thank you, Doctor. Good-bye." He turned to Pete, his gray eyebrows huge fortresses over the bright blue eyes. He smiled a short smile but was quiet for a moment, as if he were trying to phrase something in his mind. Pete and Kitty had played bridge with Jonas Kardos and his wife the week before. Now he had to change roles from friend to physician, and like so many medical men before him, he was finding it difficult—very difficult.

"Good morning, Kitty, Pete." He paused to light an old, dirty meerschaum pipe that had gone out. "I just don't know how to say this except to get straight on with it. I found a mass yesterday on Kitty's left breast. The films show a small tumor of some kind. It's located on the extreme left side, about three inches from the armpit." He was pointing to his own anatomy—speaking in short, clipped phrases unnatural for the normally voluble Jonas Kardos. "I've made arrangements for Kitty to go to Harkness tomorrow afternoon, and Dr. John Sangford will operate early Friday morning."

Pete was stunned. "So soon?"

Jonas looked at him. "Pete, we can't wait any longer than we have to on this. I tried to get surgery for tomorrow but I couldn't. I went to school with John Sangford—he's one of the best there is."

Kitty had been silent. She fidgeted with the strap of her purse. In almost a whisper she said, "Jonas? Is it . . . cancer?"

He looked at her with all the compassion that ever was in the world. "We don't know, Kitty."

Pete was getting angry. He wondered why the medical profession always used *we* when a problem got rough. For him, as a captain, it was always *I*, not *we*.

"The surgeon will open the breast," the doctor was saying, "and remove a section of the tumor and freeze it. They will do an immediate biopsy while you're in the operating room. If the tumor is benign, they'll remove it and sew the incision back up. If the tumor is malignant, they'll have to remove the entire breast." He didn't know how to soften the news.

Kitty went pale, the only other sign of her emotion the white on her knuckles as she gripped the purse strap. "I see." The words were barely audible.

There was little to say after that. They rose, and as they walked to the door, Jonas was saying to Kitty, "I'll be at Harkness waiting for you at three tomorrow, Kitty. We'll check you in and I'll explain the procedure to you with Dr. Sangford." He took her hand and held it for a minute. Then he turned to Pete and extended his hand. "I'm sorry, Pete, I wish there'd been an easier way to break this." Pete shook his hand briefly, then put his arm around his wife and they walked to the car.

They drove home in silence, the bright December sun warming the hills of Hunterdon County as they drove. Pete slowed the Volvo as they wound up the half-mile driveway guarded on both sides by oaks and dogwood. He stopped the car at the steps of the house. It was a one-story farmhouse, sided with cedar shakes. Pete had built it almost by himself. They went into the living room—a long, low room paneled in walnut and cedar. The fire was still blazing in the massive stone hearth adding to the easy comfort of the room. Pete went directly to the telephone.

"Who are you going to call, Pete?"

He looked at her. "Bob Quinlan at the flight office. I'll tell him that I can't fly my trip tomorrow."

"Wait, darling." Kitty put her hand over his on the phone. "I was thinking about that in the car on the way home. One of the boys can drive me into the city tomorrow, and there isn't much you can do here." She was almost back to normal now, taking charge as she always did in a crisis. "I think you should go ahead with your trip—it'll keep your mind occupied."

Pete protested some more, but he knew that she always won this kind of discussion. She was standing next to the fireplace now, her arms folded across her breasts. The stance told him, "I have made up my mind and you are not going to change it!"

"OK, Pudge, you win." He took his hand from the phone and walked to the fire to put another log on the grate. The fire blazed. "Can I get you a drink? Or some coffee?"

"It's a little early for a drink—how about coffee and some of the cookies I made last night?" They went into the brick and walnut kitchen and started the routine they had shared a thousand times—Pete getting the cups and saucers from the cabinet, Kitty filling a plate with the rich chocolate cookies left from last night's dinner. They stood facing each other across the island in the center of the room. She was looking at him across the counter, her hands clenched into fists in front of her. Pete was pouring the coffee.

"Pete? Will you love me as much with one breast?" Her eyes were bright, the tears were rolling gently down her cheeks, splashing silently on the counter. She was looking at him—unblinking. He dropped the cup he had in his hand, spilling the coffee, and ran to her. He held her fiercely, her small head buried in his chest. She was shaking now, in great heaving sobs, feeling the horror that only a woman can feel when she knows that she may lose much of her femininity.

"Pudge . . . Pudge. You're my strength, my life—you know that you are." He sensed that the words were inadequate. They stood that way for a long time, gently rocking —drawing strength from their closeness and their love. Pete could feel her breasts against him. The breasts that had nursed three children, that had given him so much pleasure for so long.

Pete was jolted back to the present by the telephone's insistent ring. He picked it up. "Yes?"

"Hi, Pete, it's Stan."

"What is it, Stan?" His voice was quiet—controlled.

"I just wanted to tell you that I won't be around for dinner tonight. I met an old friend, and we'll be going over to Sausalito."

"Fine, Stan. See you in the morning."

"Pete?"

"Yes?"

"I heard about Kitty being in the hospital. If there's anything I can——"

"Leave it alone, Stan." Pete cut him off. "I'll see you in the morning." He hung up the phone and lay back on the bed, his hands behind his neck. He stared out the windows at the clouds above the city.

Cathy Armello browsed through the magazines at the newsstand in the lobby while she waited for Mike. She had changed into a dark blue body shirt and plaid slacks, and carried her uniform coat over her arm. She had just picked up the latest issue of *Cosmopolitan* when Mike tapped her on the shoulder. "Excuse me, Miss. Would you care to go out to dinner with a dashing young airline pilot?"

Cathy looked at him and laughed. Mike looked like anything but an airline pilot. His long hair was now combed down over his ears, adding to the already bushy appearance of his moustache. Transcon, like all airlines, was paranoid about long hair and Mike had received several warnings about the curls over his collar. Pilots, for the most part, are conservative in dress as well as politics. Since the Flight Operations Department of Transcon was run by pilots, the younger men like Mike were in a constant state of conflict. Especially the single pilots. His friends outside the airline teased him unmercifully about his short hair, and he heard constant rumblings from the Chief Pilot about its being too long. Mike somehow managed to walk the tightrope between getting severely reprimanded by the flight office and being socially acceptable to his peers on the New York singles scene. He wore a brown suede vest over a white turtleneck shirt, boots, and widely flaring double-knit pants. His outfit was punctuated by a chain around his neck with a gold ankh symbol hanging from it.

Cathy was still giggling. "You always tell us how different *we* look in clothes, but, Mike, you're too much!"

He grinned from behind the hair. "Let's go across the street to the Iron Kettle. I'm in the mood for something Italian."

"That's great for my girlish figure, Mike." Cathy returned *Cosmopolitan* to the rack, and they walked out the large front entrance to the little restaurant across the street. A large iron kettle hung over the door.

It was a small, dimly lit place with booths along the walls and tables filling the center of the room. The tables were covered with red-checkered tablecloths, and the ever-present Chianti bottle as a candle holder was centered on each table. Mike and Cathy took a booth next to the front window. A waiter appeared and took their drink order—a Scotch sour for Cathy and bourbon and water for Mike. Up until a short time ago, Transcon, along with most major airlines, had prohibited its pilots from drinking twenty-four hours before a flight. Earlier in the year, however, Transcon changed the rule as had some other airlines, recognizing that the FAA specified only eight hours, and that a cocktail before dinner would not impair a man's judgment at nine the following morning. It was a compromise, and Transcon placed a ten-hour rule on their pilots.

The waiter brought their drinks and left. Mike raised his drink in a minitoast and said, "To life, to love, and to the Iron Kettle's cannelloni stuffed with crabmeat!" Cathy laughed and shook her head as if to say, You're hopeless. Mike looked at her for a long time after she turned to stare out the window.

They had known each other for a long time. Cathy had been working for Transcon for seven years—three years longer than Mike. When he first started with the airline, Cathy had taken him to her rather ample bosom and taught him the way of the world. They first met on a commuter flight to Detroit, Mike's first regular line trip. They were to stay in Detroit for two hours before returning to New York. Mike, trying to appear very self-assured and swaggering with what he thought to be the proper attitude, had asked Cathy to have breakfast. He still remembered her answer.

"Listen, Junior," she had responded, with a little impatience at the fresh kid in front of her. "In the first place, you don't go around taking stewardesses out to eat, because you'll be broke within a month. In the second place, I happen to know how much you make during your first year's probation and it may surprise you to know that my salary is half again what yours is, so you're being stupid. And in the third place"—she had seen his shattered expression and felt instantly sorry for him—"there's a great coffee shop here, so we'll have waffles together, but on *separate* checks."

They had liked each other immediately. Their friendship grew as the years passed. They had tried dating once, about six months after they met, but something had prevented any romantic attachment. Mike would call her occasionally for a movie, and Cathy felt comfortable calling Mike if she needed an escort for one of the affairs she so frequently attended. Sometimes they wouldn't see each other for months and then they would run into each other on a trip, like this evening, and fall back to their old pattern of teasing and verbal sparring.

Cathy was an attractive woman. She had short blond hair that she kept in a pixie cut. She carried the aura of Southern California—all sunshine and outdoors—a healthy glow, coupled with an easy grace that made all her movements appear effortless. Mike had met her parents once, when they had flown a trip to Los Angeles together. Nathan and Sparkle was what Cathy had called them, and Mike had never found out what their real names were. Having dinner with them made it easy for him to see where Cathy had acquired her warmth and effervescence. It was a cozy and secure home—filled with laughter and congeniality, one that Mike enjoyed doubly because his own adolescence had been marred by fighting and divorce when he was thirteen.

Cathy took a cigarette out of her purse and Mike lit it for her. "Where did you get yourself so tan? Take some time off in L.A.?"

"No," she said, "I've been on a cruise in the Caribbean. Remember the last time we flew together? I told you I was going to be on one of those afternoon quiz shows? Well, I won a seven-day cruise and a bunch of other things." In fact, she had won over four thousand dollars' worth of prizes. "It was fabulous! I took my roommate with me. We went to Aruba, Curaçao, St. Lucia—a whole bunch of places." Her excitement was infectious. Mike could picture the two girls basking in the sensuous Caribbean sun. Her roommate, Cheryl, had been a cheerleader with Cathy at U.S.C. They both had magnificent bodies, and Mike was tempted to make an appropriate comment when the waiter arrived to take their order.

He looked at Cathy. She said, "You order for me—surprise me," and gave him an impish grin.

Mike turned to the waiter. "Antipasto for two, we'll both have cannelloni stuffed with crabmeat, and a bottle of Ruffino Rosatello, very cold."

The waiter nodded and left. They were quiet for a time, watching the people rushing by, hurrying to wherever people hurry to in San Francisco on Thursday.

Cathy broke the silence. "What have you been doing with that wreck of an apartment you live in?" She had been in Mike's apartment a couple of times. It was in an older rent-controlled building on East Eighty-third Street, and Mike wasn't one to be concerned with housekeeping on a grand scale. When he had arrived in New York, he had lived with a friend for a month, and then found the apartment. He furnished it with junk from a secondhand furniture store. When Cathy had seen it last, it looked much as it had the day he moved in.

"Well," he said with a laugh, "I've finally gotten someone to come in once a week to clean the place. Furthermore, I'm now dating a girl who claims to be an interior decorator. She works in the furniture department at Bloomingdale's, and promises to make my humble abode a castle in no time."

"Anything serious?" Cathy looked at him, amused.

The waiter brought their antipasto and two plates.

"No, not really." Mike was talking as he served Cathy some of the hot peppers and salami from the huge plate in front of him. "I really don't know what the problem is, Cathy. I can't seem to get excited about any of the girls I've met lately. God knows I'm surrounded by beautiful women—that last batch from stew school was something out of this world. But I just can't stomach all the giggling and childish reactions any more. It seems I've gotten too old to enjoy the fruits of youth. It doesn't seem worth it to put up with a lot of immature behavior just to go to bed with someone." He laughed at himself. "Listen to me . . . the old man at twenty-nine. Take Jeannie, my decorator friend—she's attractive, nice to wake up with, but there's something missing, Cathy. She's so turned on to the Upper-East-Side-New York way of life. I guess it took this job to show me that there was more to life than singles bars, and phrases like 'where did you go to school?' It gets old so quickly." He looked at her. The brown eyes had been watching him intently. "Sorry about that," he said. "There aren't a lot of people who would understand the feelings."

Cathy started to speak, but the waiter was putting down the enormous dishes of cannelloni. She waited until he had left. "I know what you mean, Mike. I can remember when I first got to New York as a brand-new stewardess. I was going to set the world on fire then. Funny how it all changes when you get a perspective by seeing the rest of the country—the world, for that matter."

The waiter returned, bringing a bottle of wine, and poured a small amount into Mike's glass. He tasted it, nodded to the waiter, then turned back to Cathy. She was looking out the window again, and Mike followed her gaze. Stan and Susan were getting into the bright yellow Shelby across the street.

"Who do you think she is?" Cathy looked at Mike.

"Beats me. Stan's a pretty straight guy—I can't imagine he'd have something going for himself here, and a fianceé waiting at home."

Cathy watched as the car swiftly left the curb. "She's a stunning woman, whoever she is. I think Stan's got his hands full."

"Hey! This stuff is going to get cold!" Mike attacked the food on his plate like a man who hadn't eaten in days.

Donald Greco looked at the soggy mass of potatoes on the stainless-steel tray. They were cold and unappetizing.

The meat had been lukewarm, but at least edible. The potatoes and limp string beans were unpalatable. He put his fork down and shoved the tray to the end of the bunk. Greco looked around him. The cell was much like most of the cells that he'd spent fifteen of the last twenty-two years inhabiting. The walls were bare, except for the inevitable graffiti—cruder than what one sees on buildings and in washrooms. One side of the cell was open, with bars floor to ceiling. An electronically controlled door took up half of the barred wall. Two bunks were hinged to one wall, supported by chains on the sides—across from the bunks were a toilet and washbowl. The washbowl had a green stain from the continually dripping faucet. The top bunk was hinged up against the wall because as an escapee, and transient prisoner, Greco was segregated from the regular prison population.

He was segregated at meals now, too, since the two fights he'd started in the mess hall. The guard who had brought his meal had been snide when he shoved the tray under the small space beneath the bars created for just that purpose.

"Greco," he had said, "we ain't gonna miss you one bit around here. I heard you was leaving, and I'm sorry I won't be here in the mornin' to say good-bye." He had taken a long look at the prisoner—a special look that he saved for those convicts he truly disliked—and walked away before Greco could reply.

The sullen man wouldn't have replied anyway, so the guard's attempt at dramatics had been a wasted effort. He sat with his head against the wall, his black hair falling over his forehead, almost obscuring the narrow black eyes that darted back and forth in constant motion. He held his large hands clasped over his knees with his feet on the bunk. When the guard had returned to his station at the end of the cell block, Greco rose and retrieved the tray from the floor. He had tried to eat the meal.

He looked at the tray again, picked it up, and hurled it against the opposite wall. The crash of metal on concrete brought the guard back at a dead run to his cell. He looked at the mess on the wall and now dripping down to the floor, then turned to the prisoner. "Screw you, Greco. I hope it smells good by the time you get up, 'cause I ain't about to worry myself over your sanitary conditions." He went back to the guard station, laughing.

Greco decided the guard was an ass. They all were. That one at Cook County Jail who had turned his back on him long enough for Greco to grab his gun—he was a beaut! The expression on his face had been one of disbelief as he had pulled the trigger. The guard was off the critical list. Greco had read about it in a newspaper while in a boxcar traveling west. The rest of the escape had been easy. He had forced the other guard to the floor—something anyone would do willingly when he saw his friend's guts all over the floor. Greco had commandeered a passing cab using the gun, and fled the city one step ahead of the police. He had still been running when they caught him in Ogden, three weeks later. The only difference was that now the feds were going to be his captors, and even Greco had to admit that federal law officials weren't dumb.

He lay down on the bunk and studied the pattern of steel strapping on the bunk against the wall above his head. He was tired of being in prison. He decided that it restricted his movement too much. The walls were starting to close in on him as they had two years ago. Then, he had stayed out of trouble because he had been up for parole in a few weeks. Now, he was facing life—with no chance of parole because of the escape. He shuddered a bit —something uncontrollable—and kicked the wall in frustration.

The giant storm crashed on toward the southeast, its wind now officially measured at fifty-five miles per hour. In Kansas City, a government meteorologist turned to the teletypewriter and started to transmit over the severe weather circuit:

Susan MacKenzie stared out the large plate-glass window at the lights of San Francisco. The Spinnaker Restaurant is built on pilings over an arm of the bay in Sausalito. The city sparkled like a diamond necklace across the water. They had been silent for almost the entire drive, Stan intent on guiding the car through the streets of the city, then onto the highway, past the Presidio, and on across the Golden Gate Bridge. What little conversation there had been had been restrained and noncommittal. It was as if each of them, after the initial excitement of their chance meeting, had retreated to regroup and assess a military situation. The silence had continued as they turned off the freeway just after crossing the bridge and drove down the winding approach road into the little community of Sausalito. The town had been a shelter for Susan during the past twelve months, and whenever she got too depressed or felt too sorry for herself she would come here—to walk along the familiar streets past the many shops and stores that were outlets for the local artists and craftsmen. It would soothe her to browse in a leather shop, looking at belts and handbags, or to explore the Village Fair—a large conglomerate of shops that sold everything from art to wine.

Stan had parked the car on the main street and they walked to the restaurant, not touching, but close. The Spinnaker dominated the point of a long spit of land reaching out into the water. As they walked along the path to the restaurant, Stan said, "I love this place—the town, its setting—it's almost a storybook place."

"I know. I used to do some shopping here."

They went in through the big front doors. The maitre d' recognized Stan. "Good evening, Mr. Burkhart, it's a pleasure to see you again." He had smiled his best professional smile at Susan and led them across the dining room

· 41 ·

to a table in the corner by the windows. He seated Susan, then turned to Stan. "Mr. Burkhart, let me know if there is anything you need." He made a half-bow and left them.

As Stan ordered drinks Susan thought, Again? I wonder when he was here before, and with whom? Was it Ellen? She stopped herself, feeling like a jealous female, and turned to look across the bay. The moon was completely hidden now, but the air was still crystal-clear. The waiter had set their drinks down quietly.

"Susan?" Stan was looking at her, holding his glass as if to toast to . . . to what?

"Oh! Sorry." She touched his glass lightly with hers. "It's just so beautiful!" She nodded toward the city.

"Yes, that's why I like it here so much." He was silent. They watched two couples in their early twenties being seated at a table across the room. Stan started to chuckle softly.

"What's so funny?" She knew the answer before she had finished the question, and joined in his amusement.

They had first met, or rather seen each other, in a little dingy bar near Stan's apartment eight years before. The unique thing about the place was that it was one of the few bars in New York that had a jukebox and a dance floor. There were booths along three walls, surrounding the dance floor, and a jukebox that played nothing but slow, lazy music. Someone once said that dancing (as it was then) was just an excuse for making love standing up with clothes on, and that's what most of the couples in the place were doing. Stan was with a girl who had been a casual date, and who was also quite drunk at the time. He had given up trying to carry on a conversation with her and was about to suggest that they leave when two couples walked into the bar and took a booth directly opposite them. He was thinking how interesting it is to place people into a category based only on observation. It was a game he often played with himself when he was bored.

He watched the two couples for a few minutes and made two observations: first, the tall brunette and her date were very close—he could tell by the way they sat with each other. They were relaxed, natural about their touch, easy with their smiles—probably married or engaged, he decided. The second conclusion was that the girl with the short red hair and her date, a guy with huge arms and hands, were either fighting or had just met, because they were sitting apart from each other and not talking much. Fascinated, he ordered another drink for himself and his date and continued to watch.

Stan assessed the redhead as she and her date danced by the booth. She was a stunning girl—about twenty—short and petite. The legs beneath the short skirt were perfect, punctuated at the ends by tiny feet. He watched her giant of a date try to pull her closer as they danced, and watched her push him away with equal force—a standoff. Somehow that pleased him. As they danced past again, he met her eyes over the giant's shoulder, and their glance locked for a long moment—much longer than strangers who make eye contact usually look at each other. He looked away. He knew that she was watching him now, too, and he tried to figure a way to make some sort of sign. But how? A crazy idea began forming in his mind, which was now a bit hazy from his fifth drink. He took a business card out of his wallet and wrote on the back, *Please call me tomorrow*, signed it *Stan*, and hid it under the table.

He sat for a while, hiding the card from his date. Finally, the giant the redhead was with got up to go to the men's room. The other couple was locked in an embrace on the dance floor. Stan asked his date to dance. She got up, a little unsteadily, and they danced toward the table where the red-haired girl was sitting alone. He saw that she was watching, and dropped the card on the table in front of her—praying that she wouldn't get up and show it to his date or, worse yet, show it to the brute she was with. Stan saw her read his message, look at it with some amusement, and quickly put the card in her purse. He had left the bar quickly after that, not looking back.

She had called the next day.

"Hi, Stan, it's me." Her voice was soft and melodic. There had been a long embarrassed pause on the phone.

"Who is me?"

"Susan MacKenzie."

They met for dinner that evening. Stan picked her up at the student nurses' residence at Columbia Presbyterian Hospital. They ate at Pete's Tavern, an old historic place near Stan's apartment, and they were in love—very much in love—by dessert.

They lived together for two years. At least, they lived together when Susan wasn't at the hospital. She was barely twenty years old, Stan only twenty-four, but the first year of their relationship was a combination of maturity and discovery—much like a rare vintage wine, tasted for the first time. A year after they met Susan graduated from nursing school and took a job at St. Vincent's Hospital near the apartment. Stan, having had a private pilot's license, decided to continue flying in order to work for the airlines. All the major carriers were desperate for pilots, Vietnam having dried up the source of military fliers, and Stan loved flying with a passion that Susan couldn't understand. That lack of understanding was probably what created the first tension between them. The friction grew, as it always will when there is a breakdown in communication between lovers, and when it was at its peak, Susan met Jack Crowley. Stan was never quite sure how they had met, but within a month she had married him. Stan converted his pain into energy and redoubled his efforts to get the necessary flying hours to qualify for an airline job. Six months later, he had been in a New Pilot Class at Transcon's training center.

Susan looked across the table at Stan. "Were you thinking about it, too?"

"Yes, I guess I was."

"Stan . . . tell me about Ellen." She was putting them back on a friends' basis, he thought. "There was one thing that you didn't say in the coffee shop at the airport."

"Oh? What was that?

She looked into his eyes without blinking. "That you love her."

"I do." Stan looked away. "I guess." The waiter brought menus to the table, and Stan was thankful for the interruption—he could gather his thoughts. "Oh, I don't know what to say about it, Susan. We've been together for a long time—almost three years—but it doesn't seem to be going anywhere. It's kind of like an old coat—it doesn't always look so good, but it's comfortable to wear, and it's warm in the cold." The waiter arrived again, and Stan ordered dinner and wine.

Susan watched as he ordered, and again was reminded of his calm, self-assured manner. She was impressed, but refused to admit it to herself. When the waiter had left she asked, "Are you living in the same place?" For some reason it was important to her.

"No, I moved about a year after you left . . . married Jack. I bought in on a little brownstone down the block from the old apartment, and I've been there ever since. Why? Is it important?"

"I don't know," she said. "Silly woman thoughts, I guess. We had so much there . . . at the old place, I mean. I just hated to think that you were sharing it with someone else."

He laughed. "You haven't changed much in eight years —still so emotional about unimportant things." He had said it kindly.

"And you don't get that way any more, I suppose? Have you seen *The Fantasticks* recently?"

The Fantasticks was a show that they had seen together many times. It was a fairy-tale kind of musical that had played in Greenwich Village for several years, and every time Stan saw it, he wept like a kid. He decided to change the subject.

"Why did you change your name back to MacKenzie?"

"Oh, I don't know . . . Too many unhappy thoughts connected with the other name, I guess. Jack and I never had any kids, so it didn't make any difference." Susan took a sip of wine and set the glass down carefully, keeping her fingers on the crystal stem. "I never told you why I married him, did I?"

Stan paused as the waiter refilled their glasses. "I just assumed that he had more to offer you than I did, and that was what you wanted."

Susan was looking across the bay, gently shaking her head. "Well, in a way that's why." She turned to him, almost angrily. "Oh, Stan! You were always so involved with flying, so dedicated to reaching for the most important thing in your life. I thought that I should have been that most important thing. When Jack came along, he made me feel like I *was* the most important thing." She shook her head again, bitterly. "What a mistake!"

"What happened, Susan?"

"Well . . . nothing . . . that was the problem. When I met Jack he was an administrator at the hospital. He said that wasn't a challenge after a while, so we moved to Denver, where he tried his hand at real estate, then to Phoenix, and on, and on. The real trouble was that he *had* no goals. As we moved from place to place, he became more dependent on me, and my salary. I finally couldn't take it any more. We had a fight—a big one—and he left. I found out about a girl he had stashed away in an apartment, and I finally called it quits. We were in Vegas at the time, so the divorce was easy and quick. My parents helped a bit financially, and when it was all over, I came here." She nodded her head toward the city. She lit a cigarette and relaxed visibly.

"I'm sorry, Susan, so sorry." He said it gently. He looked at her profile as she stared out the window and thought, You're more beautiful than ever, Susan. I'm sorry that you were hurt, but it has seasoned you well. Your eyes show a wisdom that wasn't there before. And how thick is the wall that you've built to insulate yourself?

Stan felt as if he were in a chess game. The opening moves had been played at the airport, he and Susan placing their knights and bishops—moving the pawns aside too quickly. Now they were finishing the middle game—with most of their defensive pieces gone, and others strongly positioned for the end game. And how *would* this game end? In a draw? Or would one of them topple the other's king?

Susan brought him back to reality. "Will you actually be flying the plane tomorrow?" She laughed. "I mean . . . What does a copilot do?"

"Well, he has the best job in the cockpit—all of the fun, and none of the responsibility. Technically, he's second in command, and should anything happen to the captain, he would take over the responsibility. In answer to your first question, yes, I'll be flying half the time. The captain and the copilot usually split the flying chores down the middle—the captain flying one leg of the trip while the copilot handles the radios, then the copilot flying the next leg. The only time that doesn't happen is if there's an unusual situation like weather, or an emergency. In that case, the captain takes over the flying and earns his salary."

"Are there many of these 'unusual situations,' as you call them?" She looked a little worried.

He smiled. "No, very few—one a year is a lot—usually none at all."

They talked through dessert and three cups of coffee

and tea. About Stan's career, about Susan's job and the one she hoped to find in New York, they talked on and on, bringing themselves closer together. They looked into each other's eyes and hearts, both looking hard—afraid, not of what they might find, but of what they might not find. They spoke of philosophies, and goals, and emotions, and were drawn together by what they learned.

Stan signaled for the check and paid. They sat silently for a few minutes. He was taking a last sip from the gold-rimmed cup when the two young couples got up from their table. They both watched the four people leave, sharing something new, and yet old. No checkmate for this game.

"We should go." Stan broke their silence. He looked at her for a long time. "Susan . . . will you stay with me tonight?"

She looked at her purse on the table—silent—then started to pick it up. It had been long, so long since . . . Stan covered her small hand with his.

"Yes." It was barely audible. "I want to."

Stan saw the brightness in her eyes, the lower lids brimming with tears.

She nodded her head, smiling, and louder now—"Yes."

> *"During major weather disruptions, it shall be the respon-*
> *sibility of the chief dispatcher to coordinate with crew*
> *scheduling and aircraft planning sections so as to minimize*
> *the effect of such weather over the company's system."*

> Transcon Airlines Regulations, Vol. III
> Sec. 25-I, Para. 9

3

She was running at him, her hands high in the air carrying a dark, dripping mass. She was naked. Her face had no features—only a huge mouth that was wide open in a silent scream. Where her left breast should have been there was a massive bleeding wound. When she got very close, she hurled the object at him—it was a breast.

Pete sat bolt upright in the bed. He was sweating. It was cold, and he was crying. The dream had been so real, so terrifying. He sat on the bed for a moment, his hands covering his face, then swung his legs over the edge of the bed and walked to the bathroom, the bile of fear in his throat. He threw up. When the fear had subsided, he rinsed his mouth and returned to the bed. He sat by the phone, tempted to call, but decided it was too late. Pete picked up a pack of cigarettes from the night table and lit one, dragging the smoke deep into his lungs. Calm began to return.

He thought of Kitty—probably asleep in the hospital room, lying on her side the way she always did. He thought of her strength, of her ability to see his needs before he himself could, and then to lend him the strength he felt he lacked. Pete had always felt deep down inside that women had more courage than men. Oh, they would cry easily, and seem to come unglued at trivial things. But when real stark crisis reared its ugly head, it had always been Kitty that kept life moving.

He remembered when Pete Jr. had died. He had been killed in a light-plane crash in Pennsylvania. Petey—they called him that to keep the two men from being confused —had been taking a friend to a high-school reunion when the engine quit and the plane started to descend. He had picked out an emergency landing field, and they had made it when a small child darted out of the woods into their path. In avoiding the child, Petey had put the aircraft into the trees. His friend walked away with only a broken arm —Petey had died on the way to the hospital.

Pete and Kitty had been having dinner when the call came from the Pennsylvania State Police. Pete had answered and, after a brief conversation, had said, "Yes, we'll be there in the morning. Thank you for calling." He hung up the phone and turned to his wife. "Kitty . . . Petey's been in an accident. He's dead."

She hadn't said a word. She got up from the table, visibly white, and walked to the big couch by the fireplace and sat down. She shook her head slowly back and forth, not wanting to believe. Then she looked at Pete. "How?"

"Apparently his engine failed near Wilkes-Barre. Hal will be all right, they said, only a broken arm."

"I see." Still no visible emotion. She looked around, as

if distracted. "Pete? Do you want some coffee? It'll only take me a minute to . . . " She had started to rise, then sat back down and buried her face in her arms on the end of the couch and silently sobbed.

Pete went to her, knelt down with his arm around her, and stroked her hair. They remained together for more than an hour, and then she was all right. He gave her some tea and put her to bed. He decided to tell Petey's two younger brothers in the morning. The boy had been a carbon copy of his father—tall, lean, with the same sparkling blue eyes and the same passion for flying that Pete had.

He had poured himself a brandy and sat in the big leather chair across from the fireplace and read, then re-read, the letter. He hadn't even told Kitty—it was to be a surprise for her after dinner. He poured himself another brandy. The printing of the green and gold Transcon letterhead blurred as the tears came. He couldn't read the rest again:

> *Dear Pete,*
>   *I just got a call from the Personnel department. Petey has been accepted, into Transcon New Pilot Class #43 starting on June 12. He'll get the official notification in a few days, but I wanted you to know.*
>   *Congratulations—it will be an asset to have two Douglasses flying on the line.*
>
>   *Best regards,*
>   *Bob Quinlan*
>   *Chief Pilot*

Kitty had found him in the chair the next morning, next to the empty brandy bottle. The letter was on the floor. She picked it up, read it, and wept just a bit more. Then she fixed coffee and toast, and when it was ready she gently woke her husband.

For the next week she had taken care of everything—she told the two younger boys, handled most of the funeral arrangements, and received the sorrow of their friends. She had to, because Pete had fallen into a deep depression that he wouldn't shake until long after their son's death.

And now, more than a year later, Pete realized that Kitty was his real strength. He had leaned on her—relied on her a great deal since Petey. But starting tomorrow, he promised himself, he would try to be *her* pillar of support. His renewed determination brought an inner calm, and he lay back on the bed. Just before he drifted off to sleep he noticed it was one-thirty Pacific time—it would be four-thirty in New York and the nurses would be waking Kitty soon.

The large clock on the wall in Dispatch said three thirty-five. The sign underneath it read: CENTRAL STANDARD TIME—FOR GREENWICH ADD SIX HOURS.

Lars Gunter had been on duty for almost ten hours, and judging from the papers and maps strewn on the desk in front of him, he would be in Transcon's Central Dispatch office for a long time to come. As the airline's senior Chief Dispatcher, it was his responsibility to manage the aircraft along Transcon's far-flung routes in such a way as to keep unused aircraft to a minimum. Normally, this was done by the scheduling and planning sections, but with a storm of this magnitude and resulting disruptions to service, the job was turned over to Lars. He worked in conjunction with the other dispatchers across the country, and with the aircraft planning office in a dimly lit room two stories below.

He spoke into the phone. "I'm canceling all flights into Idaho, Montana, and the Dakotas as of four A.M., Central Time. Denver will probably close an hour or so before Salt Lake, so we'd better cancel flight 456, San Fran–Denver, and operate a downline section from Wichita east."

He had a map of the United States in front of him with a clear plastic overlay on top of it. On the clear plastic, shading of different colors depicted the projected path of the storm and how far from the center of the storm the weather bureau predicted heavy snow. On the desk next to the map was a thick book that Gunter referred to on occasion. This was the *Red Book*. The red had long since been replaced by a sturdy black binder, but it still said RED BOOK on the cover. Inside the large manual were the contingency plans that Transcon had compiled for almost any eventuality. There was a section entitled *Hijacking*, with all appropriate State Department phone numbers, both office and home phones, should the airline have to contact key government people during the incident; *Missing aircraft/Overdue aircraft* cataloged proper procedures for handling families and press should that situation ever arise; *Inflight Emergency* dealt with procedures to be instituted should an aircraft become disabled in the air and require emergency handling when it landed. There were several other sections in the book, and Lars Gunter was carefully studying the section marked *Severe Weather, West*. This detailed recommended cancellations and aircraft reroutings so that half of Transcon's sizable fleet would not get stranded at airports that were closed by the snow.

He picked up the phone again. "Planning? Let's cancel flight 128 out of Salt Lake and have the crew ferry the aircraft to the West Coast—probably Portland. We could use it there because I'm canceling 127 westbound from Chicago." He put the phone down and looked at the message that a clerk had just handed him. "Shit!" He threw down his pencil and picked up the phone again.

The man in the planning room answered with patience —it was as confused down there as it was in the Central Dispatch office. "Yes, Lars?"

"We just blew our first one—they've closed the airport at Boise and we've got a 727 there." He was angry. "I wish to hell they'd get more snow equipment." Lars didn't want to realize that all the snow equipment in the world could not have kept the airport open in this storm.

"OK, Lars, I'll take it off the 'in service' board—what's the number?"

"It's plane number 709."

"Fine . . . and, Lars?"

"Yes?"

"Relax, will you?"

Lars said, half to the phone and half to the clerk next to him, "Relax, the man says! We've got the worst fucking snowstorm in fifty years and Charlie Cool downstairs says *relax*!" He sat down at his desk and ran his hands over his thin hair. He turned to one of the other dispatchers and said, "Hey, Roger—I'll flip you for coffee."

Roger got out his coin, smiling, and they went through the ritual. Lars lost.

The normally quiet dispatcher said "Shit!" one more time, kicked the desk and started for the coffeepot. As he was pouring the second cup, the severe-weather teletype rang three times and started printing at high speed:

SEVERE WEATHER BULLETIN #9—BULLETIN #8
CANCELED . . .

Lars looked at the clock—it was only three forty-five and he had already canceled twenty-seven trips. That meant twenty-seven groups of unhappy passengers, and a lot of money that would not be paid to Transcon. Christ, Lars thought, why don't I work in a bank? He went back to the big desk to answer an insistent telephone and sat down.

In Salt Lake, Donald Greco turned in his bunk. It was cold in the cell. He looked out the windows above his head—two little slits with wire mesh across the glass. The snow had started to fall in little flurries. He considered complaining to the guard about the cold, but decided it wouldn't help—the bastard would only laugh at him.

He could stand the chill anyway—his mind was too active to sleep and the cold made him more alert. He hadn't slept since the lights went out in the cell block. No . . . one more night here wasn't worth a stink. Donald Greco made a vow to himself in the cold cell: After this night, he would never set foot in a prison again.

His mind stimulated by his decision, he sat up on his bunk, his back against the cool wall. His mind started working on probabilities—the probabilities of the next day. He remembered being transferred from jail to jail in Chicago. There were weaknesses there. In and out of cars, different rooms, doors. Lots of possibilities for escape. Greco's mind worked like a calculator. He was street-wise, sensitive to slips in procedure, aware of chinks in the penal system's amor. His entire life had been spent capitalizing on others' lack of foresight. He decided that the ride from Point-of-the-Mountain to the airport was probably the weakest link in the transportation back to Chicago. Barring that, the airplane itself held possibilities. Initially, his mind, like a misprogrammed computer, spit out the airplane as an escape—too many security problems. The nation's alarm over hijacking had made the airports bristle with lawmen, federal customs men, security guards. Too risky in the airport. But he held the thought long enough to think about the airplane itself. Once on the plane he could weigh the possibilities as he had done all his life.

He tried to recall all he knew about airplanes. He had been on an airliner only once—four years before. The memory was hazy—and it was impossible to formulate a plan until he knew the man or men that would be with him to escort him. They were the key to everything.

Donald Greco pulled the gray blanket tighter around his shoulders and pressed himself against the wall. He began once more to trace tomorrow's movements, looking for flaws.

Stan moved his left arm gently, trying not to disturb Susan. His watch said it was one forty-five. Susan stirred with his movement and buried her head deeper into his shoulder. She made a sighing sound and swallowed—Stan could feel her throat muscles work against the skin of his chest.

"I'm not asleep," she said, and moved her body closer to his. Her left leg pulled him against her warmth. Her voice was soft and furry. "Do you want a cigarette?"

"Mmmm."

"What does that mean?"

He chuckled. "It means, why do people like to have a cigarette after they've made love to each other?"

Susan pressed her breasts against him and inched up to kiss his throat, just below his left ear. "You still haven't answered my question."

"OK, I'll get them." He left the warm bed reluctantly and padded across to the dresser for cigarettes and matches. He returned and sat on the bed facing her, one leg on the bed, his knee touching her hip, the other foot on the floor. He lit two cigarettes. Stan looked at her in the match glow. The sheet was across her thighs—one arm was bent behind her head, the other rested on his leg. Stan had left the bathroom light on and the door partly open so that when the match went out, he could still see her in the soft light. His hand joined his gaze as he traced the curves of her body. He said finally, "You're an incredible woman, Susan."

"You're something yourself." She said it gently.

He touched the copper hair, dark in the dim room as it lay across the pillow. "I like it this long—it's exciting."

Susan said nothing, just smiled and looked at him. They weren't shy with each other any more. Their closeness had returned, bathing the lovers in a glow that surprised both of them.

They had been shy—briefly shy when they got to Stan's room. He had opened the door and stood back. Susan hesitated, looking into the room.

Stan looked at her. "Susan . . . you don't . . . "

She shook her head, as if she had resolved the argument in her mind, and walked into the room. Stan had turned out the light and opened the curtains fully. They sat on the bed—not too close. She turned to look at him in the soft light. "Stan, what will you think?" She hadn't said it indignantly, as most women do; rather it was a request for reassurance.

"Is it important?"

"Yes." She closed her eyes. "Very important."

Stan turned to her and took her face gently in both hands. He lifted her face to his—the tears were starting to brim at the bottom of her eyes; she was blinking to keep them back. "I think . . . I think that you are the loveliest woman I have ever seen. I think that I'm very glad that you were in the airport this afternoon. I think" —she started to speak and he shook his head—"that we learned of love, and life, and a million other things from each other—and knowing that—there is no place else you should be but right here."

She buried her head in his chest and whispered, "Thank you. . . . It's been so long, so very long. And I'm scared."

He knew that she would be all right now, and he laughed softly. "There's too much between us to be scared. Come here." He stood up and, drawing her up with him, tipped her head to his and kissed her—softly, warmly. He took his lips from hers and said, "Hi there—it's nice to see you." She smiled and he kissed her again—longer, more urgently. They clung together for a long moment. Then he took her arms from around his neck and put them gently to her side. He unbuttoned her dress and slipped it from her shoulders. She shuddered and shook her hair around her neck as he touched her breast.

He was gentle—more gentle than she remembered. They undressed each other in silence and lay between the cool sheets. They explored, touched, kissed, rediscovering a long-forgotten fire that had burned so brightly in a little apartment years before. Neither of them spoke as they washed away their own hurts by glorying in each other's sensuality. It was different, and yet the same—there had been others between that time, when they had taught each other, and now. But it was like a scent recalled from a far-off childhood. They remembered. They made love slowly, soothingly, as if there were no clock and no location. Hemingway would have said that the earth moved, but for Stan there was no earth—nothing except Susan— as their passions peaked and ebbed. The fire left slowly, taking all of their fears and doubts from them.

When he left her, she had whimpered, and he pulled her close—kissing the tears away. They had lain that way for an eternity.

And now reality slowly replaced unreality. "Stan?" Susan touched his thigh. "What happens when we get to New York tomorrow?"

"I don't know . . . it's all too fast. I wasn't prepared for this."

"Neither was I."

Stan took another cigarette from the pack and offered it to her. She shook her head. Her hair flowed across the pillow. He shrugged and looked out the window. "It'll take a few days to get things straightened out when I get back."

"I know . . . I'm going to need a day or two to get my thoughts in order, too. Stan? Could it happen all over again? I mean . . . has too much gone by to, well, to try again?"

"I don't know, Susan. I just don't know."

She retreated. "Neither do I. This whole thing seems like such a dream . . . I just——"

He looked at the clock and quieted her by putting his fingers to her lips. He said softly, "Hey. It's almost two-fifteen. I've got to get a little sleep or I'll be a wreck tomorrow. Be right back." He got up and walked toward the bathroom.

Her laugh was like a crystal bell. "Good old ten-minute-bladder Stan."

He returned to the bed and put his arms around her as he lay down. They were both asleep within minutes.

At three-fifteen, the storm claimed its first victim.

Joshua Belson heaved the farmhouse door open against the drifted snow. It required a lot of force—the drifts were better than three feet, and the center of the storm had not passed Nashua, Montana. Josh plunged his way through the drifts to the barn. He was going out to check some livestock there, and to make sure that the upper shutters of the building were barred tight against the howling wind.

He looked around during the tortuous hundred yards to the barn. The visibility was so poor that he could barely make out the shapes of the farm machinery in front of the silo. They had been obscured by swirling snow, and as he approached he saw that the big tractor was drifted to the top of its tires with new snow. He finally got the barn door open and went inside. All seemed peaceful despite the swirling storm outside—there was just a small amount of snow creeping in through a broken window-pane. Josh covered the pane with a piece of plywood, and looked slowly around before returning to the house. The barn was quiet, with most of the animals either asleep or eating the hay he had rearranged. The sounds came from outside—the wind was whipping the giant tackle that was suspended from a large beam that extended beyond the roof at its peak. They used it when the hay was baled, lifting three or four bales at a time to the loft. Josh cursed himself for forgetting to remove the rope and two heavy blocks when they had finished bringing in the hay two months ago.

He pushed hard on the barn door and it grudgingly opened against the wind. He turned around, his back to the wind, to swing the heavy bar across the double door.

As he dropped the bar in place, a violent gust of wind wrenched the eye hook from the beam directly above his head. The seventy-five-pound collection of rope and hardware slashed across Josh's neck and shoulders. The force of the blow pitched him headfirst into the barn doors. He slid to the ground silently, lying parallel to the wall. The wind moaned through the loft thirty feet above where he lay.

In fifteen minutes Joshua Belson was covered by the drifting snow. It would be two hours before his body was found, and during those two hours the giant storm crashed across the Canadian border, moving steadily southeastward at a speed of thirty-five miles per hour. The Canadian Pacific reported that three of its trains were known to be stranded—one, the crack transcontinental supertrain that ran daily from Vancouver to Winnipeg, was trapped in a mountain pass in Alberta. Fortunately for the more than one hundred passengers, the Canadian Pacific always carried extra fuel and food supplies during the winter. It would take three days before the tracks could be cleared sufficiently for the train to proceed eastbound.

The storm roared on, leaving a trail of death and destruction a thousand miles wide—sealing off most farms and towns in the northern west—and the people living in its path prepared for a long period of cold and quiet.

"Each certificate holder shall have an inspection program and a program covering other maintenance, preventative maintenance, and alterations that insures that . . . (b) Competent personnel and adequate facilities are provided . . . and (c) Each aircraft released to service is airworthy and has been properly maintained for operation in air transportation."

Federal Air Regulations
Part 121.367

4

Jerry Guccione hung his trousers in his locker and slipped into the white coveralls with the green-embroidered Transcon insignia across the back. He buttoned the coveralls, kissed his fingers and transferred the kiss to the buttocks of the girl from a centerfold that was taped to the wall of his locker, and closed the door. He snapped the combination lock shut and walked out of the locker room to the mechanics' line shack nestled in the corner of the mammoth hangar.

He walked through the door. "Morning, Mac. What's the exciting news for today?"

Mac McDonald, a lead mechanic who had been with

Transcon for twenty-seven years, put down the big metal logbook he had been writing in. "Morning, Jerry. Not much of anything happening right now—only a brake change on one of the 747s, an engine change on two"—he held up his fingers—"count 'em, two DC-10s, and new tires for an airplane that blew two when it landed last night. Same old shit."

"Christ! Why do we get all the crap on the three-to-noon shift?" Jerry poured himself some coffee and sat on the corner of the supervisor's desk. He looked around the room at the nudes taped to the cinderblock walls. The room was the size of a small, one-car garage. There was a long, chest-high table running the length of one wall with several of the cumbersome aircraft logs that are kept aboard every commercial airplane strewn along its length. The logbook was a complete history of the plane. Block-to-block times, engine performance readings, and any mechanical discrepancies were written down by the flight crew after each flight. If there was anything mechanically wrong with the plane, on the page that noted the problem a mechanic had to write in what had been done to correct it and then sign his name.

Across the room from the shelf holding the logbooks were two desks. One was for the lead mechanic on duty, and the other, where Jerry so comfortably sat, was for the maintenance supervisor. Jerry Guccione was a small, muscular man. He had dark eyes that matched his long hair. He reminded one of an Italian James Cagney in many respects. There was a conflict in his personality, however; his temper did not match his Sicilian background. He was quick and energetic. No one had ever heard him complain (something that is quite unique in a mechanics shack) even when he had worked for hours, outside, on a cold wet morning when bare fingers would numb in a few minutes. He had lost his temper only once. It had been in New York before Jerry transferred to San Francisco two years ago. The cause of the fight had been long forgotten, but when it was over, Jerry had put two men in the hospital. The story had preceded him to San Francisco, as reputations often do. When the local brawler challenged him, Jerry had only laughed and offered to buy the man a beer after their shift was over. They had come to work the following day as close friends, and none of the mechanics ever knew what transpired after work. He was well liked, and had been offered a lead mechanic's job several times. Each time he had turned it down because his real love was working on airplanes, and as a lead, his time would have been divided between working and administrating. That idea didn't appeal to him at all.

He drained his coffee in one gulp and turned to the burly McDonald. "Have you got anyone on overtime, Mac?"

"Yeah. Connaly and Snyder stayed on after the night shift to help on the 747 brake job."

"Do you want me on one of the engine changes?" Jerry stubbed out his cigarette in the overflowing ashtray on the desk.

"Hell no. You worked your ass off on that 727 nose-gear retract yesterday. I've got an easy one for you. Aircraft 718 came in last night and it's due for a twenty-five-hour check. The only write-up was a leak in the hydraulic compartment."

Jerry was looking at one of the nudes on the wall—a blonde with gigantic breasts. "I remember the airplane— it was clean the last time it was out here." He had an incredible memory. The numbers of all of Transcon's airplanes were cataloged in his mind. He had an ever-present picture of every plane in his head, and could recall a minor dent in a wing or a chronic system problem whenever a number was mentioned. Aircraft 718 was a 727. The first number, seven, represented the type of aircraft. The last two numbers corresponded to the number of that type of aircraft in Transcon's fleet, and when it had been acquired. Airplane 718 was the eighteenth 727 that the airline had purchased. It was one of the newer ones in the fleet, and Jerry remembered that it had had few problems.

He hopped off the desk. "I'll get on it. How much time do I have?"

"About three hours. It has to be at the terminal at seven this morning. It's going out as flight 602 at eight."

"OK, Mac." Jerry walked to the door, looking once more at the busty blonde on the wall. "See ya later—I'll call when I'm done."

He opened the door and was flooded with a crescendo of sound. Even at this hour of the morning—darkness outside—the hangar was as bright as daylight. The glare from three hundred fluorescent lights illuminated the hangar like a tropic sun. There was noise everywhere. The accoustics in the giant building were terrible, and a wrench dropped on the floor at one end of the hangar would echo and re-echo across the vast open area. He walked past the monster 747 that was up on huge jacks, the wheels a foot off the floor. There were three jacks in all—one under each wing near the fuselage, and one under the nose, just aft of the nose wheels. Four men were huddled near one of the four massive landing-gear trucks, under the right wing. Jerry liked the 747—it was a well-designed airplane—but he felt it was a pain to work on. Everything was so big that special vehicles and tools had had to be designed to maintain it. Half the work had to be done twenty feet in the air, or higher, and Jerry didn't like heights. One of the men under the wing waved as he walked past. Jerry waved back and continued toward the far end of the hangar.

He passed one of the DC-10s—its engine cowl off and a large chain hoist rolled into position to remove the engine from the left wing. As he neared the 727 he was to work on, he noticed how it was dwarfed by the two aircraft he had just passed. He laughed to himself as he thought back to when he had first started with Transcon. The largest airplane they had then was the DC-6, a four-engine propeller type. The green queen with the golden pussy was the nickname it had because of the rather unique paint scheme. But it was the largest and best aircraft of its time. And now the 727 he stood next to was small when compared with the jumbo jets, yet it was almost twice the weight of a DC-6. He shook his head and wondered, Where will it all stop?

Jerry looked up at the airplane. He liked the 727—it was easy to work on, and most of the maintenance could be performed at ground level, or from a small flatbed truck that could be raised about six feet. The only real problem was the soaring T-tail. To work on the tail, they had to use a cherry picker—much the same kind of vehicle that telephone linemen use. The 727 was also the first jet that Jerry had trained on at La Guardia and he still had a sentimental attachment to it.

Jerry took the flashlight from his hip pocket and began the routine of a twenty-five-hour check. He started at the left front, beneath the captain's window, and walked slowly toward the tail checking the side of the fuselage for anything unusual. When he had gone only a few feet—as far as the nose gear—he ducked under the airplane and, reaching up into the wheel well, turned on the light. He stayed there about three minutes, checking carefully all the components that were in the space above, looking for loose cables, fluid leaks, anything that was not as it should be. Satisfied, he turned out the light and continued his slow walk toward the rear—out around the left wing and back to the main landing gear, where he repeated the same thing that he had done at the nose gear. He looked at the two massive tires to see if there were any cuts or worn spots, he checked the brake wear-pins—little indicators that told by their exposed length how much the brakes were worn—he scrutinized the brake lines for leaks, and so on. Again, he was satisfied and continued toward the rear, his flashlight playing on the underside of the tail-mounted engine.

He finished the exterior portion of his inspection by

opening the crew and passenger oxygen panel. He satisfied himself that the fill valves were closed properly and the two pressure gauges indicated oxygen pressure within limits and closed the door, fastening three clips that were recessed into the fuselage. Then he looked into the radar compartment directly under the nose, and was back at his starting point.

He decided to have a quick cup of coffee before going to the interior inspection and logbook inspection that would complete his job on plane number 718. The exterior check had taken more than an hour. He walked to the near wall of the hangar where the coffee machine was.

"Hi, Jer—what's Mac got you doing?" It was Ted Kowalski, the big, burly man who had challenged Jerry two years before.

The shorter man waved as Kowalski came over to the coffee machine. "I'm doing a twenty-five hour on 718."

"We sure could use you on that." He nodded to the 747 that was still on jacks. "It's turned into a real bastard of a job."

Jerry Guccione also had developed a reputation for solving difficult problems when they arose. He had a natural talent for seeing right to the heart of the problem—whatever it was—and coming up with a solution that would save time or effort. He had turned three suggestions in to the engineering department for special tools and, under Transcon's cash-bonus program, had received three large sums of cash representing a percentage of the money that the company would save in time or material by adopting the suggestion. One of the ideas had been for a newly designed engine sled and carrier that cut engine change time almost in half. The sled was now being used by the entire industry.

Kowalski had been explaining the trouble they were having with the brake change. "Got any ideas, Jer?"

Jerry drained his coffee cup and threw it into the trash can. "I'll have to see it first. I should be finished with this in less than an hour. I'll check with Mac and come give you a hand."

The big man was finishing his coffee. "Thanks, Jer—see you later." He turned and started toward the 747.

Jerry walked back to the aircraft he had inspected, dropped the airstairs that were nestled under the three tail-mounted engines, and went up into the cabin. The airplane was quiet, the noisy clamor from outside instantly shut off when he closed the rear entry door. The APU was not running because the aircraft was in the hangar. The APU is a small jet engine in the belly of the plane—an Auxiliary Power Unit—that supplies electricity and air conditioning while on the ground. It was one of the things that made the 727 such an attractive aircraft to the airlines. Because of the APU, the plane was not dependent on ground equipment, and that saved a great deal in capital outlay for those who purchased it. It also made the airplane self-sufficient, enabling Transcon to operate charters into airports that they didn't serve normally without having to rent other carriers' ground support equipment.

He made his way through the silent cabin to the cockpit, hardly noticing the rows of seats as he walked. To Jerry, unlike Transcon's management, the seats were unimportant. He saw an airplane as almost a living thing—a mass of wires and tubing—a marvel of design and engineering. To Jerry, it wouldn't have made any difference if they had been seats or sacks of wheat. He loved the machinery, not its function.

When he got to the cockpit, he sat in the flight engineer's seat, which faced the right side of the airplane. He opened the metal logbook to the last entry and read:

1) Slight leak in hydraulic compartment below "A" system reservoir.
2) Please clean windshield.
3) Captain's seat back will not recline.

He chuckled over the third entry and thought, Poor baby, couldn't get any rest at all. It wasn't a malicious thought, though, because Jerry had a good rapport with the pilots, and he liked them. He knew that each pilot had to adjust his seat for his particular frame. The seats themselves were a marvel of mechanical ingenuity and could adjust to an infinite number of positions. He looked at the underside of the captain's seat and decided it needed lubrication, nothing more. That pleased him because if the seat had been defective, it would have taken half an hour to replace.

He placed the logbook back on the flight engineer's table and left the cockpit for the rear of the plane. The hydraulic compartment referred to in the logbook was located in the airstair area, just behind the left rear lavatory. He walked past the lavatory and opened the rear door, standing just aft of the entrance to the cabin. He opened several large panels on the left side of the stairs and turned on the compartment light.

The area was about the size of a small closet. To the uninitiated, it would have looked like a confused tangle of tanks, tubing, wires, and switches. To Jerry Guccione it was a thing of beauty. His flashlight beam went right to the "A" system hydraulic reservoir and twitched over its surface. The reservoir is a shiny metal tank about the size of a half-keg of beer. There are several thick hoses connected to it, covered with a stainless-steel mesh as a protective cover. The flashlight beam traveled the length of the main supply tube that connected this reservoir with the smaller one that supplied the "B" system hydraulics, located near the wing. As with all transport airplanes, the 727 has at least two main hydraulic systems as well as a smaller backup system. The functions of each system are duplicated for most of the components so that the failure of one system is not really critical. They are connected in such a way that it would be almost impossible to have a multiple failure of both systems because of an intricate system of check valves and dual-control actuators.

He saw what he was looking for at the base of the tube

he had been following with his flashlight. There was a bright spot of light as the beam reflected from one of several large couplings. Jerry left the airplane, walked quickly to his tool box, and selected two large wrenches. Then he stopped at a large locker recessed in the hangar wall, picked up a can of grease, and returned to the airplane.

In the airstair area, Jerry opened another panel, lower down, to permit easy access to the leaking coupling. He squeezed into the space on his side. He tightened the coupling as far as it would go—about one half-turn—and attached a safety wire to it. While he wiped the fitting clean with a rag, he took another quick look around the tiny compartment. His gaze traveled the length of the parallel set of thin tubes that climbed toward the high tail. There were four of them—pressure and return lines for the "A" and "B" system elevator controls. About a foot to the right was another set of four lines. These carried fluid to the rudders, some fifteen feet above Jerry's head. They were all fastened at intervals to the bulkhead that made up the rear wall of the lavatory. Jerry finished the inspection of the compartment and crawled out. He closed the panels that were open and fastened them, then went back inside the airplane to the cockpit.

Inside the cockpit, Jerry quickly lubricated the rods beneath the captain's seat and tried it a few times—it worked perfectly. He sat once more in the flight engineer's seat and opened the logbook to write opposite the handwriting of the flight engineer who had brought the plane to San Francisco:

1) Tightened lock nut "A" system balance line
2) Notified cleaners to clean windshield
3) Lubricated recline tubes on capt.'s seat

He signed the book, JVG, and closed it. The "V" stood for Vicente, but he had never told anyone—for some reason he was embarrassed. He looked at his watch. It was almost four-fifteen. He left the 727 and went to a little room cut into the rear wall of the hangar. Lighting a cigarette, he dialed the lead mechanic's number in the shack on the other side of the hangar.

"Mac? It's Jerry. I'm finished with 718—just a loose coupling nut, nothing serious."

Mac said into the phone, "Good . . . anything else?"

"No, but Kowalski asked for some help on the 747 brake job. I thought I could give them a hand."

The lead mechanic sounded harried. "Fine, but not too long—I want you to taxi 718 over to gate number two at seven o'clock. Flight 602 departs at eight. Have some lunch at the terminal, and finish the shift over there."

"OK, Mac, will do." Jerry hung up the phone. It sounded ridiculous to have lunch at 7 A.M., but then, the airline business had always been crazy. Jerry was one of the few mechanics on his shift who had been checked out and authorized to taxi airplanes around the airport, so the decision to send him to the terminal seemed logical. He was thinking about what he would have for lunch as he walked to the 747 a hundred yards away.

The operating room at the Columbia Presbyterian Hospital was being prepared to receive Kitty Douglass.

They had wakened her at six and started to prepare her for the surgery that she feared so much. Two nurses carefully washed her entire left side from hip to ear with an antiseptic solution. Kitty trembled a little when they shaved the whole area to remove any source that bacteria might cling to. When the preparations were finished in her room, she was transferred to a rolling, stretcherlike table and wheeled down the corridor. In the room outside the O.R., she was again transferred to a similar table that was sterile. She saw Dr. Sangford standing next to her—his hands were encased in latex, held in the air away from his body.

"Good morning, Kitty." His voice was muffled behind the mask, but she was sure that he was smiling, because his eyes were kind. She nodded slowly, closing her eyes. "I don't want you to worry about a thing—just relax." It was Dr. Sangford again.

She thought, as he nodded to the anesthetist and her face was covered by a mask, how much it was like television— the lights, the people being so serious, all the gleaming equipment. She closed her eyes again and there was nothing.

Bob Quinlan had been at La Guardia Airport since six. He had been wakened by the call from Chicago at four-thirty and now, two hours later, he was talking on the telephone as he watched the airport come to life. The drive from his home in Connecticut had taken only forty minutes because of the early hour's light traffic. His office was three stories above the ramp area at the extreme end of the terminal, and he had a sweeping view of the airport and the Transcon gate area through the large windows that formed one wall of his office.

The Chief Pilot turned away from the window as he spoke into the phone. "What's the status of crews now, Glen?"

He was talking to Glen Meyer, his counterpart in the Chicago flight office. "Well, right now we figure that at least twenty-four of your crews will be out of position at midnight tonight—possibly more—depending on how fast the western airports can get back in operation after the storm passes." Normally, the crew schedulers would handle the problem of crews being out of position for their return trips, but with a disruption of this magnitude, Glen had called Bob Quinlan at his home to waken him.

The Chief Pilot in New York swiveled back to look out the window. "Glen, let's set up a briefing conference right now so we know where we stand."

"Good idea."

They set up a conference call on the vast telephone system that Transcon maintained. Included were Quinlan,

Meyer, the crew schedulers for both stewardesses and pilots, the chief Transcon meteorologist, Lars Gunter, and several other dispatchers and aircraft planners around the country.

Glen Meyer started the conference once everyone was on the line. "Brad, why don't you start us off with an updated weather picture?"

Bradley Jennings was the newly promoted Chief Meteorologist of Transcon. He was young—and black—one of the first of his race to enter the higher echelons of the airline. He was also one of the most talented meteorologists in the country. "Well, here's what we have." He was speaking from the central weather room in Chicago. He was nervous because he wasn't used to being on center stage—even on the telephone. "The storm is centered over the North Dakota-Montana border right now. The heavy snow coverage is roughly egg-shaped"—he was moving his dark hands along the map in front of him, visually describing the area even though no one could see him—"it's about a thousand miles across, and fifteen hundred miles long, the length running from northwest to southeast. It's moving southeast at thirty miles an hour, right now. The system has so much moisture that there's enough snow to close *any* airport that it passes near. There's no snow equipment in the world that could keep up with a storm having this much moisture."

"How long will it last?" It was Bob Quinlan.

The meteorologist was gaining confidence in his speaking ability. He heard a cough over the telephone. "It's hard to tell. There's a weak warm front moving northward from Arkansas. Normally, when the two air masses meet, the snow would change to rain—a hell of a lot of rain—but at least rain instead of snow. But there's a factor here that's a little unusual—the southern jet stream running in an arc from . . . oh, say Phoenix to St. Louis and then turning back to the south. If the jet stream puts more spin on the storm *before* it reaches the warm front, it'll be able to reach up into Canada for more cold air and probably overpower the warm front. If that happens, we'll have snow for another twenty-four hours." He spoke of the storm as if it were a living thing. He was sorry that it was causing so much disruption over Transcon's route structure, but as a meteorologist he was fascinated by the undulating, changing lines on his map and welcomed the opportunity to document and study them. He had started to go into a detailed discussion of the storm, much as a professor would, when Glen Meyer cut him off.

"Thanks, Brad. Would you stay on the line, please? We may need you again. Lars? What have you and the planning office done with the affected trips?"

"You want every one?"

"Yes, Lars."

Each man listening referred to the papers in front of him as the dispatcher, who had now been up for eighteen hours, detailed what trips had been affected by the storm at each airport that Transcon served.

"We've projected Denver to close around ten, Mountain Time, so we've tentatively canceled everything after that. That'll be flights 942 and 783, and anything later. Salt Lake should close about an hour after that, so we've canceled 127 and 128—128's crew will be ferrying the airplane to Portland in about an hour after they've gotten a legal rest period."

"That's another of my crews." Glen Meyer checked off a number on the sheet in front of him.

Bob Quinlan broke in. "What about 602?" He knew that it was flown by one of his New York crews.

"I think 602 will be OK," Lars responded. "The snow will be there, but they should be able to get in and out all right. It's the last trip we're going to try for at Salt Lake, though, everything after that has been canceled."

Quinlan checked the corresponding list on his desk and put a check mark next to the flight number.

Lars continued. "Everything out of Pierre has been

canceled for several hours, same with Boise—I've got a crew and airplane stranded there—it's the crew for flight 485. That's the only one that's been stuck so far."

Glen Meyer gave a grunt and checked off another of the Chicago-based pilots. They went on for a while, covering every flight that would be affected by the storm. After about twenty minutes the conference call was over and all the participants went back to the job of minimizing the problems the storm had created.

Bob Quinlan hung up the phone and stared out the window at the increasing activity below. Then he picked up the phone again and buzzed the crew desk.

"Yes, Captain Quinlan?"

"Sam, tell me who's flying 602 back from San Fran today." There was a rustle of papers as the crew man looked through the schedule.

"It's Captain Douglass. Burkhart and Fuller are with him."

"Thanks, Sam." He hung up the phone. That poor bastard, he thought as he pictured Pete Douglass. First Petey last year, and now Kitty in the hospital. He's sure had more than his share. He felt good, though, because he knew that one of his best crews would be flying into Salt Lake in the snow. He picked up a pencil and put a note on his pad to call Kitty in the hospital this afternoon.

The pilots in New York called Quinlan a good boss. He was a short, energetic man with salt-and-pepper hair and a constant elfin grin. He was tough, but fair—and the asset that made him a good boss was that he liked people—especially his pilots.

"Come on, Greco! Wake up." The guard banged his nightstick on the bars. "You have to get cleaned up and shaved by seven-thirty. The warden called—you have to leave early account of the snow." He motioned to the windows with the nightstick.

Donald Greco rubbed his eyes and sat up. The snow

was falling harder now. He must have fallen asleep sometime after two, he thought. He was hungry, and his mouth was dry. He went over to the wash basin and splashed some water on his face. The icy cold liquid brought him full awake. Then he filled the cheap plastic cup full of water and drained it in one long series of swallows.

The guard was saying, "I never been on a plane—I wonder what it's like. The warden said you have to be in his office any time after eight and have to leave for the airport before nine."

Greco looked at him—he was young. They had changed shifts sometime during the morning. The man outside the cell couldn't have been more than twenty-five, Greco thought. Almost twenty years younger than me. It was the first time he had thought of a bull as anything remotely human. The guard was holding a tray with breakfast on it. He knelt down to slide the tray through the slot under the bars.

"I see you didn't like the dinner last night." He was looking at the mess on the wall and floor in the corner of the cell. "Can't say as I blame you—the food here isn't the greatest."

Greco laughed and spoke for the first time. "You're a nice guy. What the hell are you doing being a bull?"

The guard stood up. The prisoner's remark had offended him. He was one of the new breed of correction officers. Young, dedicated, trying to change the image of prison guards and prisons. He said curtly, "I'll be here to get you at eight." He turned and walked back to the end of the cell block.

Greco picked up the tray and went back to the bunk. The breakfast looked better than the dinner had. Scrambled eggs, bacon, juice, and coffee. He started to eat, deciding to shave later—maybe they'd let him shower first.

The guard returned. "Here's your clothes." He hung a hanger on one of the cross pieces between the bars.

Greco looked up. "Hey, bull! I'm sorry about what I said before." The young guard's expression changed back to one of mild interest. "Listen, do you think I can take a shower after I eat? I mean, I'm gonna be on a plane in public, and I'd like to smell nice."

The guard nodded his head. "I'll see what I can do." He left.

Greco attacked the bacon—he was ravenously hungry, and the food on the tray was hot, even if it wasn't good.

The alarm was ringing urgently. Sam Riese stretched a big arm from under the covers and fumbled with the clock, finally locating the tiny button and silencing the alarm. He stayed in the warmth of the bed for only a moment, then swung his legs on the floor. The room was cold. He padded across to the window in bare feet and slid the pane closed. He noticed that it was snowing a little harder than it had been when he arrived at the motel.

The Federal Marshal's Office in Salt Lake City had gotten him a room in the Holiday Inn, close to the airport since there were no hotels near the prison. The room was brightly decorated with hotel-modern pieces of furniture. The bed had been large and comfortable—Sam had slept well after his flight from Chicago last night.

As he got his shaving kit from the suitcase and started toward the bathroom, the phone rang. He picked it up. "Hello?"

"Sam, this is Frank DiLaura at the office."

"Good morning, Frank."

"I hope I didn't wake you—did you sleep well?"

The big man sat on the bed. "No, I was awake. The room is fine. What's up?"

"Well, the snow is getting a little heavier, and I'd like to send the car at six forty-five instead of seven-thirty. Any problem?"

"No, that's OK. Have you checked with the airline?"

"Yes, they said they're planning on operating the flight as scheduled—I hope they don't change their mind."

"Good. I'll see you at six forty-five."

"Oh. Sam, I won't be driving—I'm tied up here. I'll send Howard Flander—he's a good man."

"OK, Frank—thanks for all your cooperation."

"So long, Sam. Have a nice trip home."

Sam Riese hung the phone up and went in to the shower. When he had finished the shower, he dried himself and started shaving with the straight razor he had used for forty of his fifty-seven years. He looked at the gray hair and slight paunch in the mirror—he had aged since his wife died a year ago, and even though he ate much less since he cooked for himself, he was still about twenty pounds overweight. He carefully finished shaving under his chin and cleaned the razor, putting it back in the shaving kit on the wash stand. He dressed quickly in a conservative gray suit and white shirt.

His shoulder twinged with a touch of arthritis as he strapped on his shoulder holster, and he winced. Riese picked up the gun from the bed and put it in the holster. It was a 357 Magnum—about the same size as a long barrel .38 but twice as powerful. He didn't like carrying the big gun—it was uncomfortable—but ever since an incident in New York, ten years ago, he had put up with it. He had always carried a snub-nosed .38 until that time. It was the only time he had ever had to use his gun in the thirty-one years he had been a federal marshal, and it had been almost disastrous. Two men had rushed him. He had dropped one immediately with three shots—the other three shots had almost cost him his life. The first missed the other man completely; the other two had hit him in the belly. He had kept coming and would have shot Riese, but for the marshal's quick reflexes. After the incident, Sam Riese had switched to the more powerful and accurate pistol that he now carried.

He patted the shoulder holster and thought, This is the

last time. No more traveling when I get back to Chicago, and no more carrying this damn extra weight. He had decided on early retirement last month, and his request had been approved a few days ago. He put on his suit jacket, altered at the armpit to accommodate the holster, closed his suitcase, and went to the restaurant for breakfast.

Sam Riese was tired of traveling—tired of countless breakfasts in unremembered restaurants and coffee shops. As he ordered, he thought of the small cabin in the Poconos that he and Ethyl had worked so hard to buy, and he thought of how he would spend the rest of his life fishing and relaxing. He watched a snowplow pass, flinging aside the two inches of freshly fallen white on the wet street.

5

The warm weight on his arm surprised Stan as he reached for the phone. "Hello?"

"Good morning, it's five-thirty." It was a pleasant female voice.

"Thank you." He hung up the phone and remembered that the warmth came from Susan. She mumbled sleepily and buried herself in his shoulder. Stan put his other arm around her and pressed his face to her clean-smelling hair, kissing it. "Hey," he said softly, "it's time to get up."

"No, not yet." It was almost a whimper as she pulled close.

He gently rolled her on her back and kissed her mouth,

tasting the sleep. He touched her breast and felt himself becoming aroused—her body was warm and exciting. "Come on, love, wake up . . . time to go to work."

"Mmmmm." She opened her eyes and gave a start when she saw him smiling at her.

"Hi there."

"How . . . ?" She had been dreaming of Jack, and airplanes, and a little apartment in New York. The memory of the dream was muddled by sleep. She lifted her head and then put it back on the pillow.

"Are you awake?"

It was coming back to her now—their evening, their lovemaking. "Yes." She stretched under the covers, her arms over her head against the headboard. When the blanket fell from her breasts, she pulled it back up to cover herself. Stan was sitting up now, facing her. She said, "God! Do you always get up this early?" She couldn't look at him.

"Yes. But then I usually don't stay up so late, either." He had noticed how she quickly covered herself and was puzzled. And yet he understood, because even though he had a fierce urge to go to the bathroom, he was reluctant to get up from the bed. He had always been comfortable with his nudity—especially with Susan—but the shyness was returning for both of them. He finally overcame his reluctance when his bladder would no longer stand it, and went to the bathroom. Susan looked at his strong back as he went in.

When Stan returned, he had a towel around his waist. Susan was out of the bed, dressing. She stood and looked at him in her panties, her arm covering her breasts. They stood for a moment, facing each other, then both laughed.

"I guess we aren't ready for the morning after the night before, not yet anyhow." It was Stan who had broken the laughter.

She dropped her arm. "No, I guess not." She was

serious again. Stan thought she was beautiful—the sight of her body did things to his brain and his stomach.

He decided, wisely, he thought, not to push things, and kept the towel around his waist. "Susan? If it means anything . . . I'm glad you're here."

She smiled and nodded—dropping her eyes. She said nothing. There was a long, uncomfortable pause. Finally Stan broke the silence.

"Susan—a lot has happened here." He gestured toward the bed. "We both need time to think. Let's not talk about it right now. All I want you to know is that I have no regrets—none at all." He had walked over to her and was holding both her shoulders, looking at her. "What comes of it is another thing, and that'll take time." He paused. "You?"

She shook her head. "No regrets, Stan, but you're right —let's talk about it later."

He dropped his hands from her shoulders. "How about breakfast?"

She hesitated. "Will the rest of the crew be there?"

"Probably." He laughed again. "But the hell with them—it's none of their business." His confidence was returning.

Susan finished putting on her dress and stuffed her hose into her purse. "OK, I'll need about fifteen minutes to change and pack." They walked to the door.

Stan touched her arm as she held the door open. He was behind it, hidden from the hallway. She turned to him and he bent to kiss her nose. "Susan . . . I'm glad it happened. It'll be right—whatever way it works."

She smiled a quick, unsure smile and stepped into the hallway.

Susan went to her room, thankful that she didn't meet anyone in the hotel corridors. Once inside, she decided to take a quick shower. Her head was spinning with questions and she hoped that the warm water would relax her.

It helped. She still wasn't sure whether she should have slept with Stan, but her mind had stopped whirling. She packed her things quickly, and put on the pants suit that she had not worn the night before. As she combed her hair in front of the mirror, she realized that she wasn't nearly so tired as she should be after getting only three hours' sleep. There was only a pleasant ache in her body as she stretched her arms above her head. She thought about Stan. She was glad that he wasn't pressing her—but then, he never had. He had always insisted, when they were living together, that she make up her own mind. It had been one of the things that had infuriated her years ago. He insisted that she was an individual, and that she make her own decisions. Their first fight had been over an election for mayor of New York. When she had asked him how she should vote, he had told her to make up her own mind—he would try to explain the issues as best he could, but would not try to sway her one way or the other. She realized now how much that attitude of Stan's had helped her to get out of her marriage. She had been able to make the decision to leave Jack primarily because Stan had forced her into a feeling of independence and self-sufficiency. She sensed that this was, again, a time when Stan wouldn't push her, but would let her know his feelings, and then she would have to make a decision. The thought relaxed her, and she was feeling happier about the night with Stan when he knocked on the door.

They walked into the main lobby from the elevator and Stan set their bags by the front desk. They walked side by side into the dining room. The three girls and Mike were already seated at a large table in the corner. The flight engineer caught Stan's eye and waved them over. As they sat down, Stan introduced Susan to the three girls, then turning to Mike said, "And this is Mike Fuller—be careful around Mike—he's incorrigible." There was a long silence as if they expected a fuller explanation of Susan's presence. Susan could tell from the creeping redness behind Stan's ear that he was embarrassed. She smiled and tried to hide behind the big menu. "Susan and I have known each other for years—I talked her into coming back to New York with us today instead of last night on the nonstop." He had said it very rapidly and it was all Susan could do not to laugh out loud.

The waiter broke in and Stan ordered breakfast for them. As he was ordering, Cathy, who was sitting between Mike and Susan, said, "That's a lovely material, Susan—I don't think I've ever seen any plaid like it before."

"Oh, thank you. It's the MacKenzie hunting tartan. My dad got it for me when he was in Scotland. It's kind of an obscure plaid though. I tried to find it in New York at one of the Scottish shops, but they didn't have it. I wanted to make a long skirt with it." She hoped that she was making a good impression. The feeling of being an outsider was beginning to come back because of all the uniformed, attractive people at the table.

"Do you sew a lot, Susan?" Cathy had finished her breakfast and was lighting a cigarette. She was appraising the woman as only another woman could. She *is* gorgeous, she decided. Calm—secure, with a good head. Watch out, Stan! Cathy knew about Stan and Ellen. She and Mike had gone out with them once in New York, and she had sensed a certain lack of feeling between the two. And now, this added force—this stunning redhead who was obviously important to Stan—added a bit of spice and intrigue.

Susan was saying, "Well, whenever I have time I do —clothes are so expensive nowadays."

As Susan spoke, Cathy decided that she liked this girl— she had life, a spark that was hard to define. Susan was explaining to Cathy why she was going to New York when Pete Douglass arrived. He obviously hadn't slept well. "Morning, everyone," he said as he sat in one of the two empty chairs at the table.

"Pete, this is Susan MacKenzie." It was Cathy, helping

out Stan's embarrassment. Pete nodded and shook her hand. "Susan is a friend of Stan's and she's going to ride to New York with us."

"It's nice to meet you, Captain Douglass." She said it seriously.

Pete laughed. "Call me Pete, Susan, everyone else does. It'll be nice to have you on board." Stan noticed that Pete was in a much better mood. "You could have picked a better day, though."

"Oh?" She looked up, not sure what he meant.

Pete looked at Stan as he spoke. "The weather's not so hot. Apparently that storm has created havoc all over the Northwest, and down through the plains. So"—he turned to Susan—"we might have a problem getting back to New York. Dispatch called me this morning to tell me about it. They've canceled every trip after 602—those whiz kids in the weather section figure that we'll be the last trip in and out of Salt Lake before the airport closes."

Mike Fuller had been listening. "What do *you* think, Pete?"

The captain spread his hands. "It's hard to tell, we'll have to wait till we get there." He looked at his watch and stood up. "If you don't mind, I'd like to leave a little early—the car's here. I've got to pay for some calls I made. Meet you in the lobby."

As he left, Mike caught Stan's eye, tipping his head toward the door as Pete left. Stan decided not to tell them that Kitty was in the hospital, and he shrugged at Mike's unasked question. He turned to Susan. "I'll leave the car here—they have an office across the street and we'll ride with this bunch of degenerates to the airport." The four girls laughed at him. Mike looked very hurt. They finished breakfast quickly and went to the lobby. Stan left Susan with Cathy as he went to take care of the rental car.

When Stan returned to the lobby from the Avis office, the two girls were standing near the door. Stan watched them as he approached. They had obviously hit it off well, and that pleased him. As he got closer he said, "Pete's in the car—is everyone ready?" They all started toward the door.

It was a gray morning outside, with a slight drizzle falling. The long car was parked in front of the door, Pete Douglass already in the back seat. They handed their bags to the driver standing by the open trunk and got in.

Sam Riese walked across the open space between the coffee shop and the lobby of the motel. He could see his breath misting in the cold Salt Lake morning. The marshal entered the lobby and sat in one of the overstuffed chairs. He had checked out before he went for breakfast, so all there was to do was wait for the car. He watched the snow falling—there was almost an inch of new snow covering the road. A truck with a plow blade moved past. Behind the plow, a black sedan followed slowly, turning into the motel driveway. The driver got out and walked into the lobby. Sam Riese rose, knowing this would be his driver.

The man was young, intense. He walked with purpose toward Sam, holding out his hand. "Sam Riese?"

"Yes." They shook hands.

"I'm Howard Flander."

"Hello." He went to get his bag. The young man's hair was longer than Sam felt it should be. Suddenly he felt very old, out of place.

"We'd better be on our way—the snow is starting to come down harder. The plows are working, though—we shouldn't have any trouble getting to the prison." Flander was already at the door.

Sam picked up his suitcase and nodded. They walked to the car. As he got in the passenger's side, Sam could barely make out the base of the mountains in the distance. Ethyl would have liked this place, he thought—it's sad that she won't ever see it. He got in and closed the door.

The crew arrived at the airport at six forty-five. The drive had been short, with almost no traffic. As they tipped the driver and picked up their bags, Stan turned to the captain. "Pete, I'm going to take Susan to the gate and get her checked in, then I'll meet you in Dispatch."

"OK, Stan—hurry though, it's going to be a long day."

Stan picked up Susan's bag and walked her to the boarding area for flight 602. As they passed the luggage check-in lines she said, "Aren't we going to check my bag?"

"No, it's small enough to fit under your seat, so you can take it on board—saves time at the other end." They arrived at the check-in counter. It was early, and there were no passengers in the boarding area. A handsome young man was just putting the movable strips in slots on the wall behind the podium. It read:

> TRANSCON AIRLINES
> GOLDEN-JET SERVICE
>
> TO:
>
> SALT LAKE CITY
> CHICAGO (O'HARE)
> POINTS EAST
>
> DEPARTURE: 8:00 A.M.

As he turned around, Stan said to him, "Hi, Art—how've you been?"

The young man smiled and shook hands. "Hey, Stan—I didn't know you were out this way." He looked at Susan.

"Art, this is Susan MacKenzie. She's going on 602 with us to New York. Would you take care of her while I go up to Dispatch?"

"Sure, I'd be happy to."

Susan looked at him. He wore the dark green jacket of

a Transcon passenger agent, with muted yellow shirt and green tie. He was about twenty-five, short, and the aviator-type glasses he wore added a professional, yet mod look to his rugged face. He was looking at her with undisguised admiration.

"Susan, if you'll have a seat for a while, I'll get to your ticket in just a moment."

She smiled at him. Stan gave her a quick kiss on the cheek, and left the boarding area, heading toward the Dispatch Office.

She took a seat in one of the comfortable leather chairs that were attached together in rows, ashtrays spaced along them on the dark green carpet.

Transcon had just redecorated their part of the terminal, using a green and gold motif. It was tastefully done, with generous use made of wood grains and rough-textured stone. While she was looking around at the boarding area, the passenger agent hung up the phone he had been talking on and came over to her. "Susan, if I could have your ticket, I'll check you in. The load is light, so we aren't going to use a seat-assignment chart today." The name tag on his lapel said *Mr. Forenzo, Passenger Service Representative.*

When he returned with a ticket wallet, all stamped with the hieroglyphics of the airline industry, she looked up and said, "Have you known Stan long?"

He chuckled. "Well, I don't really know him too well. We see each other often, like today, but that's all. Working for Transcon is like being in a club—we're all friends—it's easier to work that way. But I probably wouldn't recognize Stan on the street without his uniform, and I doubt that he'd recognize me."

She wanted to say, "You ought to know what it feels like to be a *nonmember*," but she didn't. Art Forenzo left her with a smile as a passenger arrived at the podium behind him. She watched him. He worked quickly and efficiently. He had a ready smile that was sincere, and a way with people that made them feel that they were important. He turned and smiled at her, starting to come over to where she sat, but another passenger arrived at the check-in counter, and he shrugged, turning back with a smile to the elderly woman who had just arrived.

Stan walked the fifty yards to the Operations Office at a brisk pace. He opened the door and walked down the short corridor, depositing his suitcase and picking up his flight kit from the bag rack as he walked. He stepped into the brightly lit room.

Pete and Mike were standing by the weather map to his left. He walked over to them. "Sorry it took so long."

Pete turned. "That's OK, Stan—it wasn't that long, we're just starting. And Susan *is* quite a female."

Stan thought, Well, old boy, I guess you've stopped being a bastard to everyone around you for the time being, and I'm glad. He ran his finger under the sequence weather report for Salt Lake City. "Doesn't look too bad," Stan said. "Eight hundred scattered, fourteen hundred overcast with six miles visibility, light snow. Temp's twenty-eight, wind's almost down the runway—zero one zero at sixteen knots."

Pete gave a half-laugh. "Now, my fair-haired young co-pilot, take a look at the forecast!"

Stan shook his head. Pete had taught him to look at the forecast *first*, then look at the sequence weather—that way you could see what the weather bureau *said* it was going to be like at a station, then the sequence would tell you whether the forecast had been accurate, by detailing weather at the time the sequence observations were taken. He looked at Pete. "Going to be close, isn't it, boss?" He looked at the forecast again. The present weather was exactly as predicted; however, they were forecasting a two-hundred-foot overcast with a half-mile visibility for the time of their arrival, along with heavy snow. One-half mile was the lowest legal visibility that they could land with—if the visibility was worse than that, they couldn't even start an approach.

Pete was seated at one of the tables in the center of the room. Stan left the weather board and sat down next to him. The captain was studying the many sheets of paper in front of him that made up the flight plan for flight 602. In his hand was the computer copy of the leg from San Francisco to Salt Lake City. It contained the route of flight, fuel burnout at different altitudes, the weight of the airplane at takeoff and landing, and several other important items. The plan was broken down into segments roughly one hundred miles in length, giving the crew checkpoints so that they could compare their actual progress along the route with that projected by the computer.

Stan knew that before the advent of the computer, and its infinite abilities with numbers, the copilot had had to do the figuring that was on the computer print-out that Pete held, and he was thankful that he didn't have to try. The computer could recall the route, time, winds, everything from its storage banks in miscroseconds, and print it—copilots took as much as half an hour on a long flight plan.

Pete broke into Stan's thought. "Stan? Look up the distance from Salt Lake to Vegas for me, OK?"

"Sure, Pete." He got out the operations manual that he carried in his flight bag and looked up the mileage. Since Transcon had no route between the two cities, it was not listed, so he got out the high altitude airways chart and measured the distances along jet routes eleven and nine. He turned to Pete. "Three twenty-seven to Boulder—make it about three-sixty to Vegas." The mileage he gave was in nautical miles rather than statute miles. The distance in statute miles would have been greater—about four hundred and five.

The captain was doing some quick figuring on the fuel worksheet. "That's about the same distance as Reno is from Salt Lake. I want to name Vegas as an alternate as well as Reno. I don't trust the Reno weather as much as I do Vegas."

Stan got up and went to the upper-winds map seven feet away. "Pete? That's running parallel to the jet stream. Pretty close to the southern curve of the thing. The burn-out would be higher, probably."

One of the unique qualities in Pete Douglass' personality was the way he supervised his crews. He encouraged discussion about a flight and, unlike many of the older senior captains, welcomed a comment from the copilot or flight engineer, even if the view differed from his own. His philosophy was that the men flying with him were future captains for Transcon, and he well knew that a captain had to see all points of view. Because of this, Pete had a reputation of being one of the best "training captains" in New York. It wasn't anything official, but all the copilots knew that flying with him would enhance their knowledge, and they looked forward to it.

The making of an airline captain, with its vast responsibility, is a long, slow process—filled with many hurdles and setbacks. The constant checks, schooling, physical examinations—any one of them could terminate a pilot's career if not passed. It took a long time. Three or four years as a flight engineer, then six to ten years as a co-pilot. Today's captains are the sum total of all the experiences they have had during a long apprenticeship. Pete had taken, from the captains he had flown with, all the good traits that he saw, and he had rejected the bad. In a way, it was like breeding prize livestock, eliminating bad qualities while striving to perfect the good ones.

Pete had flown as a copilot in DC-6s with a man named "Doc" Palmer for years. Doc had taught him more than any other captain. Together, they had encountered almost everything that can happen to an airplane—engine fires, snowstorms, hydraulic failures, ice—the whole spectrum of hair-raising experiences. The one thing that Doc had always done was share his thinking with the man in the right seat and request his opinion. The period with Doc Palmer was now paying off. In fact, he thought, he had *not* considered the increased headwind from the jet stream because he had been thinking of Kitty, and he was pleased that Stan had reminded him. He looked across the table at the sandy-haired copilot and decided he would be a good captain. "Good thought, Stan. I'll up the alternate fuel by two thousand pounds, to be on the safe side. Let's add it all up."

The two men totaled the fuel they wanted for the first leg of the trip—enough to fly from San Francisco to Salt Lake, hold over Salt Lake for an hour, then fly to Las Vegas, then fly for another forty-five minutes. The forty-five minutes was a required safety measure insisted on in FAA regulations. The total for the trip came to 38,400 pounds of fuel. Fuel is figured in pounds instead of gallons because a gallon is not constant—it will shrink or expand according to temperature, and fuel temperature can vary as much as a hundred degrees. A pound is always sixteen ounces regardless of temperature.

Stan looked at Pete. "How does thirty-eight, four sound?"

"On the button."

"Good." Pete signed the papers and turned to the flight engineer. "Mike, we'll want thirty-eight, four in the tanks for takeoff." That was Mike's signal to proceed to the airplane to make his preflight inspection. He picked up his bags and went to the door. Pete turned back to his copilot. "The Chicago weather is probably going to be shitty, too, but we'll take another look at it when we get to Salt Lake. We'll take what the computer says for now."

Stan nodded and gathered the papers together. He took them over to the dispatcher for his signature, requesting the two-thousand-pound increase in fuel and change in alternate airports. The dispatcher called the fuelers and ordered the increase. When the papers were all in the envelope, Stan picked it up and returned to where Pete was standing by the weather map. The girls had finished checking in and had joined him.

He was speaking to the head stewardess. "Terry, there's a fair chance that we'll have to divert from Salt Lake. Our alternates are Reno and Vegas, but don't say anything to the people—we won't know for sure until we get closer. No use in rattling them for nothing. I'll make an announcement as soon as we can tell which way the weather is going."

Cindy's eyes went wide. "Reno? Las Vegas?"

Pete smiled at the new girl. "Cindy, those are what we call 'paper alternates.' It doesn't mean that we'll go there. We may come back to San Fran if the weather closes Salt Lake—it depends on where we can go to do the passengers the most good."

"Is the weather that bad, Pete?" It was Cathy.

"Well, it's not good—they've canceled all the trips from Salt Lake after ours, and we may not get in at all."

"I've got a feeling I should call my date for tonight and tell him not to wait up." It was Cindy again, a puzzled frown covering her face.

They all laughed at the new girl and headed for the airplane.

Susan was watching Art Forenzo behind the podium in the boarding area. He was having a hard time. An irate man in his mid-fifties was waving his ticket in front of the passenger agent's nose and actually yelling at him. "Dammit, I don't *want* to stop in Salt Lake City! I want to go to Chicago—that's what this ticket says, Chicago. I was never told this wasn't a nonstop flight. What are you people running here anyhow, a railroad?"

"I'm sorry, sir, we don't have a nonstop leaving for Chicago until eleven A.M. I can check TWA or United if you like." Art, Susan decided, was doing an Academy Award job of not losing his temper.

"No, goddammit! I am not walking all over hell's half-acre now! I have just never seen such inefficiency in my life! What's your name, young man—I'm going to write the president of Transcon!"

Susan could see Art clench his fists under the counter. "Forenzo, sir, F-O-R-E-N-Z-O. Arthur Forenzo."

The man was writing furiously in a notebook he had extracted from his obviously expensive gray suit.

"And may I know *your* name, sir?"

"It's on the goddam ticket." He hurled the ticket at Art. It bounced off the counter onto the floor. "How soon before I can get on the lousy airplane?"

Art busied himself picking up the ticket and writing on it. "If you'll just have a seat, sir, we'll be boarding in about ten minutes."

Susan studied the man as he took a seat away from the other passengers in the corner of the boarding lounge. He looked very familiar. He was bald, with dark horn-rimmed glasses, and his hair was graying heavily around the ears. A big man—the seat jostled as he sat down—he looked like a professional, a doctor, perhaps. Maybe she had seen him at St. Francis—she quickly sped through the catalog of her mind. No, it didn't ring true. The face was terribly familiar, but not from the hospital. She just couldn't remember where she had seen him. She turned her attention to Art again. He had regained his composure quickly, as airline passenger agents must, and was smiling at a young mother with an infant at the counter. The woman couldn't have been more than twenty, a brunette with rather plain features. The baby was tiny—perhaps two months old. Susan felt a growing need within her— the same feeling she had whenever she would step into the nursery at St. Francis. Ah, Susan, she thought, the maternal urge dies hard.

The boarding area was becoming crowded now, filling with travelers bound for Salt Lake or Chicago, accompanied by their friends or relatives waiting to say goodbye. There were no people in front of the counter as Stan, with the rest of the crew, stopped to talk to Art. Susan got up and walked over to them.

Stan smiled. "Hi there—I missed you." She touched his sleeve, feeling warm and needed after watching the scene that Art had just gone through.

The passenger agent was saying to Terry, "It's a light load, six up front and twenty-three in the back—no problems except one." He jerked his thumb over his shoulder at the man Susan was trying to remember.

"What's with him?"

"Don't know for sure, just angry at everything. He's in the back cabin."

Terry gave a mock sigh of relief and turned to Cathy. "Go to it, babe, turn on that California charm and rescue Transcon's good name."

They cleared a path for an elderly couple stepping up to the podium. Art Forenzo smiled and took their ticket. Stan said to him as he was stamping the ticket, "Art, we're going to take Susan on early, is that OK?"

"Sure, go ahead." He turned to the two U.S. Customs men standing by the jetway door and waved. The crew walked to the door, and one of the uniformed men, made necessary by the recent wave of hijackings, opened the door. As they passed, the other made a brief inspection of Susan's ticket and waved her through the door with them.

They walked down the jetway to the open door of the 727. Cathy watched Stan and Susan from behind, their conversation punctuated with smiles and knowing looks. Cathy knew there was something very special between them, and was pleased with the thought. Stan had an eagerness to him this morning that the stewardess had never seen before, and she thought that it suited him.

Stan, Pete, and Susan entered the cockpit. Stan had said, "Why don't you stay up here for a while—it might be interesting." Mike was already seated in the flight engineer's seat and greeted Susan's presence with a broad grin, his moustache spreading across his face.

"Welcome to my humble abode, fair lady."

Susan laughed. She stood in the doorway as the two pilots hung up their uniform jackets and climbed into the two seats in front. She looked around at the small space, surprised that it was so cramped. Pete was sitting in the front seat on the left, Stan in an identical seat on the right side. Between them was a large pedestal covered with levers and two large wheels. Immediately behind it, extending between them to the backs of the seats, was a long, low, box-shaped platform, covered with dials and switches. Mike sat at a seat which faced a large panel extending from the ceiling on the entire right side of the cockpit. It, too, was a maze of gauges, lights, and dials. There was a narrow table in front of him at the base of the panel. It was covered with a book, papers, and a computer-type slide rule that Mike had taken out of his bag.

The flight engineer slid his chair in and said to Susan, "Have a seat behind Pete."

There were two more seats facing forward, one behind the other, on the left side. With Mike's seat pulled in toward his panel, there was barely enough room to slide into the seat directly behind the captain's. "What are these two seats for, Stan?"

"Oh, they're the observer seats—used whenever one of us is getting a flight check, or for instructors on training flights. Susan? Give us about two minutes and we'll be able to talk, OK?" He turned back to the panel of dials in front of him and began checking each instrument. Pete was doing much the same thing, and Mike was busily positioning switches on the engineer's panel.

Stan reached over his head and turned on a speaker so

that Susan could hear. "San Francisco clearance, this is Transcon six oh two, IFR to Salt Lake."

A voice from the speaker answered, "Roger, Transcon six oh two, cleared to Salt Lake airport as filed, maintain three-seven-zero. Sacramento six departure, departure control frequency will be one-twenty-four point four, squawk zero five two six."

Stan had been writing quickly on a pad of paper taped to the right windowsill. He repeated the clearance back verbatim, then turned to Susan. "Well, what do you want to know?" He smiled and gestured around the cockpit.

"What was all that?" She looked confused.

"That was the clearance to go to Salt Lake City—it was filed with the Air Route Traffic Control Center an hour ago, and now we have a slot in the sky to get there in. It's a little oversimplified, but that's the general idea."

"How do you know what all these dials are?"

"That's because we are true geniuses!" It was Mike talking. He had swiveled his chair to face forward between the two pilots. "Actually, Susan, there's a lot of duplication in the cockpit. The instruments in front of Pete and Stan are identical, just powered from different sources so that there's always a backup should one source fail. The only difference between the captain's and co-pilot's seat is that Pete"—he pointed to Pete's left knee—"has the steering wheel."

She laughed. "The *steering* wheel?"

Pete shifted in his seat so that Susan could see the black, half-circle wheel attached to the wall. He turned over his shoulder and said, "It steers the airplane on the ground by turning the nose wheel—in the air, it doesn't do anything."

They were interrupted by a booming voice from the door. "Hey! What is this? I always knew you pilots were a worthless bunch, much given to hanky-panky."

Stan turned in his seat. "Jerry Guccione, you old lecher, how are you?" Susan looked and saw a short, stocky man in white coveralls filling the lower two-thirds of the doorway, a metal book in his hand. He handed the book to Mike and squeezed between Susan and the engineer to shake hands with Stan.

"Jerry, this is Susan MacKenzie. Susan, this is Jerry Guccione. He's an old friend who has saved me from the ravages of the Upper East Side more than once." He turned to the mechanic. "Hey! It's good to see you. What are you up to?" He introduced him to Pete and Mike. They nodded hello.

"Oh, not a lot, I just bought a house up in Marin—why don't you call the next time you're here? We can make like old times in New York." He looked at Susan, as if asking permission. She smiled and watched Stan, who was obviously happy at seeing the man.

"Hey, you guys—make this a very smooth flight. My sister and her new baby girl are going to Chicago with you. Her name's Julia, and she's a gorgeous Italian type—like me —so stay away from her! They're going to see my folks— the first time they'll see their new granddaughter."

After a few more words, the mechanic turned serious. He said to Pete, "Captain, there was a write-up about a hydraulic leak aft. I looked at it, and tightened a lock nut on one of the balance lines. Should give you no trouble. I put some grease on your seat, too." Pete looked surprised and the bull-necked mechanic laughed. "I meant on the recline mechanism, not on the fabric."

The conversation went on in the cockpit—an easy, relaxed banter. In the rear, the three stewardesses were preparing the cabin to receive the first passengers. Terry and Cathy busily checked the meal and drink supplies in the galley, insuring that there were enough meals for the planned passenger load. Cindy went efficiently through the cabin checking that all first-aid kits, fire extinguishers, and oxygen bottles were in place and properly fastened down. The passenger agent came on to tell the girls that he was about to board the people. Terry grabbed him by the arm as he went out the door.

"I want some more cans of coffee. There's a good chance

we'll be holding over Salt Lake for a while, and I don't want to run out. Can you get me five more cans?"

"I'll try, but I can't promise." He walked back up the jetway to the waiting passengers.

Terry stayed at the front door and called back to the other two stewardesses, "People coming!"

Jerry Guccione heard her. "Stan, I've got to run. I want to say good-bye to Julia, then it's time for lunch. Will you call me when you're back?"

"Sure, Jer—take care."

"Nice meeting you, Susan. 'Bye." He left the cockpit. Susan moved to get up as the passengers started going by the cockpit door.

Pete turned to her. "Stay here, Susan, we've still got fifteen minutes, and you can run back and sit down in a while." She nodded and smiled at him. Her smile is like Kitty's, Pete thought, so fresh and honest. A stab of uneasiness coursed through his gut. His wife should be out of the operation soon.

Art Forenzo poked his head inside the cockpit. "We got six and twenty-four, Captain—picked up one more than we expected. Have a nice trip." He stopped at the forward entry door and handed Terry Dunlap the passenger manifest.

She gave him the tickets she had collected and said, " 'Bye, Art, see you next trip."

The passenger agent smiled, thinking she was pretty, and that it was too bad she was married. "So long," he said.

Then he grabbed the polished steel handle and leaned against the heavy door's weight. The big door closed silently, the only sound that of the locks engaging, making the door pressure-tight. Inside flight 602, the ringing bell on the jetway was very faint as it pulled back from the aircraft.

> *"Flights will be planned to take advantage of tailwinds and jet stream effect, if any, where consistent with safety, to maximize fuel savings where possible."*

Page 75, Para. 7

> *"During winter operation, braking reports are to be used in an advisory sense. Be alert for rapidly changing conditions on runways and taxiways."*

Page 114, Para. 3 (a)
Transcon Flight Operations Manual

6

"Good morning, Warden." Sam Riese followed Howard Flander into the office.

The warden looked up from his desk at the two men. "Morning. Which one of you is Riese?" The warden wasn't overfriendly. He had a distaste for federal employees—one he had retained ever since he had been rejected by the FBI.

"I'm Riese." The older man spoke.

"If you don't mind"—the warden motioned for the two federal marshals to sit down—"may I see your identification?" Riese handed him the small Moroccan leather case with the plastic identification card and picture. The warden studied it for a long moment, then handed it back to Riese, satisfied that the man in the picture and the man sitting before him were one and the same. He turned to Flander with his hand out.

The young man was surprised, but reached into his breast pocket and produced the same kind of leather folder and handed it to the man behind the desk. Again, the warden studied it, comparing the picture and the face. He handed the wallet back. "Sorry if I appear a little cautious," he said finally, "but this Greco is a real beauty, and I don't trust anything about him."

The two marshals looked at each other, a little dubiously. "No problem, Warden." It was Riese. "You can't be too careful—I read the dossier on him on the plane last night." He looked around the office. There were photographs on the wall. One of the warden and Robert Kennedy in some sort of conference room. Another in front of the Mormon Temple—the warden shaking hands with a very old and distinguished-looking man, while a plump woman looked on. Must be his wife, Riese thought. There were other pictures—the remnants of many years of service in correctional institutions. Sam Riese wondered why, ever since his wife had died, the whole idea of criminals, prisoners, and prisons had depressed him so. He found his mind wandering back to the little cabin in the mountains near Hazleton. The fishing in the trout stream that ran by the cabin was good. But what would it be like alone, without Ethyl to comfort him? He dragged his mind back to the present with great effort.

"Before you bring Greco in, I'd like to call the airline and set things up. They know we'll be on the flight, but I want to check with the station manager just to be sure. Mind if I use the phone?"

The warden lifted the phone across the desk and placed it in front of Riese.

He picked it up and spoke. "This is Riese, Federal Marshal. Would you please get me the Transcon Airlines station manager at the airport?" There was a pause. "Fine, I'm in the warden's office. Thank you." He put the phone down.

The three men sat in silence for about two minutes. The warden finally spoke. "I'll be glad to get rid of Greco. He's been a troublemaker since he got here." He picked up a sheet of paper and looked at it. "He started two fights in the mess hall. We segregated him at meals after that. Last night he threw his tray against the wall and messed up the cell pretty bad. I don't need that kind of trouble here."

Riese looked at the man without blinking. "We got here as soon as we could spare the manpower, Warden."

"Well, he's a federal problem." He said it with a conservative Westerner's contempt for big government. "The people of the State of Utah don't need his kind to waste their money on, even for a day. And . . ." The phone's ring prevented him from finishing.

Sam Riese picked up the phone. "Hello? Yes, is this the station manager? Fine, Mr. Burnick, I'm Sam Riese. I'm the marshal that's going to transport a prisoner on flight 602 to Chicago." He listened for some time. "Fine, thanks a lot for your cooperation." He looked at his watch and spoke again. "It's almost nine o'clock now—if we leave soon, we should be able to meet you by a little after ten, will that be OK? . . . Good." He looked out the window at the snow. "Is the flight going to be on time?" There was another pause. "Fine, Mr. Burnick—see you in an hour at your office."

As he hung up the phone, Howard Flander, who had not spoken until now, said, "Everything OK, Sam?"

"As far as they know, the flight's on time. They want us there an hour early so we can get on before the other passengers. The station manager, Burnick, sounds like a competent man—it should all go smoothly." Sam Riese's gut was beginning to tighten, as it always did. He turned to the warden. "If you can bring Greco in here now, we can get going—the snow will probably slow us down on the way to the airport. I don't want to be late."

The warden pressed a button on his desk and a guard appeared at the door. "Bring Greco up here." The guard disappeared. The warden appeared to soften, now that he was sure that the prisoner was leaving his charge. He looked at the two men across the desk. "I'm sorry that I blew off steam before. It's rough keeping these outsiders in line. You understand, I'm sure." His eyes were requesting reassurance.

Howard Flander busily lit a cigarette, not looking at the warden. Sam Riese ignored him as well. There was a stony silence in the room until the door opened and a guard walked Donald Greco in ahead of him.

He was dressed in a dark, cheap suit. The white shirt collar was wrinkled around the throat where a sickly maroon tie was knotted. The dark eyes darted nervously between the two men seated in front of the warden's desk. His hands were shackled together in front of him by a heavy set of handcuffs.

Sam Riese stared at him for a moment, then rose. "Mr. Greco, my name is Sam Riese." He had always treated prisoners with dignity—long before the cries of "no respect" had risen from prison populations across the country. He felt that they were still human beings, even if they had broken the law. He didn't consider himself soft because of this, only fair. He continued, looking directly at the sullen man, "It's my job to transport you from here to Chicago, where I will deliver you to federal authorities there. I anticipate no problems." He softened his voice a bit. "You and I will be together for some six hours—let's make it at least civilized, shall we?"

Greco's eyes narrowed slightly, but he said nothing. The marshal stepped closer to him. He was taller than Greco, and bigger. He motioned for the guard to remove the handcuffs. When the guard started to protest, Riese reached into his pocket and produced another pair. "I have my own," he said with a small smile.

The guard stepped in front of the prisoner and unlocked the shackles. Greco stood rubbing his wrists. Riese looked at him. "You right-handed?"

"Yes." Sam was surprised at the deep voice coming from such a small frame.

"Good, this'll work out well, then. I'm a lefty myself." He locked one cuff on Greco's left wrist, the other on his own right. "These stay on for the next six hours."

The prisoner looked surprised. "What if I got to go to the bathroom?"

"You'll go once when we get to the airport, and again when we get to Chicago. The flight's about two and a half hours. If you can't hold it on the airplane, you'll have to wet your pants!" His voice had hardened again. Greco just shrugged.

Flander got up. "Sam, we'd better go." He gestured out the window. "Looks like it's getting worse."

They left the warden's office and went down a long narrow corridor to a heavily secured exit door. The warden watched them leave with a mixture of envy and disgust. The damn feds, he thought, always in their natty suits with their fancy credentials. I'm glad they're gone. He was surprised that the older marshal was taking Greco—he felt that it should have been the younger one, Flander.

Outside, the snow was falling steadily. Not heavily, the visibility was pretty good, but it was a constant snowfall—not the flurries that had been. Howard Flander opened the rear door and the two men got in awkwardly, because of the handcuffs. They settled themselves on the back seat with Greco on the right, away from the driver's side. Flander closed the door and walked around the car to get behind the wheel. The engine roared to life, hinting at power that was surprising for such a sedate-looking automobile. The car swiftly left the curb and accelerated out the open gates of Point-of-the Mountain Prison. The snow muted the sound of the tires as it drove away.

As the gates flashed past, Donald Greco canceled one of the possibilities in his mind. He was looking at the back of Howard Flander's head. The man had a bull neck, and drove with quick, sure movements. Greco's intuitive knowledge of people ruled out any attempt at escape between the prison and the airport. It would have been futile. He glanced briefly at Riese. He had noticed Utah plates on the car—perhaps Riese would be the only one on the plane with him. He studied Riese until the marshal turned his way. He quickly looked out the window, his mind churning with the next set of probabilities.

"San Francisco ground, Transcon six oh two for taxi."

"Roger, six oh two. Cleared to Runway one right, follow a United DC-10 coming from left to right."

"Six oh two, Roger." Stan let up on the mike button and turned around to look at the right wing tip as the 727 started to roll out of the gate area. As they cleared the gates, waiting only momentarily for the big DC-10 to pass, Stan reached to the center pedestal, moved the flap handle to the fifteen-degree position, and watched the annunciator lights wink yellow, then turn steady green, showing that all the flaps and leading edge devices were in proper position. Pete Douglass reached above his head and tested the antiskid system, the release lights going on and off. At the flight engineer's panel, Mike Fuller was busily preparing the aircraft's systems for flight. The cockpit of a 727 is fifteen feet or more ahead of the nosewheel, and the motion is much like riding in the back of a bus. The three crewmen were gently bouncing up and down in unison as they rolled across the uneven surface of the taxiway.

There had been no conversation since the airplane started to taxi, each pilot busy with routine preflight duties. The nosewheel groaned as the captain leaned on the steering wheel, making a right turn to parallel the runway. Mike broke the silence.

"Ready for the list?"

Stan turned around and said, "Go ahead, Mike."

"OK. The weights are the same, takeoff speeds are the same. Trim setting is twenty-one point five."

Stan flicked a button on the control yoke and the big trim wheels in the center of the cockpit whirred around and stopped at the new setting that Mike had received from the Transcon Load Planners. Pete had stopped fifty yards behind the DC-10 ahead, yet the blast from the giant engines rocked the airplane gently.

Mike had to raise his voice as a 707 roared by them on the runway, its engines at takeoff power. "Trim?"

Stan checked the three trim indicators between the pilots' seats. "Three set!"

"Start levers?"

The copilot put his hand on the small gray knobs. "Three in idle!" They read through the eleven items carefully, even though they knew the list by heart and could have recited it from memory. They both knew that memory was human, and therefore fallible, while a printed card did not forget anything.

Mike said to Pete, "First part of the list is done, boss." He put the white card back on the small table. The DC-10 ahead was taking off. They would be pulling onto the runway as soon as the plane was in the air.

In the cabin, Terry Dunlap had just hung the handset in its bracket. She was finished with the announcements about seat belts and oxygen and all the other required items in the passenger briefing. She sat down on the small jumpseat by the front door. Cathy was seated in the center of the cabin, next to the coat closet. Cindy, being the most junior of the three, had a takeoff station at the extreme rear of the airplane, between the two lavatories.

The passenger address system came to life. "Ladies and gentlemen, we in the cockpit would like to add our welcome to Transcon's flight 602. We'll be taking off momentarily and I'd like to ask the cabin crew to proceed to their takeoff stations. Captain Douglass will have more details of our trip when we're airborne." That announcement was made on all Transcon flights, not so much for the passengers as for the stewardesses. It gave them time to be seated before takeoff so they wouldn't be caught by surprise and be thrown down the aisle by the acceleration.

Pete's muscled hands gripped the throttles. When the clearance came, he pushed them forward—more roughly than usual, Stan thought—and yelled to the copilot, "Line 'em up, Stan!"

He leaned over and, studying the gauges on the instrument panel, manipulated the throttles until they were all even. "Looks good—RPMs and temperature normal."

Pete put his hand back on the throttles and the 727 hurtled down the runway at an ever-increasing speed. Stan watched the airspeed indicator slowly move clockwise. When it passed one-twenty-five he called out, "Rotate!"

Pete took his right hand from the throttles and pulled on the control column with both hands, holding the left wing down a bit to compensate for a slight crosswind. His feet were juggling the rudder pedals in coordinated movements with his hands. The nose reluctantly climbed into the air, until the cockpit was twenty-five above the ground. They could see the end of the runway coming closer, the waters of San Francisco Bay beyond. The airplane hung there for just a moment, then the main gear shook itself free of the runway. With the increased speed, the fan-jet engines took a bigger bite, and using what seemed like a second wind, the graceful machine soared skyward.

Pete watched the altimeter for a rise and, when he saw it, threw his thumb up between the seats. "Gear up!"

Stan reached forward and pulled on the lever, and the wheels thumped into their wells, the automatic braking mechanism stopping the spin before they nestled into the fuselage.

At fifteen hundred feet the captain called for climb power and Stan adjusted the throttles back, reducing the power by ten percent. Mike announced from the flight engineer's seat, "After-takeoff checklist is done."

The airplane gently rocked as they entered the low overcast about two thousand feet above the ground. The turbulence was light as they neared the Sacramento VOR station, the first radio checkpoint on the flight plan. Pete Douglass turned to Mike. "Give Terry a call—tell them they can start serving now. I'm going to leave the seat belt sign on for a little while. Tell 'em it shouldn't get any rougher than this."

Mike picked up the handset that was used for both P.A. announcements and cockpit-cabin communications, and pushed the button overhead marked *Cabin*.

Terry heard the two-tone chime and looked at the ceiling. A red light was on, indicating that the cockpit was calling. She picked up the phone next to her seat. "Go ahead, Roger Ramjet, it's your dime."

Mike laughed. "Terry, the boss says it's OK to start serving—it shouldn't get any worse than it is now."

"Thanks, Mike. You guys want any coffee before I start?"

Terry could hear him asking the two pilots. "Two with cream and sugar, one black, love."

"OK. Be right up." She hung up and walked back toward the galley area in the center of the cabin, signaling to the other two girls that it was all right to get up. Cathy joined her in the galley. "The guys want some coffee. I'll take it up, then get started." She stuck her head out in the aisle. Cindy was stopping halfway to the buffet, talking to the elderly couple on the left side. "We're going to have to teach that girl that on an hour-and-ten-minute flight, you get the trays out first, *then* talk to people."

Cathy shook her blond head, laughing. "Come on, Terry, you want to spoil her enthusiasm?" She stuck her head out and signaled to the new girl to come into the galley.

Terry was pouring three cups of coffee as Cindy arrived

and Cathy gently began to tell her the facts of life. She took the coffee on a small tray to the cockpit and rapped on the door. She could hear Mike get up and check the peephole before he opened the door. She went in and set the tray down on Mike's table. "Will it be smooth?"

Mike looked at her. "It should be, Terry, we haven't had any turbulence reports. It might be a little bumpy just before we land."

"Thanks. Call if you need anything." She smiled and left.

Mike Fuller handed the green cups of steaming liquid to Stan and Pete, then turned back to the logbook on the flight engineer's table, starting to fill in their time and altitude. Stan was sitting casually, his feet up on the metal bar in front of the instrument panel. The cockpit was quiet. Pete concentrated on the instruments before him, holding the 727 to a steady two-thousand-foot-per-minute climb. They broke through the clouds into bright sunlight at twenty thousand feet.

The clouds below produced a bright white glare. Stan reached for his sunglasses and put them on, adjusting them carefully to fit his earphone. He turned to Pete, remembering that the captain never wore sunglasses. He could see the creases deepen at the corners of Pete's eyes as he squinted against the morning sun. As flight 602 neared thirty-three thousand feet, Pete eased back on the power and began leveling off, trimming the aircraft for cruise speed.

Stan was puzzled. "Pete?"

He turned to the copilot, waiting. They hadn't spoken much since the takeoff from San Francisco, except for the normal radio transmissions. "What is it, Stan?"

The copilot pointed to the altitude reminder on the center panel. "We're cleared up to thirty-seven thousand."

Pete's error caught him by surprise. He quickly pushed the throttles back to climb power and continued upward. He made a chuckling sound and said to Stan, "Sorry about that. I was thinking about something else." He turned his attention back to the instruments, and smoothly leveled the aircraft at their assigned altitude.

Stan keyed his mike. "Transcon six oh two, level three-seven-zero."

The Center controller replied, "Transcom six oh two, Roger."

Pete's error had caught Stan by surprise, too. Pete was a pilot's pilot—smoothly professional, thorough, and precise. His mistake could not be termed critical—leveling at the wrong altitude could, but rarely did, occur, and the consequences wouldn't normally be dangerous, but when Stan considered Pete's action in relation to the man, it became a startling occurrence. First there had been his distraction during the approach into San Francisco last night —now this. He decided to bring it up again, but wasn't sure how to start.

When three men spend long periods within touching distance of each other, a strange thing occurs. They develop, on the surface at least, an intimate relationship, shaped by their different personalities. This was the second month that Stan had flown with Pete and Mike. For the first few trips, their conversation had been confined to where they lived, the cars they drove, the status of negotiations between the pilots and Transcon's new management—surface topics, neutral. As the weeks passed and the trips became routine, the three men delved deeper into each others' thoughts. Politics, relationships, desires for the future, Stan's possible marriage (and his dissatisfaction at the thought) all became topics of conversation in the bright sunshine.

At the end of their first month, Pete had invited them out to his farm for dinner. Mike had another engagement, but Stan and Ellen had gone, and thoroughly enjoyed the evening with Kitty and Pete.

Thinking of that evening, and the lasting friendship that he felt had been established, justified Stan's question.

He could picture Kitty as she served coffee and brandy to them from the big coffee table by a blazing fire. They had been silent since they had leveled off, and Pete had pulled the engines back to cruise power. "Pete?"

The captain turned away from the side window and looked at Stan. His eyes were reddened from not enough sleep. He looked tired—harassed. When Pete didn't reply, Stan said, "Pete—is there anything I can help with? I mean about Kitty."

Pete shook his head and tried an unconvincing smile. "Thanks, Stan, there isn't much to do but wait and see." The captain paused while Stan answered a routine call from Salt Lake Center, then continued. "How did you know about Kitty?"

"I ran into Harry Jensen in Dispatch last night."

Pete nodded. "I see."

Stan was dissatisfied with the conversation. "Pete? I feel that we know each other well enough—do you want to talk about it?" He wanted to yell: Come on, you pious bastard, open up! It helps. But the captain-copilot barrier, coupled with the difference in ages, prevented him from saying more. Pete took his airways chart from the glare shield and studied it, signaling silently for a change of subject.

Had Pete been of Stan's generation, with its emphasis on communication and openness, he might have continued. But he had been brought up to believe that a man didn't admit to weakness—and his thoughts about Kitty's operation he saw as a weakness. The gut-busting fear that she would lose her breast returned as he looked across the wide expanse of cloud below. He had talked to enough other pilots about a mastectomy. The scar was a hideous thing —red and ugly from armpit to navel. He involuntarily shuddered as the memory of his dream returned.

Intellectually, Pete Douglass knew that his relationship with his wife didn't revolve around the bedroom. They had so much—so much else that they shared. A mastectomy wouldn't end their sex life. He knew all of that, yet he had grown up in the era when sexuality switched sides—suppressed before the war, then flaunted without being open after the war. It wasn't a subject that was to be discussed with any but the most intimate friends—and Stan didn't fit that category. He couldn't bring himself to talk about it, even though he desperately wanted to.

His mind wandered. He thought of what the mastectomy would do to their lovemaking. He was sure now that it *would* end in a mastectomy, and for the first time thought about Kitty without a breast as they made love. On their wedding night in Honolulu, he remembered how she had walked into their bedroom fresh from a shower, a towel wrapped around her body. He had been sitting on the bed waiting with his bridegroom's nervousness. She walked to the window and drew open the drapes that Pete had carefully closed, then turned to him and dropped the towel to the floor. The moonlight over the ocean played across her breasts—high and proud, erect with anticipation as she walked toward him. He had started to rise to her, but she kept him seated with a gentle hand on his shoulder, then circled his head with both arms, pulling him close to her . . .

"Pete." Stan touched his arm. "They want us to turn to a ninety heading. Vectors around southbound traffic." He pointed out into the clear blue. A contrail hung gracefully in the sky ahead and to their left. Pete hadn't heard the controller. As he reached for the autopilot control knob, Stan saw an unsteadiness in his hand. The 727 banked slightly to the right and steadied on the new heading. Stan decided to stay extra alert, still wishing that his captain would open himself up.

Terry closed the cockpit door. She paused for a moment, surveying the cabin. She heard a click as Mike checked to insure that the door was locked. Her passengers were quiet, looking out the window or reading. As she walked toward the galley to start the breakfast service, a man in his mid-forties stopped her. He put down the San Francisco *Chron-icle* that he had been reading. He was well dressed in a business suit, his smile friendly.

"Will we have any trouble getting in to Salt Lake?" His voice was deep, calm. "I heard on the radio about the storm."

Terry sized him up quickly, deciding that he was a frequent traveler and was used to the problem of weather. She knelt down and kept her voice purposely low. "Captain Douglass thinks we'll get in—we might have to hold, though. He'll make an announcement as soon as he knows for sure." The man smiled and thanked her. She stood up and went back to the buffet.

Cathy and Cindy were efficiently working as a team—Cathy was taking beverage orders and then returning to the galley where Cindy would have the two trays ready to be taken back to the passengers. Terry and Cathy arrived at the door to the galley at the same time. Cathy said to Cindy, "One with coffee, and one with tea and lemon." She turned to Terry. "No one's drinking this morning." She pointed to the open liquor drawer—it was untouched.

Terry laughed. "I'd worry about anyone who was drinking at eight o'clock in the morning anyway."

Cathy had worked back to the middle of the Coach cabin. She took the two trays that Cindy had set up and walked back, giving one of the trays to a young girl travel-ing by herself, and the other she put on a table next to the mother holding her lovely little daughter. Cathy stopped for a moment to look at the infant. She was wrapped in a crocheted pink blanket, the little ball of blond fuzz on top of her head barely visible. The stewardess smiled and said, "She's beautiful. If there's anything you need, be sure to tell me." She paused. "The copilot told me your brother works for Transcon."

The young girl nodded shyly. "Yes, he does—he's a me-chanic in San Francisco." Cathy smiled. The girl con-tinued, "He gave me this trip as a birthday present so that

Jennifer could see her grandparents for the first time." Julia looked at her daughter proudly.

"Well," Cathy said, "that makes you doubly special!"

She turned to the other side of the cabin, looking out the windows as she moved back two rows of seats. They were still in the clouds. The man that Art Forenzo had pointed out was sitting on the aisle. When she approached him, he said quite loudly, "Is there any booze on this lousy airline?" The tone startled Cathy, who took a step backward. She saw Susan sitting two rows behind him.

"Yes, sir. Would you like a drink?"

"It took you long enough to get here! Bring me a Johnnie Walker Black with soda!"

"Would you care for breakfast?" Cathy was amazingly unruffled.

"Of course I want breakfast—and hurry, I've been starving ever since I got on this blasted airplane!" A few of the passengers had turned to look at the source of the loud voice. The balding man had dismissed Cathy with a wave of his hand, as if he were Nero dismissing a tribune from the throne room.

She walked back two rows and stopped next to Susan. "Would you like breakfast, Susan?"

The redheaded girl could tell that Cathy was making a strong effort to control her anger. "If it's not too much trouble, Cathy."

The stewardess smiled. "No trouble. You drink tea, don't you?"

"Yes, I do." She was surprised that Cathy remembered. "Does this happen often?" Susan had said in a low voice, nodding to the back of the man's head.

"No, fortunately. Just once in a while. You get used to it—occupational hazard." She smiled quickly and walked back up the aisle to the galley. She told Cindy to fix a tray with tea for Susan, and rummaged in the liquor drawer for the Scotch. "Oh, shit!" Cindy was startled by the oath. "There's no Johnnie Walker Black Label, only

Red. This is going to be quite a day!" Cathy put the two bottles on the tray, picked up Susan's tray as well and started back down the aisle. She set Susan's tray down first, walking past the Scotch drinker, then returned and put the tray in front of him.

"Sir, I'm sorry. We only have Red Label. We also have J&B, Dewar's, Teacher's . . ."

"Goddammit! Can't a person get anything out of this stinking airline! That's ridiculous!"

Cathy stood for a moment, then decided that she wouldn't even attempt to charge the man for a drink, because he was just the type to pull the fifty-dollar-bill-I-don't-have-anything-smaller trick. It meant having to write up a special report to attach to the liquor forms, but she didn't care. She quickly finished serving breakfast and decided to go to the quiet of the cockpit for a cigarette.

Susan MacKenzie watched Cathy leave through the curtain and go up to the front. She was glad she had declined Terry's offer to sit in First Class. She liked Cathy, and felt that she was getting some insight into the people that Stan worked with by sitting back here. She felt sorry for the blond stewardess. One thing that could be said for nursing was that your customers weren't usually in a position to be chronic complainers. Oh, there were some real beauties among the hospital set—those people who came to the hospital for the joy of complaining to their friends, doctors, nurses, and anyone else who would listen about how sick they were. But she never ran into the kind of verbal abuse that she had just seen. She felt sorry for Cathy because the stewardess was really trapped—that much she understood. In a highly competitive industry like the airlines, the only thing that a company could offer was service and the people who provided that service were often in the middle, as Cathy was—torn between providing courtesy and service on one hand, and on the other sometimes having to withstand a torrent of abuse from someone like the man with the horn-rimmed glasses.

Thinking about Cathy like this also made her think of

Stan—how he had changed. He had acquired a calm, self-assured exterior much as the stewardess had just shown. She liked it in him. It made her feel secure, knowing that he was capable of taking charge of things if necessary. Susan's thoughts drifted to the possibility of establishing, or rather, reestablishing the relationship they had had before. She looked around the airplane. Stan was in a different world now. As the passenger agent had said, it was like a club. Could she be comfortable with Stan knowing that he was a member of this club—surrounded by attractive people, away from home often? He had said at dinner that pilots had one of the highest divorce rates among occupational groups, yet the marriages that worked, worked so much better than the average nine-to-five-job-house-in-the-suburbs kind. Her train of thought was broken by a voice from the speaker overhead.

"Good morning, folks. This is Captain Douglass. We're at thirty-seven thousand feet, our cruising altitude to Salt Lake this morning, and we've just passed over Battle Mountain, Nevada. We expect to arrive in the Salt Lake City area in about thirty-five minutes. As some of you probably know, there is a rather large storm in the center of the Great Plains, and Salt Lake City has received more than its share of snow. We just checked the latest weather —they're reporting overcast skies, the wind is from the north at twenty-five miles per hour with some higher gusts. The temperature is twenty-seven degrees and it's still snowing. The visibility is down to one mile with the snow. However, that's well above our landing limits, so we don't expect any difficulty in getting in to land. If there's any change, we'll certainly let you know." The P.A. clicked off and Susan turned to stare at the grayness out the window.

Pete Douglass hung up the handset he had used for the announcement and drained his cup of coffee. Cathy sat on the first observer's seat directly behind him. She had just lit a cigarette. "Lying to them again, Pete?"

He was studying his chart, then changed the course

selector on the instrumental panel as he tuned in the Bonneville VOR station. He laughed. "Guilty by omission, Cathy. I told them what the weather is, not what I think it'll be when we get there. It's deteriorating pretty fast."

Stan looked across the cockpit at her, perched on the seat with her knees together. He could see halfway up her shapely thigh. "How's Susan doing back there?"

"Oh, she's fine—seems to be enjoying it. It's the bastard that's sitting two rows in front of her that ticks me off."

Mike had swiveled his chair around to face forward. He said, "Is it the man Art pointed out in the boarding area?"

"Yeah, that's the one—I can't figure it out. He's well dressed, obviously wealthy—he's got manicured nails—you'd think he would have enough breeding to be a little civil." She shook her head. "You guys have it made! I think I'll take flying lessons and get out of this racket—become a pilot for Transcon."

The flight engineer rubbed his hands. "Oh boy! Back to double rooms on layovers!"

Cathy grabbed his left ear, the one that didn't have an earphone over it, and twisted. She stubbed her cigarette out in the green paper cup she had been using as an ash-tray and stood up, bending her head slightly to avoid the slanting panel of the cockpit ceiling. "Well, back to the troops—you guys want anything?"

The three of them shook their heads. Pete and Stan turned back to look out the window. As she started to leave, Mike swiveled his seat around to face to the rear and grabbed her hand.

"Cathy? I had a nice time at dinner last night. I've been thinking about it—if we're not too late tonight, want to try again? . . . Dinner, I mean."

The girl looked at him for a long moment, her hand resting on the doorknob. "I don't know, Mike. I enjoyed it, too—let me think for a while, OK?" She opened the door and was gone. The wondrous scent of Estée Lauder left with her.

Stan was repeating the clearance he had just received on the radio. "Roger, Transcon six oh two. Descend to two four oh, check leaving two nine."

Pete disengaged the autopilot and gently nosed the 727 toward the ground six miles below.

Cathy Armello stepped into the cabin, hearing the door lock behind her, and sensing through her feet the change in the pitch angle as they started to descend. She walked slowly to the rear, automatically checking the First Class passengers on her way back to see if they needed anything. The well-dressed businessman was reading the newspaper again, and Cathy picked up his breakfast tray and returned it to the buffet. Cindy was talking to Terry as she stood munching on a left-over Danish pastry.

The older girl turned as Cathy edged into the galley. "Feel better?"

"Yep—thank God there's a place to hide on these airplanes once in a while." She turned to Cindy. "How's our star complainer?"

"He hasn't said a word. I picked up all the trays except the one from the girl with the baby, his, and what's her name . . . Susan's?"

Cathy thought that Cindy wasn't very sensitive to people —she should have remembered the name of the girl they had met this morning.

"Do you want me to get them?"

Cathy shook her head. "No, you relax—I'll pick them up." She left the galley and walked back into the Coach cabin, stopping at the row of seats where the mother and child were sitting. The young girl had put her baby on the seat next to her—the little girl was asleep. Her mother was just setting down her coffee cup.

Cathy smiled at the infant, so peacefully asleep. "Would you like some more coffee?"

Julia Pilero shook her head. "No thanks, I'm finished— it was very good." She was quite shy.

"Fine. Let me take this out of the way." The stewardess

picked up the tray and walked toward the rear. She passed the man with the horn-rimmed glasses and noticed that he was quiet—deeply in thought, staring into his glass of Scotch. The first miniature bottle was empty, and the second was half gone. The meal on the tray before him was untouched.

Cathy sat on the armrest across from Susan, holding the tray with both hands. "Can I get you some more tea, Susan?"

"Oh, no thanks, Cathy." They looked at each other for a moment.

The stewardess said with a nod of her head, "He's going to be drunk before we get halfway to Chicago."

Dr. Joseph Mannheim stared at his second Scotch and sighed. It was a time for introspection, for self-analysis. What to do when he got to Chicago, that was the biggest problem—a hundred-and-fifty-thousand-dollar-a-year practice down the drain. Oh, he still had his license, that was something. But the word would get around, the referrals would start to ebb and eventually dry up, and radiology was not the kind of medicine that could survive without referrals.

He moved his drink in a circular motion and watched the ice cubes swirl around. They were like the words that were spinning in his head—the words that had been spinning ever since the jury had reached its verdict at eleven last night:

"Has the jury reached a verdict?"

"We have, Your Honor."

"Would you give the verdict to the bailiff, please?"

The bailiff had taken it and handed it to the judge. He read it without a trace of emotion. "We the jury find for the plaintiff, and award damages in the amount of eight hundred and fifty thousand dollars."

Joseph Mannheim's attorney had closed his briefcase without a word to his client. The balding doctor had looked at the dead girl's parents standing behind the other long table. They were shaking hands all around and animatedly congratulating one another. He shook his head—the vision blotted itself out, only to be replaced by other parts of the story swirling like the ice cubes of his drink.

He almost laughed as he took another sip of the Scotch. It had been a classic story—one he had heard at med school a dozen times. He had been in San Francisco for a radiology convention, and taken an afternoon to drive out to the Napa Valley. He passed a car that had careened off the road and smashed into a pile of large sewer pipes—the steam was still rising from the hood. He had stopped and run to the wreck. A girl, a very pretty young girl (they had shown pictures to the jury), was lying face down across the front seat, her nose and mouth a mass of blood from the steering wheel. He turned her over slowly and made a superficial examination. She was pale, but there was a faint heartbeat. The big problem was that she wasn't breathing —smashed teeth and blood were blocking the airway, and to live, she had to have air. He had quickly tried to clear the airway, but it was no good.

Other people were gathering around the wreck, and he had yelled for one of them to call an ambulance. As a radiologist, he never carried a bag, but he did have a small penknife. Mannheim remembered a woman scream, "He's killing her!" as he plunged the knife through her throat for the tracheotomy she had to have. He didn't think anything of it at the time. The girl started to breathe then, and he remembered being concerned for the scar that she would have at the center of her throat, and how she'd have to wear scarves to cover it.

Despite her improved breathing, she became more pale, and was dead before the ambulance arrived. The dead girl's parents had sued him, claiming that her death was a direct result of his clumsy attempt to save her life. His whole career had been brought out at the trial—Northwestern Medical School, internship at Cook County; his residency at the University of Chicago had been a high point at the trial. The parents' attorney had been cross-examining him:

Q. Ah! After your one-year residency, you went into a *surgical* residency for one year?

A. Yes.

Q. But, Dr. Mannheim, doesn't it take many years to complete a surgical residency? (This accompanied by knowing looks at the jury.)

A. Yes. I left after a year to go into general practice.

Q. I see. (Arms folded, more knowing looks accompanied by nods at the jury.)

His own attorney had tried hard to repair the damage on re-direct:

Q. Dr. Mannheim, did you ever return to the surgical field?

A. Yes, I did. In nineteen fifty-one, I was drafted into the service, and because of my residency, I worked in a surgical tent just behind the front lines in Korea.

Q. Performing surgery?

A. Yes.

Q. How long did you practice surgery in the service?

A. Almost three years.

But the parents' attorney, returning to the point in his summation, had ignored his service in Korea, saying, "And this man, with *one year* of surgical residency, took it upon himself to stick a penknife, a *penknife*, mind you, into young Gloria's throat, in hopes, he says, of getting her to breathe again!" He had just shaken his head and walked away from the jury box.

During the defense's case, they had brought many prominent medical men to testify that the girl had died from massive internal bleeding—a torn aorta, crushed spleen, dozens of other things, and that even with the best possible care her chances of life would have been slim. But his attorney had told him that juries have a strange dislike for the medical profession when they themselves are healthy, and particularly in California, with an out-of-state physician, are very likely to ignore the evidence and award large sums of money in negligence cases. They would appeal, of course, but that didn't help to counter the massive depression he was slipping into.

He took another sip of his drink and set it down, watching the liquid warmth slosh back and forth in his glass as the plane passed through some light turbulence. The money wasn't a problem—at least the eight hundred and fifty thousand, because his malpractice insurance would adequately cover it, but oh, yes, the word would get around. He sighed and took another sip of Scotch. He knew that he had been stupid to get involved—that's the problem, he decided, getting involved—motives mean nothing any more. He turned and looked out the window. He could tell that they were entering clouds—the sun was beginning to dim as its brilliance was diminished by the passing gray. It would sparkle on the curved Plexiglas of the window by his seat, then disappear, to return in the same peculiar pattern of light. The curve of the window, the light playing over its slightly scratched surface, jogged Mannheim's memory. He studied the curve of the plastic—the light pattern. Korea.

It had been the spring of 1951, a surgery tent—Charlie med station, they had called it. What was the town? Chorwon, that was it. He had been attached to the first Marine Division. Able Company, First Infantry Battalion, had been advancing when the North Koreans launched a savage counterattack—they had flown the casualties in by the dozens in helicopters—a funny Plexiglas bubble covered half the stretcher on each side of the chopper. He had run to one of the helicopters and looked through the plastic cover —a young Marine, he couldn't have been more than eighteen, had lost half his face. It had shaken him badly. He didn't know why, because he had seen plenty of horror in the emergency room at Cook County—carnage from the streets of Chicago.

Joseph Mannheim had just stood immobile at the sight of the young soldier beneath the plastic bubble. A colonel, the commanding officer of the medical detachment and a career officer, had seen him and walked rapidly to the side of the helicopter—Mannheim relived the whole scene as if it had happened yesterday. He could even hear the whistling sound of the chopper blades as they swished overhead.

"Captain Mannheim?" The colonel was standing in front of him. He hadn't responded. The colonel looked around, conscious of the enlisted men watching. He grabbed the younger man's lapels. "Captain! This is Colonel Ramsey! Get on with your duties!"

He had shaken his head, the anguish violently written on his face. "They didn't want to be here . . . look at that poor kid—he'll never be whole again . . ." He gestured like a puppet toward the boy on the stretcher.

Colonel Ramsey had exploded. "*They* didn't want to be here—*none* of us want to be here!" He lowered his voice so that only Mannheim could hear. "Mannheim, you're a doctor—and an officer—so get to work, you bastard!" He had pulled him close as he spoke, then thrown him against the side of the helicopter—hard! "Captain Mannheim, *you have no choice!*"

You have no choice.

He hadn't, of course, and he had performed well, receiving two citations for merit while he was in Korea. It was Colonel Ramsey who had steered him to radiology after the war, with letters of reference for a residency at Mayo.

Mannheim sighed audibly as his thoughts returned to the present. He poured the remaining Scotch into his glass, mixing in soda from the small container on the tray. He knew that he shouldn't be drinking so much—he didn't even like it, and the headache from last night was still there. But despite the dull ache behind the bridge of his nose, he decided the Scotch was helping. He drained off the drink in two swallows.

You have no choice.

He chuckled to himself. He hadn't had one at Chorwon, but he had had a choice in the Napa Valley—all his training, his belief had been to try to help people, to care for them, and his choice had been to help—the best way he could. Look what it got me, he thought—an eight-hundred-and-fifty-thousand-dollar pain in the ass, a practice that may go to pieces. His mind projected, played games with itself: Would he get involved again?

His immediate reaction was violent—*never*! He shoved it out of his mind and began toying with the omelette on his tray. It was cold. He decided he wanted another drink.

Susan was looking at the blond stewardess. "I know that man from somewhere—I just can't place him. I've seen his picture, something like that. I want to tie him in to the hospital in my mind, but it doesn't fit." She shook her head, puzzled. "Have you got a minute to talk?"

Cathy said, "Sure. Let me take these trays back, then we'll have a few minutes before landing." She got up, took Susan's tray and walked to the galley.

Susan watched her go, and was reminded of a television commercial for panty hose, where the men on the airplane leaned out of their seats to watch a stewardess's legs go by. Cathy had beautiful legs, that was certain. She found herself wondering about Stan—and Ellen—wondering if Ellen's legs were as appealing.

Cathy returned quickly and sat on the armrest across the aisle again. Susan offered her a cigarette.

"No thanks, we're not allowed to smoke in the cabin—it's unladylike, they tell us." When Susan started to put them away, Cathy laughed. "Oh, no, go ahead—it's a rather antiquated view, I've always thought, but I suppose it makes sense. We can always go to the cockpit."

Susan felt a twinge, thinking of Stan. She finished lighting her cigarette. "Have you been a stewardess long, Cathy?"

"Almost seven years now." When she saw the look of surprise on the other girl's face she smiled. "It's a pretty good job after a couple of years. The salary is as good as most secretaries', and the time off is fantastic—I've got enough seniority now so that I only work about fourteen days a month."

"That's amazing—I don't know if I could put up with the people, though."

Cathy was quiet for a moment. "I guess you basically have to like people in this job. Scenes like this one"— she gestured to the passenger two rows in front of Susan —"don't happen very often, and I've found that the best way to deal with them is to be as nice as possible—sort of a 'kill 'em with kindness' approach. Another advantage to the job is the travel—we get discount privileges with other airlines, so we can go almost anywhere in the world." She paused for a moment, self-conscious about talking so much. "How long have you known Stan, Susan?"

The redheaded girl inhaled and blew the smoke out in a long sigh. "About nine and a half years, I guess. We were dating—no, we were engaged without a ring—before Stan went to work for the airlines. He must have started about the same time you did."

"Yes, I remember now—I flew with him as a new stewardess. He was a brand-new flight engineer." She wondered if Susan knew about Ellen.

She sensed the question in Cathy's mind. "Stan told me that he was engaged to Ellen last night at dinner. Do you know her?"

"I've flown with her a few times." She was relieved. Cathy didn't like to hide things from people. "What happened?"

Susan looked puzzled.

"With you and Stan, I mean."

"Oh. Well, I met someone else and married him. It didn't last too long, though. I divorced him a year or so ago and went to San Francisco—a nursing job. I just decided to go back to New York last week and was leaving last night when I ran into Stan. We hadn't seen each other in seven years, it was quite a jolt."

"I'm glad that you ran in to him, Susan. I like you. Maybe I'm talking too much—Mike tells me that I do—but he needs something more than Ellen can give. I hope you'll be in the city. I think I'd like to get to know you more."

Susan was surprised, and pleased. She liked this blond, carefree woman, and she'd need some female companionship when she got to New York. "I'd like that, Cathy." She stubbed out her cigarette. "Thanks."

"I've got to check the cabin. We'll talk more when we get on the ground." Her smile was sincere—she touched Susan's arm and got up. As she walked forward to the buffet, she stopped at the seat two rows ahead of Susan. The man looked up at her. He seemed a little softened, she thought. Not so.

"This breakfast is cold—and was terrible! I want another drink!"

"Sir—we'll be landing in a very short while, and we've closed the galley. I'll have one for you first thing after we take off from Salt Lake."

He glared at her as she took his tray, but had no reply. As she returned to the buffet, a chime rang, and the fasten-seat-belt signs above each row of seats came on. The P.A. system clicked into life.

"Folks, this is Captain Douglass again. We're presently fourteen miles from the Salt Lake City airport, descending through twelve thousand feet. We should be landing in another six or seven minutes, so I'd like to have you all take a seat and fasten your seat belts at this time. The weather is much the same. The visibility has dropped a bit, however, to three-quarters of a mile."

Cathy made a quick trip through the cabin, checking the passengers' seat belts. Everyone was sitting quietly.

The older couple were smiling and holding hands—Cindy had found out that they were returning from a second honeymoon in Hawaii, and had stopped in San Francisco for a few days before returning to Salt Lake. Cathy warmed at the sight. They looked like two young lovers at some secret rendezvous. She saw that Cindy was already strapping herself in on the rear jump seat. She walked back to the center of the airplane, just forward of the galley area, and sat on the center stewardess seat. The small jump seat was located next to the coat-room, and it pulled out on tracks for takeoff and landing. She buckled the lap belt, then fastened the shoulder harness over her chest, attaching the ends to the big center buckle of the seat belt. The center seat is the only one from which the cabin attendants can get a view out the windows. Cindy, in the rear seat between the lava-tories, and Terry, next to the front door facing to the rear, could not see out the tiny window in the door. Cathy looked to the left, and could see out two of the windows lining the side of the cabin. There was nothing —only a gray-white color, darkening slightly as the air-craft descended.

Pete Douglass looked at the windshield wipers three feet in front of him. They were beginning to cake with a coating of rime ice. As he hung up the handset for the P.A. system, he turned to the flight engineer. "Mike, let's turn on the wing anti-ice. We'll leave it on until we break out—and turn it off if we have to make a missed approach."

"OK, boss." Mike reached above the copilot's head, turning on two switches and watching the lights blink green. The temperature needle indicated a hundred and ninety degrees—hot air from the engines was being forced along ducts in the leading edge of the wings, pre-venting the ice from forming there and changing the aerodynamic shape that was so necessary for lift. "Lights are green, Pete. The approach descent checklist is complete, too."

"Thanks." There was silence in the cockpit now. Not tension, really, just an increased alertness because of the difficult approach to Salt Lake, and excess chatter among the pilots could be distracting.

They heard Salt Lake Approach Control speaking to them. "Transcon six oh two, turn left heading zero one zero. Cleared for an ILS approach to Runway three four left, you're four miles from Riverton intersection. The Salt Lake weather is three hundred, sky obscured, three-quarters of a mile. The RVR is four thousand, variable to four thousand, five hundred." RVR is an electronic means of measuring visibility—six thousand is roughly equivalent to one mile, twenty-four hundred roughly equal to a half-mile. "Contact tower on one nineteen two passing the outer marker."

Stan keyed the mike button and spoke into the mini-tel mike that was part of his headset. "Roger, cleared for the approach, tower at the marker. Six oh two."

Pete banked the 727 to the left. "Flaps to fifteen, gear down, final descent check."

Stan moved the flap handle and could feel the airplane decelerate, then slow even more as the landing gear extended. Mike turned on the *No Smoking* sign and started to read from the checklist in his hand.

Both pilots were studying the approach charts that were clipped on a small board fastened to the wheel in front of them. Salt Lake City airport is 4,221 feet above sea level. They were studying the procedure for a missed approach. The lowest they could fly legally on the approach was 4,421 feet—if they could not see the runway at that altitude, two hundred feet from the ground, they would have to pull up and go around.

The captain spoke as he was looking at the chart. "Stan, be sure to give me a call at a thousand feet above the field, and another a hundred feet from minimum altitude."

"OK, Pete." They could hear Terry giving her announcement in the cabin prior to landing—telling the passengers to extinguish smoking materials and check their seat belts.

A blue light blinked on and off on both sides of the cockpit as they crossed over the outer marker, almost six miles from the runway. Pete had the crossbars dead center as they descended toward the ground. Stan changed to the tower frequency and spoke into the mike. "Salt Lake Tower, Transcon six oh two is by the marker, inbound."

"Roger, six oh two—cleared to land. The wind is three six zero at fifteen, occasional gusts to twenty-five."

Pete cut in, "How's the braking?"

"Six oh two, the braking's been reported fair to poor by a United 727 about, oh, ten minutes ago. The runway was plowed and sanded a half-hour ago, full length and width—there's about an inch of snow on it now."

Stan replied, "Roger cleared to land—we'll report the lights."

The airplane was starting to be tossed about now, as it got closer to the ground, and closer to the gusty winds. They flew down the glide slope, Pete keeping the crossbars perfectly centered—occasionally adjusting the throttles as the airplane pitched in the turbulence.

"A thousand feet above the ground!" Stan called out as the altimeter slowly unwound past 5,221 feet.

The aircraft continued to descend, wallowing slightly with the wind gusts as they slowed to almost landing speed. Mike Fuller stared intently out the windshield into the darkening gray. Stan and Pete's eyes were glued to the instrument panels in front of them. The copilot watched the altimeter and called out "A hundred to minimums!"

At the same time, Mike's eyes picked out the flashing

strobe lights running like a rabbit down the approach light system to the end of the runway. "Lights in sight! Just off to the left." It always amazed him how close three hundred feet was to the ground when you hadn't seen it for a long time.

Pete looked up from the instruments, transitioning his eyes to the visual cues outside the cockpit. They were right on the center line of the runway—the lights appeared off to the left because of the correction for the slight crosswind. The snow gleamed like a thousand points of light as it sped by, reflecting in the bright glare of the landing lights.

The 727 descended the last two hundred feet, thundering over the end of the runway and touching down hard. Pete pulled up the spoilers, gluing the airplane to the runway, and threw the three roaring engines into reverse. The airplane slowed perceptibly. Pete Douglass' feet worked furiously on the rudder pedals as the big 727 yawed on the runway, trying to keep it in the center of the one-hundred-and-fifty-foot-wide strip of snow-covered concrete. The nose swerved slightly to the right as a gust of wind acted as a lever on the high T-tail. He quickly took the engines out of the high power setting, back to idle reverse, and stood on the brakes.

"Eighty knots!" They were more than halfway down the runway. The little lights on the antiskid panel blinked on and off rapidly as the system metered the brake pressure to each wheel and released the individual brake as the wheel approached a skid. They slowly swung back to a direction parallel to the runway lights, and at the slower speed, the brakes took over fully. They stopped, having used almost nine thousand of the runway's available ten-thousand-foot length.

The three pilots breathed an inaudible sigh of relief. Mike broke the silence. "Very nice, boss. The people might not like the hard landing, though."

"The hell with 'em." As a captain, Pete had long ago

given up trying to explain why a soft landing is not always the best landing—particularly in conditions like these. The idea was to get the airplane on the ground—*positively* on the ground. He had planted the 727 as close to the approach end of the runway as was safe, and had he taken the extra thousand feet to make a soft touchdown, they would be in the desert now, off the far end. The dialogue was a standing joke among the three men.

Mike said, "I'll tell 'em the copilot did it." Stan laughed as he started setting up the cockpit for shutdown.

The snow was coming in great blankets as the wind whipped at the airplane. They taxied slowly, the ruts in the snow causing a jostling ride to the terminal. As they approached the building, they could make out the ground crew muffled in parkas against the wind and snow. Pete caught sight of a man with two yellow wands, illuminated in the half-light, waving him along a yellow line that was now buried under white powder. As they braked to a stop, they saw the loading stand moving toward the side of the plane. There were no jetways at Salt Lake—the people would have to walk to the terminal through the snow.

Stan grasped the three start levers and pushed down. The engines died instantly, and there was quiet. He thought, One down, and three to go.

"Passengers with concealed firearms will be permitted aboard Transcon flights provided they are officials of a municipal, state or federal government and have proper credentials authorizing them to carry arms."

Page 17, Para. 1
Transcon Flight Operations Manual

7

The black Ford sedan passed through the airport security check and rolled quietly to a stop outside the door marked TRANSCON OPERATIONS. Howard Flander set the parking brake and got out. He lifted his collar against the snow and walked around the car to the right rear door. His overcoat and suit jacket were unbuttoned, despite the heavy snow, for easier access to his pistol should he need it. He thought, Greco seems docile enough—he hasn't said a word since he got in the car an hour ago.

The drive to the airport from the prison had taken twice the normal thirty minutes because of the storm. Several cars had been abandoned along the route—Flander had wanted to stop to help one young woman who obviously needed aid, but he knew that he couldn't. They hadn't been able to go much faster than twenty-five miles an hour, and the marshal had been relieved when he finally drove through the gates at the airport.

A Transcon 727 was rolling up to the gate marked #3. The engine sound was muffled through the snowfall. It must be 602, he decided, and opened the car door, stepping back two or three paces after he did so. Greco got out first, then stood awkwardly as Sam Riese followed him, their wrists linked together. The two men walked toward the entrance. Howard Flander followed two paces behind, listening to their footsteps make crunching sounds in the snow. He watched Sam Riese's stooped shoulders rise and fall as he walked, and wondered why the office hadn't sent a younger man for the job of transporting Greco back to Chicago. But Sam Riese had been the only available marshal, and the U.S. Attorney wanted Greco back for a speedy trial.

Riese and his prisoner went in the door with Flander following. They stomped their feet free of the clinging snow on a dirty rug just inside.

A man who had been seated at a computer keyboard rose as they entered. He was about forty, a big man with reddish hair—he looked harried. He walked to the three men, Flander still standing behind Greco and Riese. "Are you Riese?"

The older man spoke, "Yes."

"I'm Steve Burnick." He held out his hand, then noticed the handcuffs and dropped it, somewhat embarrassed.

"This is Howard Flander, from the Federal Marshal's office here in Salt Lake." Riese gestured behind him with his free hand.

The station manager didn't know whether to shake hands with the other man, and decided not to. "Flight 602 has just landed, and should be leaving on time."

"Good. We noticed a plane coming in when we got out of the car—is that it?" Sam Riese spoke concisely, without emotion.

"Right. One of the passenger agents will brief the stewardess. I'd like you and your prisoner to board as soon as the passengers are off and we've serviced the aircraft, if that's all right."

"That's fine—thanks for all your help, we appreciate it. Is there a men's room close by?"

The station manager pointed down a hall leading from the main operations office. "There's one down there—help yourself."

They walked down the hall. At one point Greco hesitated, pulling on the handcuffs. Sam Riese spun around, his normally bland face turning to stone. "You do that one more time, and I'll kick your balls off!"

Flander, watching the scene from behind them, quickly reassessed the older man. He looked at Greco, slightly cowed from the exchange. He may not be too young, Flander thought, but he sure as hell isn't soft. They went into the small men's room, Flander waiting in the corner, his hand on the gun at his belt. There was no need. They finished at the urinals quickly, though clumsily, and walked back into the Operations room.

It was a rather large room, divided in half by a low counter. On the side that they entered, there were several desks with chairs and some electronic equipment. A long shelf held books and manuals on one wall. There was a television screen in the near corner with several flights listed. The first was flight 602, indicating gate #3, and an eleven-ten departure time. All the rest of the flight numbers had one word after them—CANCELED.

Howard Flander spoke for the first time, gesturing toward the television screen. "Looks like we got here just in time." He was speaking to Burnick.

"What? Oh, yeah. Everything's canceled after 602 because of the storm." He looked out the window—the snow was falling even faster. At that moment, two men walked in, covered with snow. One wore the cap of a Transcon captain, the gold scrambled eggs on his visor almost obscured by the melting snow.

Steve Burnick went over to the counter, turning back to the marshal as he walked, saying, "If you'll wait for just a minute, we'll be ready to board you first." He walked over to where the two pilots were studying the weather board on the other side of the counter. "Captain, the company wants to know what the braking action is like."

Pete looked at the man for a moment. "Terrible, if you really want to know—I'd call it nil, but that would suspend all operations, so I'll call it poor and leave it at that till we leave."

"OK, I'll tell them poor. By the way, there's a federal marshal with a prisoner going back to Chicago."

Pete looked up from the weather. "Oh?" At that moment, Howard Flander was walking toward them.

"Captain? Are you in command of flight 602?"

"That's right."

The man extended his hand. "I'm Howard Flander, a U.S. marshal." He felt better talking to someone in uniform than he had to the station manager in his green jacket. The feeling was a carry-over from his days with the Military Police. He held out his identification wallet. Pete studied it and handed it back.

"What's the story?" Stan had joined them, to listen in. He nodded at the marshal.

"His name is Greco. He escaped from custody in Chicago a month ago, and we're taking him back. The marshal that's accompanying him is Sam Riese, from the Chicago office. He's the one in the dark coat and hat. He's armed—carries a three fifty-seven Magnum in a shoulder holster."

The station manager cut in. "They'll be seated in the last row, Captain. They won't be a bother to the other passengers back there. The load's light—only twenty in the back cabin—I'll have the agent seat them all forward."

"Fine." Pete was already bored with the conversation. He looked at the clock on the wall. Ten-thirty. It would be twelve-thirty in New York, about the time Kitty should be waking up. He wondered if he should call now, but decided that she wouldn't be completely awake yet. He turned to Steve Burnick. "I want to leave early—at eleven."

The station manager was startled. "We can't—I'm sure that all the passengers aren't here yet."

Pete stared him down. "Look out the window—if the visibility gets much worse, we won't be able to take off. Call the tower—see what they're giving now."

The station manager went to the hot line. "This is Transcon Operations. What's the visibility?" He waited. "OK. Thanks." He turned back to the captain and Stan. "They're still giving three-quarters, but the RVR is down to thirty-five hundred, steady."

"Well, if we can't leave early, even with a few less passengers, we probably won't leave at all. Get me the sector dispatcher on the phone, would you?"

Burnick picked up another phone and dialed direct to the dispatcher in Chicago. He handed the phone to Pete. While the captain talked, he picked up another phone and paged one of the Transcon passenger agents to come to Operations.

On the airplane, Terry Dunlap stood in the center of the First Class cabin with the other two girls. A passenger agent was talking to them. "They'll be handcuffed together. We've given them the last row of seats on the right side. I guess the only other thing is to remind you to check the silverware on the trays after they've eaten—especially the knives and forks—they may not even eat at all. I don't know. And of course, no booze."

The girls were listening intently. Cindy's eyes were wide. She had never realized that prisoners were carried on airplanes before, and it scared her a bit. Cathy sensed her apprehension. "Relax, Cindy," she said, "there's nothing to worry about." The young girl smiled a little nervously.

The passenger agent left the airplane. Cathy Armello returned to the rear cabin and sat across from Susan. "Hi. I've got a minute before they put the passengers on. How's the trip so far?"

Susan smiled. "It's terrific—I guess it's one of those things where it helps to know the management." The two girls laughed together.

Cathy turned serious. "Where are you going to stay when you get to New York?"

"I've reserved a room at the Barbizon temporarily. I'll get an apartment as soon as I get a job and know where I'll be working."

"I was thinking while we were landing—would you like to stay with me? I have a roommate, Cheryl Eastlund. She's a stew also. We've got loads of room, and it would be nice to have a nonairline face around the place for a change. Do you know the city?" Susan nodded. "Well, our place is in a high-rise at Sixty-ninth and Second. It's a new building."

Susan looked at the stewardess. She was surprised, and flattered at the offer. After a long moment she said, "Cathy—thanks. That'd be great. I'd insist on paying my share of the rent. It would be nice to have people around—there haven't been too many lately." She dropped her eyes. "Are you sure it wouldn't be too much trouble?"

Cathy smiled. "No trouble. We've talked about getting another roommate for a long time now, and this will give Cheryl and me a chance to see if we like it. As for the rent—we're happy to take any money we can get." She opened her mouth to say more, but a chime rang in the cabin, and she heard the head stewardess calling.

"People coming!"

Cathy got up and went forward to the center of the airplane, ready to hang up passengers' coats as they came aboard.

Outside, Mike Fuller had finished his preflight inspection—a duty that he enjoyed as a flight engineer only in good weather. He was required to make a brief but thorough walk-around inspection of the aircraft at each stop, and the snow had made it a long, cold ten minutes. He was about to climb the boarding ramp to return to the warmth of the cockpit when four men approached the stairs. He stood back to let them go first. He recognized one as a Transcon agent. The other three were walking slightly ahead and he noticed the handcuffs linking two of the men together. He followed them up the stairs wondering what the poor bastard had done to be transported that way. He'd seen prisoners before, but rarely did they keep handcuffs on while they were on the plane.

In the Operations Office, Pete Douglass hung up the phone. He turned to the red-haired Burnick. "Dispatch says it's OK to leave at eleven. They're worried about getting this airplane stranded here. Can we make it?"

The station manager looked at the wall clock and shrugged. It was just another problem added to his already problem-filled day. "We'll try. Can't say as I blame you for wanting to leave." He turned to look out the window, thinking of all the people he would have to deal with when they found out that their flights had been canceled. He picked up another phone and dialed a number that would patch him into the speakers all over the terminal. "Ladies and gentlemen, may I have your attention for an important announcement. Because of the weather, Transcon Airline's flight 602 to Chicago will be leaving ten minutes early." He could hear his own words echoing throughout the building. "Would all passengers for Transcon flight 602 proceed immediately to Boarding Area three on the main concourse. All passengers for Transcon flight 602 . . ."

Pete turned to the teletype machine. It had finished printing a message from Transcon's Central Dispatch:

OPERATIONS ADVISORY—ALL STATIONS: ALL ROCKY
MTN. AIRPORTS CLOSED AT THIS TIME EXCEPT SLC AND
DEN. EXPECT REMAINING TWO TO CLOSE WITHIN THE
HOUR. ADVZ PASSENGERS DESTINED FOR GRT. PLNS STA-
TIONS, SAME PROBLEM—CHECK W/CENTRAL DISPATCH
BEFORE RELEASING ANY DEPRTR TIMES OR INFO.
                          CHICAGO DISPATCH—GUNTER

Pete shook his head in frustration. Of all the days to have a storm. He normally didn't concern himself with trying to make up time, but today he wanted to be in New York as fast as possible. He wondered if his insistence on an early departure was truly because of the weather, or whether his subconscious was urging him home on Kitty's account. He looked at the clock—it was ten minutes to eleven. He turned to his copilot, "Let's go, Stan—I want to get the hell out of here."

They walked to the door, buttoning their coats up around their chins, preparing for the wet icy blast that would greet them outside.

Cathy watched the three men move down the aisle—Riese was leading Greco, Howard Flander following. They took a seat on the right side of the airplane in the last row —just in front of the lavatory. She watched as the two men sat down and clumsily buckled their seat belts. The younger man was standing up, talking to Riese, who had taken the aisle seat. They spoke only briefly; then the third man left them and headed for the front door of the airplane. He smiled at Cathy as he passed—a brief smile. Cathy thought that he seemed worried—there had been a flicker of apprehension in his eyes.

She walked to the back, looking at Susan as she passed. Susan asked a question with her eyes, tilting her head toward the rear. Cathy just said "Later" as she walked by.

When she got to the last row of seats, she said, "May I take your coats?"

The older man shook his head. "No, we'll have to keep them on—I know it's a little awkward, but these don't come off." He held up his right wrist, dragging the prisoner's arm up with it. Cathy started to say something, but he stopped her. "We'll be fine."

Cathy looked at them for a moment, then turned and walked toward the front of the cabin.

Greco looked at the federal marshal, speaking for the first time since they had been shackled together. "Mr. Riese, can't we take the overcoats off? It's going to get pretty warm in the two hours or however long it takes. I ain't gonna try anything."

Sam Riese stared at him, then looked around the cabin. He finally saw what he was looking for on the rear entry door—a sturdy handle located about halfway up. He said, "OK, get up." The two men rose and Riese steered Greco to the door. He told the prisoner to turn around and, when he could not see, reached into a small slit inside his belt and withdrew the key to the handcuffs. "Put your face up against that door!" When Greco was flat against the door, Riese carefully unlocked the handcuff from his own wrist and closed it around the handle on the door.

"OK, Mr. Greco, take your coat off slowly, all but your left arm." Greco clumsily obeyed, shaking his arm free of the right sleeve. The coat hung from his left arm, dragging on the floor. While Greco was struggling with the overcoat, Sam Riese quickly slipped out of his own and put it in the overhead rack. As he watched his prisoner work to get out of the garment, he wondered why he had decided to do this. Coats had never bothered him, and he hadn't really cared whether they bothered his prisoner—then why this silly little act of compassion for a man he'd never see again? Getting soft in my old age, he decided. He chuckled to himself.

"Now—put both hands against the door and spread your feet backward!" Greco obeyed, taking the familiar pose of a man about to be searched. The marshal slowly unlocked Greco from the handcuffs. The coat slid to the floor in a heap, sliding from the handcuffs now hanging from the door. "Put your hand back up on the door!" Greco complied, and Sam Riese refastened the cuff to the prisoner again. "Pick it up!" He indicated the coat on the floor. Greco stooped and grabbed the coat. "Put it on the seat over there!" He did, and the two men once more sat down. Cathy Armello had stopped to talk to Susan. "Well, you really are getting the full treatment today—that was a prisoner being transported to Chicago." Susan looked surprised. "It happens every once in a while—they seat them all the way in the back, so they don't bother the other passengers—this is the first time I've seen them keep handcuffs on, though." She looked toward the rear of the airplane and saw Greco and Riese sitting down again, after removing their coats. The marshal saw her and signaled with his free hand. "Be right back," she said to Susan, and went to them.

"We changed our minds on the coats," Sam Riese said. "Could you put that one in the rack for me, please?"

The stewardess smiled and picked up the coat, wondering how they had managed to remove them with the handcuffs. As she returned to where the redheaded girl was sitting, the passenger agent walked to her.

"Did any of the through passengers get off?"

Cathy took a quick look around—the only throughs that she had were Susan, the mother with her child, and the bald man with the horn-rimmed glasses. They were all in the cabin. "No, no one got off."

"Good. We're going to leave early—apparently your captain is in a hurry." He pointed out a window. "Can't say as I blame him. I'm putting the people on now. It looks like you'll only have about seventeen or so in Coach because of the early departure."

"OK—I hope the next time we're here the weather is better."

The passenger agent laughed and headed for the front door. Cathy walked after him, waving at Susan, and stopped in the galley where Cindy was checking the supplies in the newly arrived buffet units. The two girls started working as a team—Cindy checking meals, Cathy checking the liquor count. She was relieved to find several bottles of Johnnie Walker Black Label in the drawer.

Terry had returned to the front door, ready to greet the passengers as they came out of the snow. Just as she got there, another Transcon agent was coming aboard the airplane, followed by a small boy of twelve. The agent stamped his feet to clear the snow off them. "Are you the first stewardess?"

Terry said, "Yes. And who is this?" She looked at the boy.

"I have an unaccompanied child here—his mother is meeting him at O'Hare. He's riding First Class today." The agent handed the ticket to Terry and left quickly, ducking his head into his parka as he went outside.

She looked at her new passenger. He was a head shorter than she, his blond hair was tousled and wet from the snow. She bent down, getting her eyes level with his. "Hi! My name's Terry. What's yours?" She had her hand on his shoulder.

He stood silent for a moment. Without smiling, he said, "My name's Kevin." He wore thick glasses—dark-colored frames that contrasted sharply with his pale skin. His brown eyes, large behind the lenses, stared at her unblinking. He seemed almost bored.

Terry stood up, taking her hand from his shoulder. "Well, Kevin," she said, moving him into the warmth of the cabin, "you can take any seat in this cabin that isn't occupied. Is this your first time on an airplane?"

He laughed, almost to himself. "No, this is the fifth trip this year. My dad lives in Salt Lake City, my mom lives in Chicago. I kind of hop back and forth." He hesitated by a seat. "Could you help me with my coat, please? I have a little trouble with my arm." He shrugged his jacket off his shoulder. His left arm was in a cast from wrist to biceps.

As she helped him off with the heavy coat she asked, "What happened to your arm?"

He seemed unconcerned, shrugging his shoulders. "Dad took me skiing—I fell."

Terry was determined to win the boy's affection. "That's too bad. Skiing can be a lot of fun. My husband and I do a lot of it—mostly in Colorado."

"Uh huh, I guess so." His voice trailed off. He was settling into a seat by the window, buckling his seat belt awkwardly, the cast hampering his movements.

Terry reached across the empty seat and helped him. "Well, at least you'll be home for Christmas." She smiled at him.

Kevin looked at her for a long time, his eyes devoid of emotion. "Yeah." He raised the cast. "Dad didn't tell Mom about this, though. She doesn't even know that we went skiing." He dropped the cast in his lap and turned his head.

Terry's throat tightened. "I have to go now—there are more people coming. You just call me if you need anything, OK?" She left him and walked back to the front cabin door. The boy upset her, angered her as they all did. She had seen so much of it. Small children being shuttled back and forth between parents like Ping-Pong balls, living in a limbo world of one parent or the other—mini travelers in the world of divorce. To Terry it seemed as if they cried out for love, and tried to shut out the world at the same time. She shook her head, thinking how glad she was that she and Dave had decided to wait, perhaps not to have children at all.

Mike was in the flight engineer's seat when Pete and Stan walked into the cockpit. The door was open, and as they took off their coats, they watched the trickle of passengers boarding the airplane, bundled against the slanting snow outside, relieved to be in the comparative warmth of the airplane.

As the captain eased himself into the left seat, Mike said, "Outside's pretty good. I didn't see any ice or slush stuck in the landing gear—I've ordered a de-icing truck to stand by. I thought you'd want one quick spray before we left."

Pete talked as he put on his headset, adjusting the wire-like microphone to fit directly in front of his lips. "Good, Mike—we'll want more than a quick spray, I think. Another thing—don't forget to close the pack cooling doors when we taxi, OK?"

"Sure, Pete."

It was five minutes before eleven. Stan called Salt Lake clearance delivery and requested, and got, their clearance to Chicago.

At the same time that Stan was talking on the radio, the airport manager at Stapleton International Airport in Denver was talking on the phone to the crew chief of the maintenance department.

"What's the status, Charlie?"

"Pretty bad, sir. The plows can't keep up on Runway thirty-five—we're going to have to call it quits, I'm afraid."

"How long until you can get the runway open again?" The airport manager was a very harassed man.

"If the wind doesn't get any stronger, an hour after the snow slacks off."

"OK, Charlie. Tell your men thanks, I appreciate the job they did keeping us open as long as they have. I'm going to close the airport." The manager was depressed—Denver had some of the best snow equipment in the country, and he always felt as if he had lost a fifteen-round bout by decision whenever he had to close the field. He picked up another phone and sent the appropriate messages to the FAA, the airlines, and anybody else who would be affected.

". . . maintain seventeen thousand, expect flight level three three zero within twenty miles. Departure on one twenty-five seven and squawk a thousand on the transponder."

There was some static on the radio as the controller working clearance delivery answered: "Transcon six oh two, readback is correct—have a nice trip."

"Thanks, we'll see you next week." Stan let up on the microphone button and bent forward to dial in seventeen thousand on the altitude warning instrument. Their first assigned altitude would keep them clear of the rugged granite peaks that surrounded the Salt Lake airport. He turned to Pete. "I haven't seen a prisoner in a long time— I guess I thought all crime had stopped or something." He shook his head at his own joke.

Mike started to say something but the passenger agent had entered the cockpit. "Captain? We're ready to go if you are—the de-icing trucks are standing by outside. We didn't get many people—only four in the front and seventeen in the back."

Pete turned in his seat and looked at the agent. His head was covered with snow. It was melting and dripping onto the shoulders of his parka in little rivulets. "OK, let's go now or we may not go at all."

The agent left the cockpit and closed the heavy door. Terry Dunlap stuck her head into the cockpit and confirmed the passenger count. As the pilots were reading the prestart checklist, the windshield was blanked out by a torrent of pinkish liquid accompanied by the roaring sound of liquid being sprayed at high pressure on metal.

Outside, the de-icing truck was moving slowly around the airplane. A man stood in a basket at the end of the boom arm bundled against the blowing snow. He was directing a hose back and forth along the sides of the airplane, spraying it with a mixture of Glycol and water. He watched the stream carefully, despite the snow blowing into his face—making sure that there wasn't a patch of fuselage, wing, or tail surface that escaped the heavy spray.

In the cabin, Cindy ran to the galley after the oxygen

announcement—Cathy was closing the doors on the ovens and checking that they were secure for takeoff. She stood up as the younger stewardess entered.

Cindy's eyes were wide. "What's that noise? And all that stuff on the windows?" She pointed across the cabin to where the pinkish fluid was oozing in waves down the side windows.

Cathy realized that this was probably the first time that Cindy had ever seen a plane de-iced. She laughed to herself. "That's a spray to get the snow off the wings. They always do it if it's snowing hard outside. Didn't they tell you about it in stew school?"

Cindy's eyes lost some of their astonishment. "Well . . . I guess they did. I just forgot about it."

They could feel the airplane vibrate slightly as the number three engine was started. The sound increased noticeably as each engine started in turn. Cathy said to the younger girl, "Come on, let's sit down—it'll probably be bumpy while we taxi." Cindy walked back to her takeoff station on the rear jump seat. Cathy pulled the middle jump seat out and sat down.

Pete Douglass looked across the cockpit, watching Mike transfer electrical power from the APU to the airplane's three generators. When all the generator breaker lights were out, he spoke into the microphone. "They're all running, you can disconnect."

The mechanic on the ground, his headset plugged into a little hole in the side of the fuselage, said, "OK, disconnecting—have a good trip."

The pilots watched him walk to the front of the aircraft. He was hunched over against the force of the wind. He turned and raised one of the flashlights that he held to his forehead. Pete saluted out the window and pushed the three throttles forward slightly. The airplane grudgingly began to roll.

Stan pressed the mike button. "Transcon six oh two ready to taxi."

"Transcon six oh two cleared to Runway three four left. Wind is three-thirty at twenty, gusts to thirty-five."

The copilot answered and turned to his right, peering through the snow to see if there was anything in their path as the 727 turned from the gate and headed toward the runway. The blue taxiway lighting was barely visible through the snow that was being driven almost parallel to the ground by the gusty wind.

In Chicago, Lars Gunter was looking out the big windows in Transcon's dispatch office. He was sitting in his chair, his elbows on his knees, his chin cradled in his big Swedish hands. It was a gray day. The drizzle that had started before dawn was heavier now, bordering on rain, but not quite. The temperature had been dropping steadily—it had been thirty-nine degrees at 6 A.M.—and was hovering at the freezing mark as the cold front swept into the Chicago area ahead of the storm. Lars watched, momentarily hypnotized, as the first flakes of snow began to fall. They were barely visible—little specks of light only a few degrees brighter than the drizzle—but it was snow.

A weather clerk stood at his desk, not wanting to disturb the reverie. After a long moment, Lars sensed the other man's presence and looked away from the window. "What great tidings do you bear now?" He held out his hand for the slip of paper that the clerk held. He took it and read quickly, then shrugged. He swiveled his chair around and spoke to the man at the desk to his left. "Carl, Denver's closed down—call flight 683 and have them return to Chicago. I was hoping we'd get this one into Denver—it must be a hell of a storm."

Carl Rudischaur, an assistant dispatcher, picked up a telephone from the console in front of him and pressed a button. He spoke into the phone. "This is Transcon dispatch, sector three. Would you selcal our flight 683? I'll stand by for a phone patch." He drained the bitter-tasting half-inch of coffee from his cup as he waited.

Selcal is short for "selective calling"—a system using four-letter codes assigned to each commercial aircraft. Using these individual codes, the Arinc operator can call a flight much like dialing a telephone. In the cockpit of Transcon's flight 683, a DC-8 en route from Chicago to Denver, a blue light flashed on the radio console and simultaneously a two-tone chime rang.

The flight engineer switched receivers and picked up his microphone. "Transcon six eighty-three answering selcal."

"Transcon six eighty-three, this is Denver Arinc. Stand by for your dispatch."

"Standing by." The flight engineer tapped the captain on the shoulder and indicated that the message was other than routine weather. The captain also switched receivers and waited.

"Transcon six eighty-three from Dispatch, sector three."

The captain recognized Rudischaur's voice. "Go ahead, Carl—this is Cliff." The two men had discussed the flight only two hours before in the dispatch office.

"OK, Cliff. Denver's closed. Too much snow. If you're agreeable, we'd like you to return to Chicago."

The captain paused, reaching for a computer copy of his flight plan and taking a long look at the fuel gauges. After a moment, he pressed the mike button. "Carl? How about continuing westbound—Vegas or even Reno?"

"Well, Reno's already full of airplanes—diversion from the northern stations. We'd like to keep Las Vegas as a last resort for some other trips. We'd really like to have your aircraft back here."

Cliff Brogan, recently divorced, sighed heavily. He'd had a date lined up in Denver for that evening. Barring that possibility, Las Vegas would have been fun. He spoke into the microphone. "OK, Carl—the engineer will stand by for a new flight plan. We'll turn it around."

"Roger, Cliff. We'll work the plan out now."

The captain signaled the flight engineer to take the rest of the message, then turned to his copilot. "Tell them we want a new clearance to return to Chicago." As the copilot started to call for a return routing, Cliff sighed again and mentally waved good-bye to Denver and the beckoning glitter of Las Vegas beyond.

Nine minutes after the decision to close Stapleton Airport was made, flight 683 gently banked in a 180° turn and started the one-hour flight back to Chicago. In fourteen other cockpits above the earth similar decisions were being made on the basis of the storm's victory at Denver.

Lars Gunter looked at the papers strewn on the desk in front of him. The list of canceled trips was growing long enough now to cover two sheets of paper. He thought for a long moment, then picked up the phone and dialed the number of the station manager for Transcon in Denver. It rang for a long time, then a man answered, obviously busy.

"Hello, Transcon."

"Brad? This is Lars Gunter at Central Dispatch."

"Oh, hello, Lars."

"Can you give me an estimate as to when the airport will open?"

There was a pause on the other end of the line. A hand over the receiver didn't quite muffle the tirade streaming from the station manager. "Now how in hell does he figure Transcon Airlines is responsible for his car breaking down? Tell him to shove his car and his ticket wherever it'll fit." The voice was directed back into the phone. "Sorry, Lars— we've got a few problems here. The roads leading to the airport are impassable and I've got a makeshift Boy Scout camp in front of the ticket counter—passengers who can't get on an airplane, and now they can't get out of the airport." He paused for breath. "Oh, the airport. Well, the airport manager has closed the field for twelve hours. We just got the word. If the snow stops soon, that estimate will hold, but when I talked to him, he said he figured at least twenty-four hours. That'd be around ten A.M. tomorrow morning."

"OK, Brad—thanks."

"Anything else?"

"Yeah . . . good luck with the bivouac." The dispatcher held the button down on his phone, then let it up and started to dial again. In a surprisingly short time, Lars Gunter had talked to seven station managers along Transcon's system between the Rockies and the Mississippi River. The replies were all much the same. He sighed as he hung up the phone and rubbed his eyes with balled-up fists. He had been up for over twenty hours now, and it was beginning to show. His eyes looked like road maps—and were almost glazed over besides. He hesitated, not wanting to make the call that he knew he had to make. The decision was bigger than his authority. He picked up the phone and dialed a number at Transcon's executive offices. A secretary answered.

"Mr. Dorcek's office."

"This is Lars Gunter at Central Dispatch. May I speak with him, please?"

"Just a moment, Mr. Gunter."

Lars realized while he was waiting that he disliked the management side of the airline business. It was too divorced from the pulse of day-to-day operations. Most of the executives were not real airline people any more. They had gone to business school, jumped from position to position, and ended in the hierarchy of the executive suite. Lars had been with Transcon for almost thirty years. He had started as a weather clerk in New York, then worked his way up the ladder—somehow managing to get a degree from NYU night school along the way. The president of Transcon at that time had been a man named Lester Matson. He had started Transcon as a small line—Matson Air Service—flying mail north and south; then, with luck and a small inheritance, had built Transcon into the giant it was today. Matson had been of the same breed and character as Paterson at United and Rickenbacker at Eastern—dedicated to air transportation more passionately than to life. It was Matson who had read a paper that Lars had written about making the dispatch function more efficient, and had come to New York and instantly put him in Chicago as assistant dispatcher.

He sighed audibly as he remembered the man. The breed had all but vanished. Airlines had succumbed to the call of big business, corporate policy committees, and marketing analysis. Vice-presidents didn't load mail in a snowstorm any more, as they had in the beginning.

Ralph Dorcek was an exception to Lars' philosophy. He had been a line captain for eighteen years. When a heart condition took away his license, he had made a name for himself in Flight Operations by cutting corporate red tape and reshaping the entire concept of the department. Lars was glad that he was the number two man—especially when the dispatcher was going to make a request like this one.

His thoughts were cut off by the firm voice on the phone "Dorcek."

"Mr. Dorcek, this is Lars Gunter at Dispatch."

"Yes, Lars. How's the storm affecting us? I assume that's why you're calling."

"It's not good, sir."

"Mmm. I see that Denver's closed."

The bastard doesn't miss a trick, Lars thought—he's right on top of everything. Lars could see him sitting at his desk, looking uncomfortable in the lush surroundings of his office. He would be in shirt-sleeves, with the ever-present cigar either in his mouth or resting on a piston from an R-2800 engine that had almost killed him years back on a DC-6 trip. The engine had come apart, almost taking the wing with it—the piston had buried itself in the fuselage.

"Mr. Dorcek, I'd like to cancel all operations between Chicago and the West Coast for at least eighteen hours. Operate only in the East and transcontinental."

There was a pause on the other end of the phone. "Whew! That's an awful lot of money down the drain, Lars. Give me the reasons."

The dispatcher gave Dorcek a concise rundown of the

situation to the present moment, including his discussions with the station managers.

The vice-president listened without interrupting, thinking of the poor jerks who had to fly in the stuff. When Lars had finished he paused before answering. "OK, Lars. Do it. I'll call the boss. And, Lars?"

"Yes."

"How long have you been on duty?"

"Oh, I don't know—since eight last night, I guess."

Ralph Dorcek's normally tight voice softened. "Go home and get some sleep, Lars."

The big Swede hung up the phone. He felt as if a giant weight had been removed from his shoulders. Juggling trips to keep airplanes from getting stranded, watching which airports were closing, keeping track of the several diversion points—it was exhausting. With the authorization to cancel for eighteen hours, there would be a reprieve of sorts. He picked up the microphone and announced over the P.A. system, "All dispatchers—report to Central Dispatch on line four. All dispatchers, line four." He put down the mike and watched several men pick up their phones. He picked up his own and punched the button marked "four."

Lars Gunter cleared his throat. "Gentlemen," he said after insuring that all sector dispatchers were on the line, "I've just spoken with Ralph Dorcek. He's agreed to cancel all flights into or out of any stations between Chicago and the West Coast. We're only going to operate the transcontinental and eastern trips, so until seven A.M. tomorrow, the following airports will be closed to all Transcon operations." He slowly read from a list he had prepared. The dispatchers from different sectors were writing quickly as he spoke. "So that's it. Please notify your respective stations."

He put the telephone down slowly, realizing now just how tired he was. He thought of Dorcek's request for him to go home—the bed in his house in Crystal Lake beckoned and he allowed himself the luxury of thinking about it only a moment. He was running the palms of his hands over his bare head when he saw the weather clerk tear something off the teletype and come toward him. He took the message and read it. There were two parts; the first was a severe-weather warning that contained nothing new, just the location of the storm's center. The second part was the one that brought an involuntary "Oh, shit!" to his lips. Those were rapidly becoming his favorite words. The message read:

REVISE FORECAST FOR CHICAGO AREA—INCREASING SNOW, DEPTHS 6–10 INCHES BY MIDNIGHT. SNOW HEAVY INITIALLY, TAPERING OFF BY MIDNIGHT LOCAL TIME. WINDS SOUTHEAST 20 KTS WITH GUSTS.

TRANSCON METEO.

Lars tossed the paper on the desk and looked out the window. The rain was not there any more—it was all snow, and the snow made it seem darker outside, in spite of the fact that it was just after noon. He decided to wait until he was sure that flight 602 had taken off from Salt Lake City before he went home. It was the last trip that he had in the storm's area, and he felt that once it took off, his responsibility would end. Chicago had had many snowstorms before, and he realized that he was too tired to do anyone much good.

The young weather clerk was still standing by his desk. Lars took a coin from his pocket and turned to him. "Flip for coffee?"

The weather clerk looked at him for a moment, then grinned and reached for a coin. He tossed it in the air and called, "Even!"

Lars felt good as he flipped his coin—he was using a quarter instead of a dime. His change of tactics didn't help much. He lost. He rose and strode past the young clerk, who was grinning broadly.

> *"The Captain will inform the cabin attendants as soon as possible after takeoff when they may safely begin the cabin service."*
>
> Page 103, Para. 4
> Transcon Flight Operations Manual

> *"As a cabin attendant, you are the number one representative of Transcon Airlines in the public's eye. A gracious nature and efficient performance of your duties will do a great deal in furthering our reputation of superior service aloft."*
>
> Preface
> Transcon Airlines Stewardess Manual

8

The airplane creaked as they lurched and bumped over the rutted snow. They were almost to the run-up pad at the end of Runway 34 left when the ground controller called them. "Transcon six oh two, we've lost sight of you through the snow—the RVR is reading a steady twenty-eight hundred. Contact the tower on one nineteen two at the end of the runway."

Stan hit the mike button. "Transcon six oh two, Roger."

Pete turned to the copilot. "Put the flaps down, Stan—we're almost there. We shouldn't get too much slush on them now." He turned back to the flight engineer. "Mike? In your pretakeoff announcement, tell the people we'll be dropping the gear after takeoff to remove any snow or ice—make it sound reassuring. Stan? You ready?"

Stan nodded, and changed frequencies on the radio. "Salt Lake tower, Transcon six oh two's ready."

"Transcon six oh two, cleared for takeoff, Runway thirty-four, maintain runway heading for vectors on course."

"OK, cleared to go." Stan put his left hand on the three throttles and inched them forward slowly. When Mike had finished the checklist, he threw the white card on his table and swiveled his seat forward, watching the banks of instruments as the needles on all the gauges crept to the maximum limits and stabilized there. Stan took his hand from the throttles to be replaced by Pete's in case the takeoff had to be aborted. The 727 reluctantly accelerated, pitching and jolting. The landing gear struts compressed to the bottom as they sped over the encrusted ice patches on the runway. The seven landing lights, brighter than auto headlights, created a blanket of white in front of the windshield as the snow sped by. The windshield wipers were jerking back and forth at high speed, adding to the crescendo of sound—the engines at full thrust, the struts bottoming with loud bangs—and Pete had to yell to be heard: "Rotate!"

Stan eased back on the control wheel, his hands and feet working in swift coordination to keep the big jet in the center of the runway. The nose hung in the air for a moment, then most of the sound stopped abruptly as the main wheels left the earth. Mike reached up and turned off the wipers—the silence was drastic in contrast to the noise of seconds before. The blur of runway lights disappeared as they rose rapidly. Stan's gaze swiftly moved from out the window to inside the cockpit, scanning from attitude, to airspeed, to altitude, and back to the attitude indicator in a pattern long established. He threw his thumb up to the middle of the cockpit. "Gear up!"

Pete reached across the cockpit and pulled on the gear lever, then continued the motion on up to the overhead panel, hitting the "No Smoking" sign with the same movement. The airplane picked up speed as Stan called for the flaps to be retracted. If he had thought about it, Stan would have realized that this was the reason he loved his job so much—each takeoff was the same, yet each was different.

The airplane was tossing in turbulence created by the strong surface wind. Pete said, "Hold it at two hundred knots, Stan, I'm going to drop the gear." He reached across and pushed the handle down. The noise returned as the doors just below and behind the cockpit opened—the wind noise at the increased airspeed making speech momentarily impossible. The captain waited with his hand on the gear handle until he felt sure that the wheels were cleared of snow and slush, then pulled up. Once again the noise, followed by three thuds as the wheels returned to their wells, then silence.

The wind played tricks with the mountains and caused a capricious kind of turbulence as they climbed through the gray-white clouds. Stan's eyes rarely left the instrument panel as he worked to keep the airplane level against the sudden shifts in air movement. At sixteen thousand feet, they slipped from gray cloud to bright, bright sunlight—it was like plunging up through the surface from the bottom of a swimming pool. The cloud deck stretched as far as they could see—uniform and white as the sun shone down on it. The turbulence stopped abruptly as they climbed through the bright sky. Pete looked at the cloud layer below and to the left; he could see what is called an aviator's halo—a completely circular rainbow on the surface of the clouds with the shadow of the airplane in the center. He reached up and turned the seat-belt sign off, knowing that the ride would be fairly smooth for a while, at least until they got closer to the storm's center.

Terry Dunlap saw the FASTEN SEAT BELT sign flick off from her front jump seat. She got up and knocked on the cockpit door. When it opened, she stepped in. "You guys want any coffee before we start?"

Stan held up his hand, Pete smiled and nodded. Mike said, "Two black, one with cream and sugar, Terry—thanks."

She left and walked to the galley. Cathy and Cindy were already setting up the cocktail equipment. Cherries, lemon twists, olives, all in a compartmented tray. Cathy was going to run out the trays, Cindy set them up as she got the drink orders.

The blond girl left the galley and went to the nearest row of seats that was occupied. A young couple, in their twenties, were sitting holding hands, gazing out the window at the bright sky. "Would you like a cocktail before lunch?"

They both looked up, embarrassed at having their closeness discovered unexpectedly. Cathy noticed two shiny new wedding rings. On an impulse she said, "Honeymoon?"

The couple smiled at each other, and the young man said, "Well, yes. At least we're returning home from one. We spent two weeks skiing in Salt Lake."

"Well, congratulations—the drinks are on Transcon."

They were pleasantly surprised. The man said, "We'll have Scotch, then, with water. Thanks very much."

Cathy left and returned with the trays holding miniatures of J&B. "Where did you ski? Alta?"

The girl was obviously pleased at Cathy's interest. "We were there for a week, then went to Snow Bird—it was terrific!"

Cathy smiled and said, "Let me know if you need anything else." She left them and worked quickly through the cabin, taking drink orders and returning with the trays. When she got to Mannheim, she didn't even ask—she just brought him two bottles of Johnnie Walker Black on a tray and left without a word. She brought Susan, still sitting two rows behind him, a Bloody Mary. After setting the tray down, she sat on the armrest across the aisle. There were no more passengers between Susan and the rear row of seats where the prisoner and his escort sat, and Cathy wasn't in a particular hurry to get back there. She smiled. "Everything OK?"

Susan tasted her drink. "Delicious!" They were quiet for a short time. Then Susan said, "Cathy? I've been thinking about your invitation to stay with you and Cheryl. Are you sure it wouldn't be too much trouble?"

Cathy became serious. "No, Susan—it wouldn't be any trouble. We'd really enjoy it, and I know that you and Cheryl would get along."

"Well, I think I'd like to try it. I'll stay at the Barbizon the first night—tonight—then bring my things over tomorrow if it's OK with Cheryl."

Cindy had left the galley and joined them. "Cathy, there are four meals left. Do all the passengers have a meal?"

"Oh! No, I haven't checked back there yet"—she nodded toward Greco and Riese—"and the mechanic's sister, the girl with the baby, is going to eat a little later." She turned to Susan. "I'll be back in a minute."

Cathy walked the ten feet to the last row of seats on the right side of the airplane. The two men were sitting quietly. The dark-haired one was in the middle seat, staring blankly out of the window. The older man was busily engaged in manipulating a button on his jacket. "Excuse me, would you like to eat?"

Riese answered quickly, "No thank you, miss—we won't be eating at all."

Cathy started to leave, then stopped when the prisoner said, "Wait a minute, Miss, please?" He turned to the marshal. "Mr. Riese, couldn't I have lunch? The prison food was lousy, and I'm really hungry. You don't have to worry about me, honest."

Sam Riese looked at his prisoner. He was annoyed—he had been thinking about Ethyl, about the plans they had had, and how the plans didn't mean anything now, and the interruption annoyed him. He sighed and thought, What the hell. Greco was right about the food. Even the coffee in the warden's office had been unpalatable. Cathy was still standing in front of them. "OK, Miss. Bring him a meal. I'd like a cold drink—ginger ale if you have it, please." He looked at Greco. It was against his principles to have a prisoner eat on an airplane, but he didn't want to think about the trip today, he just wanted to get to Chicago and get it over with. The stewardess left, and Sam Riese stretched and settled more comfortably into a seat that wasn't really designed for a man of his bulk. He started looking forward to meeting the two men who would take charge of Greco when they stepped off the airplane at O'Hare.

Greco hadn't seen all of it when the marshal stretched, only the butt end and part of the holster, but it was enough. He knew guns. He decided that Riese must carry a .38. It could have been a Magnum of some type, but he doubted it—cops didn't usually carry such big artillery. He had known that the marshal would be armed, he just hadn't known where he carried the gun. Shoulder holster, under the right armpit. Greco filed the knowledge in the back of his mind, storing it like a computer filing data in memory banks.

The stewardess returned with the tray. She set the ginger ale in front of Riese, then deftly lowered the table in front of Greco with one hand and set the tray down. There was an awkward moment as the prisoner unrolled his napkin and the silverware rattled to the tray. Riese didn't hesitate. "Cut the meat, then give me the knife."

This bastard doesn't miss a trick, Greco thought. He cut the meat somewhat clumsily, because his left wrist was shackled to Riese's, then turned the knife around and handed it to the older man. Riese took it and threw it on the seat across the aisle. Greco brushed his hair from his eyes and started to eat in silence.

Cathy walked back toward the front and stopped to look around the cabin. The passengers were either eating or asleep. She decided to go to the cockpit for a cigarette.

She stopped at Susan's seat. "I'm going up front. Any messages?" Her eyes told Susan a lot about her thoughts.

The redhead smiled. "Just say hi, OK?"

"Sure."

As Cathy walked up the aisle, Julia Pilero stopped her. "Miss?"

"Yes, can I get your lunch now?" Cathy sensed that the girl was a little afraid of flying.

"No. I'm not going to eat, but I'd like to feed the baby."

"Fine. Give me the bottle, I'll warm it."

The girl looked embarrassed and hesitated, then said, "Well, I'm nursing her—can I go to the lavatory?"

Cathy frowned and looked to the rear of the airplane. The two men in the last row were sitting quietly. She looked around the cabin. Nobody was within two seats of the girl. She made a decision and smiled, reaching in the overhead rack for a green blanket with Transcon woven into it with gold thread. She handed it to the young mother. "Here, why not nurse her here—no one's around, and you can use the blanket to . . . to keep her warm."

The girl showed her gratitude in her face and took the blanket. She started to unbutton her blouse—Cathy could see the flap of the nursing bra. She was mesmerized for a moment, wanting to stay and watch. The girl hesitated for a moment, and Cathy realized that she was embarrassing her further by standing there. She smiled quickly and left. She walked through the First Class cabin, sidestepping around Terry, who was seated across the aisle from the good-looking man who had gotten on in San Francisco. Must be the businessman that Terry told me about, she thought. I wish all passengers could be like that—undemanding, familiar with the routine of airline travel. It sure would make life easier.

As she reached for the cockpit door, a heavy older woman got up from her seat at the front of the cabin and heaved and squeezed herself into the front lavatory. Cathy and

Terry exchanged amused looks, and she knocked on the cockpit door.

Donald Greco watched the marshal out of the corner of his eye. The man seemed preoccupied—almost drowsy—as if he were a thousand miles away. The prisoner's mind shifted into high gear. He calmly surveyed the cabin in front of him, deciding that it was nice of the airline to put them in the last row. Nothing could happen in the cabin without his seeing it. He tried a quick, sharp movement of his right hand. Riese didn't react.

Greco, sensitive to people as only the hunted can be, had also noticed that one of the stewardesses seemed unsure. She was younger than the others—slightly nervous. His mind probed and molded an idea that was forming. He briefly thought of a hijacking in the real sense of the word, Cuba, South America, but tossed it aside. His strength for an escape lay in the friends he had in Chicago—not in venturing to a place he had never been. A hostage, a car, it could work. The plan was simple, the best kind of plan.

With a sidelong glance at Riese, Greco took the last bite of roast beef and slowly put it in his mouth. He casually dropped his right hand to the tray, then continued the downward motion, sliding the small fork beneath his leg. It seemed too easy. He looked again at Riese, turning his head this time—Riese was staring at his glass, his eyes half-closed.

Cathy Armello stubbed her cigarette out in the coffee cup and stood up. She said, "I've got to go pick up the trays—I'll call you if we have any meals left over. Oh, Stan?" The copilot turned in his seat—he was smoking a cigarette, sitting relaxed behind the control column, the autopilot turning the wheel as necessary to keep the 727 on a selected heading. One foot was up on the iron bar that spanned the lower part of the instrument panel. He looked at her with raised eyebrows. "Your friend said to say hi. She's a nice girl, Stan. I've asked her to stay with my roommate and me until she finds a place."

"Thanks, Cathy. Say hi back."

The stewardess turned on the California sunshine look, and then left the cockpit.

The three men were silent for a while, immersed in thought as they watched the sun on the clouds below; then Pete slid his seat back and climbed out, standing by the door to the cabin. While he was slipping into his jacket, he said, "I've got to get rid of this coffee—be back in a minute." He put on his hat, checked his tie in the mirror attached to the inside of the door, then stepped into the cabin.

The lavatories have a lock that works from the inside. When the door is unlocked, a small window has the word *Lavatory* displayed. When someone inside locks the door, the window changes to read *Occupied*. Rather than look a little foolish, standing by the door waiting, he walked slowly through the First Class cabin to the galley. Cathy was standing there, eating a salad from one of the meal trays.

"Hi, Pete—everything all right?" Since the beginning of the hijacking problem, pilots were rarely seen in the cabin.

"Everything's fine, Cathy—just have to use the lavatory."

The blond stewardess stuck her head out of the galley, and saw that the "Occupied" light was still on. She turned to Pete and laughed. "There's a fat old lady in there. She's been in there for about ten minutes, and will probably be there for another ten. Why don't you try the back? You can take a look at the guy that's been giving us such a hard time—he's sitting in twelve-C."

"Want me to say anything to him?" Pete was serious—he didn't like people giving the stewardesses on his trip a hard time.

"Oh, no, he's not that big a deal."

"OK, see you on my way back." The captain left the galley and slowly walked through the Coach cabin, looking at the seventeen passengers scattered throughout the airplane.

The young newlyweds were the first passengers he passed, sitting on the right side of the airplane. Their fingers were entwined as they gazed at each other without noticing him. He walked past a few more passengers without really seeing them. He was looking at the man sitting in 12-C, the aisle seat on the left side of the plane. He looks inoffensive enough, Pete thought. Most of the hair was gone from his head, dark horn-rims, and an obviously expensive suit. Pete marked him as some sort of professional man. He was sitting quietly, studying his glass. He looked up at the captain without emotion, then returned to the visual safety of his drink. Pete gave an unseen shrug and looked to the other side of the cabin. In the next row a young girl was sitting, holding a large bundle in a Transcon blanket. She snuggled the blanket close to her chest as he passed her. He decided the girl must be Jerry's sister. He smiled, and she shyly returned the smile.

In the next row, two seats behind the man that Cathy had complained about, he saw Susan. She had been watching him as he walked through the cabin. He stopped next to her. "Everything all right?"

She was looking up at him, and he thought again how much her smile was like his wife's—warm and open. She said, "Just fine, Pete."

At the thought of Kitty, he gave an involuntary shudder and walked toward the rear of the cabin. He passed five empty rows of seats before he came to the prisoner and the marshal, on the right side in the last row. He saw Greco look at him furtively, then look away. Riese seemed relaxed, barely noticing the captain as he walked by. Pete Douglass was surprised at the marshal's age. He hadn't really noticed him in the Operations Office since he had spoken to the other man. He had just assumed that they would be the same age. He was going to stop for a moment, but his bladder was sending urgent signals to his brain, and he decided not to delay.

As Pete passed the two men, his attention was momentarily distracted by a green-and-gold stewardess jacket carelessly thrown over a small door behind the last row of seats. He made a mental note to tell Terry about it. Pete didn't normally concern himself with the problems in the cabin unless they were brought to him, but the jacket looked out of place, sloppy—there was no reason for it to be there.

Both lavatories were vacant. He went into the one on the left side, opposite Greco and Riese, deciding that the jacket probably belonged to Cindy, the new girl. As he locked the lavatory door from the inside, he noticed that the engines were slightly out of synchronization, producing a slow throb. He made another mental note to correct it when he returned to the cockpit.

In the galley, Cindy said, "I'll start picking up the trays."

Cathy turned to her. "Why don't you eat first, Cindy—I'll start. I want to talk to Susan anyway."

Cindy said "OK" and turned to the rack holding the lunch trays.

Cathy left the buffet area and walked toward the rear, stopping next to Julia Pilero. "Would you like lunch now?" She noticed the gentle swell of the girl's breast, milk white; the baby was peacefully moving her mouth, her little eyes closed.

The girl smiled. "No thanks, I don't think I'll eat anything—breakfast was pretty filling."

Cathy straightened up, looking once more at the infant, snuggled so warm and secure against her mother. The funny sensation in the stewardess's stomach returned. Just as she started to go to the two men at the rear of the airplane, Joseph Mannheim raised his hand and snapped his fingers twice, sharply.

"Waitress? I'd like another drink here!" He pointed to his tray.

That was it! Cathy blew—she lost her sense of self-restraint. She whirled around in the aisle. "Sir. That's not my table! You'll have to ask your own waitress." She was furious—trembling—the transition from one emotion to the other was too much for her. She walked rapidly to the rear of the cabin, grabbed the tray from the prisoner, and ran back to the galley. Susan watched her go, surprised at the speed at which the girl moved.

Cathy almost tripped going into the galley. She slammed the tray she was carrying down on the counter so hard that the silverware and a cup spilled onto the floor. She started to speak to Cindy, to blow off steam, then stared at the floor, then looked to the counter—"My god! *The silverware!*" She looked quickly again—two spoons—only two spoons! The knife and fork weren't there!

Cathy grabbed the edge of the galley door for leverage as she whirled out of the tiny space, almost at a run. She had taken but two steps when she knew she was too late—she would remember it later as a slow-motion film. The fork in Greco's hand was lodged against the marshal's throat—a struggle in the last row of seats as Greco fumbled with his free hand, putting the gun against Riese's side. She didn't remember the sound, only a little ball of smoke.

The prisoner rose in his seat, his eyes wild pools of hate and desperation. She saw his eyes register her presence, the muzzle of the gun pointing forward. Another shot, the sound louder now, red hair pitching forward in front of Cathy, hitting the seat back with a sickening thud. Another shot in her direction as the gray-suited man rose from his seat, wilder now, the bullet shattering the oxygen unit above Julia Pilero's head—glass flying—a pain in Cathy's head as the bullet ricocheted. She stumbled to the floor as a merciful blackness took her away from the terror.

Pete Douglass had his hand on the doorknob when he heard the shots. He flung the lavatory door open in time to see Cathy stumble in the aisle, to see Greco turn toward him, his face a mask of fury. Pete's momentum carried him out the door as Greco fired again, the bullet smashing into the rear wall of the lavatory, leaving a hole the size of a baseball. The prisoner moved quickly to shoot again, but the handcuffs prevented him from positioning himself effectively. His one second of indecision gave Pete time to think.

The captain held out both hands, palms toward Greco, toward the gun. *"Don't shoot! You need me!"* His peripheral vision told him that one of the stewardesses was coming rapidly down the aisle. Greco remained frozen as he stood —the gun steady, pointed at the captain, his eyes darting nervously. Pete took a chance and motioned to Terry to stay where she was. Fortunately she did.

Pete's mind churned, grasping for anything that would give them time. He looked straight at Greco, his voice firm but subservient. "There's no need for any more shooting. We'll do whatever you want. You're the boss." He motioned to the gun. He could hear a whistling sound as air escaped through the hole in the lavatory wall. There was a pungent smell—something mixed with the acrid scent of gunpowder. Pete recognized it as Skydrol, the fluid used in the aircraft's hydraulic system.

"Each emergency procedure in this section is divided into two parts: Immediate Action *and* Reference Action. *Immediate Action* items will be committed to memory. *Reference Action* items will be accomplished by referring to the flight manual emergency section upon completion of the Immediate Action* items in the procedure."*

Preface to the Emergency Procedure Section
Transcon B-727 Flight Manual

9

"What the hell was that?" The shots, loud in the rear of the airplane, were muffled pops in the cockpit. Stan quickly scanned the engine instruments, suspecting a compressor stall in one of the engines. They were all normal—all the needles on the fifteen gauges were where they were supposed to be. He turned to Mike, who was quickly checking the engineer's panel.

At a pressure of three thousand pounds per square inch, it took less than ten seconds for the four hydraulic pumps, two for each system, to pump all the fluid out through the torn steel tubing clamped to the rear lavatory bulkhead. Stan was just returning his gaze to the engine instruments when Mike caught a flicker of yellow light from the hydraulic pump lights—the placard under the light read: "LOW PRESS."

Mike yelled, "Pressure and quantity falling! Both systems!" He had seen the quantity gauges move toward zero and frantically reached for the pump switches to preserve whatever precious fluid was left, but he couldn't have moved fast enough—the wound to the system was too massive, and by the time the switches were off, the last of the hydraulic lifeblood had spurted from the torn lines in the rear. Both quantity gauges read zero.

At the same time, Stan had seen six lights, all yellow, illuminate on the panel in front of him—they were the annunciator lights indicating low pressure to the elevators, rudders, and ailerons—two lights for each, A and B systems. The copilot yelled: "Mike! Get the pumps!" The words were futile because the engineer already had turned them off with no effect.

At the same time that he was yelling to Mike, Stan was running through the procedure for loss of hydraulic pressure: control wheel centered and neutral, check-speed brake forward, spoiler switches off. He completed the procedure in four seconds. It was not because the two men were superintelligent human beings that they were able to react so quickly and correctly to the emergency; rather it was because of Transcon's training program. Transcon's pilots spent many hours yearly at the airline's Training Center being checked and rechecked on their ability to perform under stress situations. The flight simulators used for their recurrent training were capable of reproducing any type of inflight emergency, and flight crews were continually called upon to deal promptly with those emergencies under frighteningly real conditions.

It was pure reflex, then, that took control when the eleven lights in the cockpit indicated a massive hydraulic failure. The atmosphere in the cockpit, relaxed and easy a moment before, changed to one of calm appraisal. There was no panic—they had both been in the same situation a dozen times in training. The only difference was that now it was for real. Yet fear, if there was any present, was suppressed by the knowledge that they were still flying and, in fact, flying quite well. Stan looked at the red light that was on over the autopilot servo switch—the autopilot was doing a good job. The plane responded sluggishly to changes in attitude caused by a little light turbulence, because the flight controls had no hydraulic power to assist them, yet they were holding a heading and their altitude with what seemed little trouble.

Stan's thoughts briefly turned to an incident he hadn't thought of in years. As a student pilot he had come close to being killed in a mid-air collision with another small plane, emerging from the experience shaken and unsure. His instructor, older, wiser, and somewhat amused, had told him something that had stayed with him ever since. "Stan," he had said, "there's one thing to remember about flying, especially if you're going to become a professional. The environment in which you exist is mercifully quick. If you're going to die in an airplane, the chances are that you'll never know how or why you died. If an emergency occurs and you're still in the air thirty seconds later—you'll live to talk about it. That is, if you stay calm, and don't hurry. More pilots die from being too fast than from being too slow."

In the cockpit of flight 602, recalling those words, Stan Burkhart said, "Get the book."

"What was that, Stan?" Mike was leaning forward because he hadn't heard the copilot.

"I said, let's get the book out, and see what the hell we're going to do." He paused for a minute. "Where the hell is Pete?"

Mike was reaching into his flight bag for the thick 727 flight manual and plopping the heavy book on his table. "I don't know—I'll take a look. Here!" He had opened the book to the red-tagged section marked *Emergencies* and handed it to the copilot. Then he unbuckled himself from his seat and looked through the peephole into the cabin. "Holy shit!"

"What's going on?"

"I don't know." Mike's vision was excellent, but the distortion through the fish-eye lens of the peephole blurred the scene in the rear cabin. There were several people standing in the aisle, but no one was moving. "I can't tell what happened. There are a bunch of people standing in the aisle about halfway back. Nobody's moving—they're standing like statues."

"Is Pete back there?"

Mike strained against the lens again. "I can't see him. I'd better get back there!" He started to get his uniform hat.

"Wait, Mike! We've got problems up here—check your panel first, see if there's anything else we can do."

Mike sat down again and quickly went over the engineer's panel. With the exception of the four yellow lights on the hydraulic section, everything else was as it should be. Stan was quickly scanning the procedure for hydraulic failure. He reached above the captain's seat and turned off the rudder switch—the airplane had started to roll to the left, then the right in a constant motion. This was caused by the loss of rudder control—a characteristic peculiar to swept-wing jets called a Dutch roll. (Stan briefly wondered where in hell the name came from.) He turned to Mike. "Tell me if the standby system is working." Turning off the rudder switch for system A also turned on a smaller, standby system. A green light shone near Mike's right hand.

The flight engineer watched it for a long moment. "It's working, Stan. The quantity's holding steady." The Dutch roll lessened perceptibly.

Stan realized that they would have to descend soon because of the decreased capacity of the standby hydraulic system. Goddam, he thought, it works just like it's supposed to. The Dutch roll had stopped. He said, "OK, Mike—go back and see what's going on. And tell Pete to get up here —we've got problems."

Mike put his hat on and left the cockpit. He had been taught that a uniform hat would lend authority in stress situations. Without it, he would have been just another shirt-sleeved passenger. As Mike left the cockpit, Stan turned back to the heavy manual on his lap—reading and rereading the hydraulic pages. His mind started going over the possible airports that were close by for an emergency landing, and the equipment they would require—he wanted to be ready to discuss the options with Pete when he returned to take charge.

As Mike stepped into the cabin, a sixth sense told him to move slowly, deliberately. One by one, he told the passengers to return to their seats as he worked his way toward the rear cabin. He was surprised that people weren't talking, weren't making noise. As he moved the last person aside, he saw why. The tableau was as frightening as anything he had seen in Vietnam. Terry was standing directly in front of him in the aisle. Cathy lay unmoving at her feet, head down, her straw-colored hair hiding her face. Cindy stood in a vacant row of seats on the right side of the airplane, her knuckle clamped tightly between her teeth.

Pete was across the aisle from Greco, his face strained with worry. He was speaking slowly, and looked up as Mike gently moved Terry aside and walked slowly around Cathy's prostrate form toward the two men.

Greco followed Pete's glance and looked at Mike. "Who's this?" he demanded as he swung the muzzle of the pistol halfway between the two pilots.

Pete's voice was calm, but sounded strained. "The flight engineer." His eyes told Mike not to approach any closer.

"Who's flying the plane?"

Pete didn't hesitate. "The copilot."

Mike spoke for the first time, ignoring Greco. "Pete? Are we being hijacked?"

"Not really. The gentleman wants to go to Chicago. He just wants to take one of us along as insurance."

Greco was standing in an awkward position, his left hand still shackled to Riese's inert body. His eyes flicked back and forth between the two men. Mike noticed the smell of Skydrol now—a distinct sweetish smell. Pieces of of the puzzle were falling into place. He could hear the air rushing through the torn lavatory wall. It was all making sense. He continued talking to Pete. "We've got problems up front."

He noticed Greco's eyes jump with interest. He continued, "A and B system hydraulics are shot—standby system is working, but it'll be a sonofabitch getting it on the ground." He thought he saw the gun barrel waver slightly. He wasn't sure. He decided to keep pressing. "Pete, Cathy's hurt—and Susan, she's bleeding badly. They need help." He looked at Greco for the first time.

Pete hadn't known about Susan's wound; he had been too busy dealing with the immediate danger that the gun represented. When Mike mentioned her, Pete slumped, dropping his hands. It was too early for that.

"Don't move!" Greco motioned with the pistol. Pete raised his hands chest high.

"Can we at least try to get a doctor?" Mike broke in, trying to ease the pressure off Pete. He was thinking about the conversation he had heard in the cockpit two hours before, afraid that Pete might do something to provoke Greco and unleash another fusillade of bullets.

"*No.* Nobody does anything!" Greco, for the first time since Mike's intrusion, seemed unsure. Julia Pilero's baby started to cry, deprived of her mother's breast. The shrill cry pierced the stillness in the cabin. "*Shut that kid up!*" The gun waved wildly to the front of the airplane. Two people who had stood up quickly sat back down.

"Will you at least let *me* try to help?" Mike's tone was

almost that of a friendly conspirator. "The baby's mother is hurt, too. It shouldn't make any difference to you—we'll do whatever you want."

Greco made no reply. The three men stood in their small triangle of tension, minds racing at breakneck speed, waiting for something, all unsure of the outcome. The prisoner looked at Pete as if he were expecting the captain to make a decision. He hadn't planned this far in detail—things were occurring too rapidly.

Mike heard a low moan behind him, almost a whimper. He turned slowly, cautiously, and saw Cathy raise her head from the cabin floor, then put it back down. He looked at Greco. "For God's sake, let me try to help these people!" It was a plea, quietly spoken. Greco still said nothing. He seemed to be staring beyond Pete, his expression uncertain. The big flight engineer took an unsteady·step to the rear, his eyes never leaving Greco's face. Another step backward—still no reaction. He quickly looked over his shoulder. Cathy was stirring now, trying to clear her head. She started to rise from the floor. With one hand on a seat back, Mike slowly knelt down and gripped her arm close to her armpit. His eyes never looked at her, never left the area of danger in front of him. He steadily helped her to her feet. As she stood, an involuntary cry started deep in her throat, escaping as a hoarse, high-pitched gasp.

The sound startled everyone. Greco leapt from his trance, his eyes darting again—threatened. He pointed the pistol at Cindy, his decision made. "You! Get over here!" Her eyes widened. She was unable to move except for the involuntary trembling in her legs. *I said get over here!* He waved the gun at the young girl, pointing to an area directly in front of him.

"Do what he says, Cindy." It was Pete's voice. "He won't hurt you."

The stewardess stepped into the aisle in front of Mike and Cathy and walked shakily to where Greco wanted her. He rested the gun on the back of her neck, then looked at Mike. His voice was steady once more, his plan taking shape. "This girl is going to get me out of this. You go help your people if that's so important, but I'll be watching every step. If I don't like what I see, you think about what this gun will do to her head." He looked quickly at Pete, remembering that he was behind his line of vision. "You don't move. Understand?"

Pete nodded.

Mike released his grip on Cathy's arm, realizing for the first time what a tiny girl she was as he sat her on an armrest of the seat, her legs in the aisle. She looked dazed, groggy. The crease on her forehead had stopped bleeding. He slowly moved to Susan, one row farther away from Greco. There was a dark stain on the green carpet beneath her. Her head rested oddly on the seat back in front of her. Her mouth was slightly open. She wasn't moving. He thought crazily about what a hard time the airplane cleaners would have getting the blood-stains out of the carpeting. He eased Susan back into her seat. She looked like hell. Her left shoulder was a mass of blood and fabric, her face starkly pale next to the copper hair. He could tell that the bullet had gone through the back of the seat, then through her shoulder. He could see a large entry hole on the seat in front of her, ringed with darkening stain and bits of flesh. He started to look at the wound again, but was distracted by whimpering behind him. Turning around, he saw Julia Pilero holding a bundle of pink in one hand, looking at the other, holding it in front of her face. Like Susan's shoulder, her hand was bright red. Her face had dozens of small cuts, mostly on her forehead. He saw that the overhead reading light had been smashed directly above her. "Don't touch it!" he yelled. The young mother had started to rub her forehead. Her hand stopped in midair. He left Susan and went to her quickly. "Are you hurt anywhere else?" She shook her head, dazed. Mike saw her exposed breast, still wet from the infant's mouth.

This is like a dream, he thought. It really isn't happening. Psychiatrists wouldn't have been surprised, but Mike was stunned at the idea that he could have a flash of sexuality race through his mind in the midst of this carnage. He told Jerry's sister to sit still, then walked back to where Susan lay. As he probed at her shoulder, she moaned slightly from half-open lips, her eyes fluttered perceptibly. Mike's emotions hit a peak—she was alive!

He gently pulled at the fabric of her green wool suit. It was too strong to rip, he needed the first-aid kit with its scissors, gauze, tape, he didn't know what else. He was frustrated, angry with himself for not remembering more of the first aid he had been taught, first by the Army, then by Transcon. He looked at Greco ten feet away, the gun still pointed at the base of Cindy's skull. The prisoner's dark eyes never wavered as Mike stared. "I'll need a first-aid kit—there's one in the rack right above your head."

Greco tightened his grip on the gun, pushing it harder against the terrified young stewardess. Cindy's eyes were filled with tears, she had cried out when Greco shoved the muzzle against her. He looked above him, then to Pete, back to the flight engineer. "Sorry"—his lips twisted into a malicious sneer—"you'll have to do without it."

Mike Fuller felt defeated. He looked at Greco for a long second, then returned to the shattered shoulder in front of him. He thought about Stan, alone in the cockpit, not knowing what had happened. He knew that only four or five minutes had passed, yet it seemed like hours. He looked again at the rear of the cabin. Pete was standing a few feet closer to Greco.

Pete Douglass was outraged. Statistically, one of every seventy-five airline crew members in the United States has faced a hijacker over the past ten years. Pete had faced one only a year ago. A wild-eyed frightened young man had commandeered his airplane on an Atlanta trip, demanding money and a trip out of the country. Seven hours later they had terminated the hijacking using a careful combination of negotiation and pleading. The man had been AWOL, not wanting to go to Vietnam to be one of the last there to be killed. Pete remembered talking with the young GI—he had been frightened, confused, anxious to solve his problems. He could be talked to.

The man that Pete faced now, the second time in twelve months, the man with the gun, could not be talked to. That was obvious from his reaction to Mike's request for the first-aid kit. While they had been talking, Pete had inched toward him, unnoticed. Pete's mind was in a turmoil, enraged at the thought of what was happening. He saw Cindy's green-and-gold coat hanging a foot from his right hand. He looked at the girl's terrified face. Kitty.

He had to get home!

In one swift movement Pete grabbed the coat at the collar and threw it like a matador's cape at Greco. The jacket flew through the air. Predictably, the gun swung from Cindy toward the movement of the coat, and was fired, unaimed. The sound was deafening.

Pete felt a white-hot pain in his upper thigh as the bullet ripped through it. His lunge carried him forward, his hands clawing wildly for the pistol as he fell. His forearm smashed across Greco's wrist. The gun clattered to the cabin floor. Pete was aware of screams as he hit the carpet. He opened his eyes. The gun was inches from his head. He grabbed at it desperately, his brain screaming *survival!*

Pete rolled over on his back, looking above him. The green-and-gold jacket partly covered Greco's head. The prisoner struggled with his free hand to remove it, hampered by the handcuffs that kept fighting his effort. The jacket was away from his head now, and Pete could see panic in the man's eyes as he aimed at the green cloth and pulled the trigger until the gun was empty.

"In the event of a serious medical emergency in flight, the crew will attempt to locate a physician from among the passengers. . . ."

Page 38, Para. 12
Transcon Airlines Stewardess Manual

10

Mike was the first to react. For several seconds no one had moved—frozen in their positions, playing a game of statues. He jarred himself into action and reached Pete in three long strides, kneeling, helping his captain to a sitting position. At the same time, he yelled to Terry, telling her to call for a doctor. She was already on the P.A. system: "If there is a doctor on board, would you please identify yourself." The sound of her voice mobilized everyone on the airplane. They sensed the shift of control and talked excitedly, milling in the aisle. Terry was looking out of the galley, the handset still in her hand. She couldn't see to the rear of the airplane. *"Will you people please sit down?* We desperately need a doctor! If there is one on board, please identify yourself!" She looked again and saw some passengers moving to their seats. The man in the gray suit hadn't moved at any time, however. Now he sat motionless, staring straight ahead. She hung up the handset and returned to the last row of seats.

Mike was looking at Pete's leg. Blood was oozing from the top of his right thigh, his leg was twisted at a strange angle, his face was a sheet of pain. Mike looked at Terry hopefully. She shook her head, "No doctors."

"Shit! Keep trying, Terry—keep trying." She left quickly. Mike turned to Cindy, still standing alone, small and frightened. "Get the first-aid kit!" She didn't move. "Don't just stand there like a fool. *Get the first-aid kit!*" His voice was harsh; he had seen the same kind of shocked look at the airfield at Phouc Vinh and knew that the only way to get a reaction was to break through the shock. The girl shuddered, then turned to the overhead rack. She stopped once, gagging. Mike looked at the last row of seats. Greco was sprawled against the wall, his left hand stretched out, still manacled to the marshal's. His eyes stared sightlessly, his mouth open above Cindy's jacket, which was still at his throat. The jacket was stained a dark, sickly brown in two places—at the throat and lower down. Donald Greco was dead.

Cindy managed to get the first-aid kit and bring it to Mike. He looked at Pete. "That was a dumb thing to do, boss—with all respect, I mean." He tore open the first-aid kit as he spoke. His words were kind, full of admiration.

Pete tried to smile through clenched teeth but couldn't. "Get . . . seat belt . . . extension . . . tourniquet!" His hands held his leg tightly above the wound. It was bleeding profusely.

The flight engineer stood up and reached into a compartment below the magazine rack and brought out the extension, used for passengers whose girth was too large for a normal seat belt. As he knelt next to Pete, he heard once more the hissing as air rushed out the shattered lavatory wall, out and around the torn hydraulic tubing. Fortunately, the hole wasn't large enough to cause a decompression. There were several holes purposely built into an airplane—to suck out odors from the lavatory, for instance—and one more the size of a baseball didn't make any difference.

Together, Cindy and Mike put the belt around Pete's leg. God, there's a lot of blood, Mike thought.

When it was tight, Pete spoke. Easier now, his leg was becoming numb. "Who else?" He was looking forward. Most of the passengers were seated, many turned to watch the two pilots. Mike noticed that Terry had given up on the P.A. system, and returned to where Susan lay wounded, opening the other first-aid kit.

Mike looked at the captain. "No one who wasn't hurt before. The prisoner's dead, I think. Cathy got hit on the head—just a scratch. Stan's friend is in pretty bad shape. Shoulder, lots of blood. She's alive, but I don't know how badly she's wounded."

"Go see!"

"But, Pete! . . ." His training said, Take care of the crew first, then the passengers. Without the crew, the passengers didn't have a prayer.

"Go see, Mike!" He pointed to his leg. The bleeding had lessened noticeably after they put the tourniquet on. "This won't get any worse for a while."

Mike touched his shoulder as he got up. "Nice shooting, boss. Be right back." He walked to where Susan was seated. As he came up the aisle, he could see the bullet hole in the seat back. Terry moved aside as he approached. She had reclined the seat as far as it would go so that Susan was lying almost on her back. She was pale, a deathly white, her mouth slightly open, her breathing light, erratic. Remembering that he had left it with Pete, he yelled to Cindy, "Bring the first-aid kit up here!" She had been standing halfway between Mike and Pete, unmoving, making no effort to wipe her tear-stained face. He said to her, "Come on, girl, it's all over—bring the first-aid kit." She nodded dumbly and turned to get it. Mike spoke to Terry. "Go see what you can do for Jerry's sister, then call Stan—tell him I'll be up there in a few minutes." As she started to leave he said, "And check on Cathy's head—don't let her run around if she's not up to it, OK?"

Terry smiled, then went quickly to Julia Pilero.

Mike shook his head, amazed at her composure. The Rock of Gibraltar, he thought. Thank God for mature women! He turned back to Cindy, standing behind Susan's inert form with the first-aid kit in her hand. He took the box from her and said, "Give me those two headrest covers!" Mike pointed to the seats behind her. She took off the rectangular linen covers and handed them to him. He folded them, one on top of the other, into a six-inch-square pad and pressed them to the wounded girl's shoulder. He looked at Cindy. "Here! Hold this down for me—hard!" He assumed, he didn't know why, that direct pressure on the wound might help stop the bleeding without aggravating anything. The stewardess held the pad in place gingerly. "Press *hard*, dammit!" She did. Mike picked up the first-aid kit and opened it. Small scissors, adhesive tape, gauze pads—nothing that would be of any help on such a massive wound. For the moment he felt complete frustration, angry at his own helplessness, worrying about Pete, about Stan alone in the cockpit, completely in the dark about what had happened. To add to his frustration, he dropped the largest roll of adhesive tape from the metal box. It rolled up the aisle, stopping two rows away.

It had rolled under the seat, and Mike had to kneel down to retrieve it. As he knelt, he noticed that the man with the gray suit hadn't moved—he was still staring straight ahead. Mike was puzzled. He reached under the seat. The tape had stopped against the man's brown leather briefcase. He saw a large white identification tag on it with a staff, stamped in gold, with two snakes entwined around it. A bell went off in Mike's head. He turned the tag over; it read:

JOSEPH MANNHEIM, M.D.
1100 LAKE SHORE DRIVE
CHICAGO, ILLINOIS

Still kneeling, Mike looked up at the man. He was still staring straight ahead—not even blinking. He was shaken, pale. "Is this your bag?" The pilot said it slowly, deliberately. The passenger didn't respond. The big flight engineer stood up, directly in front of the horn-rimmed glasses. *"Are you a doctor?"* His voice was brimming with anger.

The man started to shake his head. His words were almost inaudible: "No . . . No . . . not again, I can't . . . not again. . . ."

Mike was as strong as he was big. He grabbed Mannheim by the lapels of his expensive gray suit and lifted him steadily out of his seat. His face was inches away. "Answer me, you son of a bitch! *Are you a doctor?*"

"Yes." It was almost a whimper.

"Then why didn't you answer when we needed you?"

"I can't . . . you wouldn't understand, I just can't . . . *I can't help you!*"

"You worthless bastard!" Mike was shaking the man violently by the lapels of his jacket. "Whatever happened to that physician's responsibility? I always suspected the precious Hippocratic oath you bastards take was a bunch of horseshit, now I know it. How nice it must be! To say, 'I can't help you,' to be able to pick and choose the time to suit yourself. I'll tell you what, Mr. Doctor, after we try to stop all that bleeding, and can't do it because we don't know how, we'll decide *we* can't help any more, and *you* can land the fucking airplane!" The man was spluttering meaningless words. Mike stopped shaking him. "I know what it is—you haven't paid for your malpractice insurance—you don't want to take the chance!" Mike shook his head and threw Mannheim back into his seat. "You poor, miserable bastard." He spoke the last words softly, suddenly embarrassed by his own venomous speech. By throwing the doctor into his seat, Mike had knocked his glasses off.

He turned away from the doctor and said to Terry, "When you're finished there, go back and check on Pete —he's in bad shape." He turned without waiting for a reply and went to where Susan was lying back on her seat. Cindy was still holding the makeshift pressure pack. It had become bright red.

Joseph Mannheim looked out the window. They were in bright sunshine. His mind was reeling, screaming, protesting the treatment that he had received from the pilot. How dare he! What does he know about anything? He smoothed the lapels of his suit. The dull ache across the bridge of his nose was throbbing. He rubbed his temples with both hands, hoping that it would clear away some of the fogginess. He glanced back into the cabin. Two of the passengers ahead and to the right were looking at him, open disgust on their faces. He quickly looked out the window. The question rose again in his mind, even though he tried to push it back down: Would he help again? He shook his head, trying to halt the conversation in his mind, his conscience fighting every step of the way.

Even without yesterday's verdict he would have been reluctant to help, he hadn't practiced any general medicine in almost twenty years. Yet, that hadn't stopped him on the highway in California. Why couldn't he do what he knew he must? Simple, he decided. There were now eight hundred and fifty thousand reasons why he couldn't help, all of them dollars. Besides, he'd been drinking, he was shaky, he had a hangover, a headache. There were lots of reasons.

"We the jury find for the plaintiff and award damages in the amount of eight hundred and fifty thousand dollars."

Mannheim looked away from the bright sunshine into the cabin, watching the dark-haired stewardess dabbing gently at the face of the young woman he had watched board the airplane in San Francisco. It bothered him to see the stewardess doing that—she was being too gentle— she would never get the cuts clean using so little pressure. He fought the urge to tell her. Instead, he reached into his pocket for the linen handkerchief his wife had given him at Hanukkah, one of a set that he treasured. He wiped his glasses and replaced them, adjusting them on the bridge of his nose.

The conversation was still going on in his head, conscience slowly getting the best of it: Would he get involved again?

"Captain Mannheim, you have no choice!"

But eight hundred and fifty thousand dollars! A practice that's going to go to hell! Once burned, twice learned! (Now where did that come from?)

"How nice to be able to pick and choose . . ."

Oh, shit! He had almost said it aloud. He watched Terry, still dabbing at the young mother's face. *You're doing that all wrong!*

Joseph Mannheim rose from his seat, a little unsteady, and crossed the aisle. The stewardess looked at him with surprise. "Let me look at her—you're not doing that right." His voice was abrupt, blunt. Her eyes told him that she didn't trust him. He said, "It's all right—I'm OK now." For some reason, the admission of weakness didn't bother him. Terry smiled briefly and moved so that he could stand in front of Julia Pilero. He tilted her head back, noticing that his hand was trembling slightly. His head was still throbbing. He said to the stewardess, "You'd better get me some black coffee." Terry nodded, knowing, and left. He returned his attention to Julia.

The cuts were mostly superficial—small bits of glass were still imbedded in her forehead, but he wasn't concerned about them. "Are you hurt anywhere else?" The girl shook her head. He went to take the baby from her arms. There was broken glass on the pink blanket. She recoiled, holding the baby tighter to her chest. Mannheim didn't change his expression. "It's all right—I'm a doctor." She reluctantly gave him the infant. The blanket had protected the baby, there wasn't a mark on her. He laid the baby on the seat next to her mother and returned his attention to the cuts on the girl's face. She winced as he started to apply medication none too gently.

Mike Fuller replaced the bloody pad on Susan's shoulder with a clean one that Cindy had made from two more headrest covers. The bleeding seemed to have slowed somewhat, but the girl looked so pale. Again Mike felt frustrated—he didn't know what else he could do, and the feeling was foreign to him. In the cockpit, there was a solution for all problems, easily handled if one had the knowledge. But this . . . this was beyond his abilities, and he was again angry at his own helplessness. He looked toward the front of the cabin. The doctor that he had so recently humiliated was bending over Jerry Guccione's sister. He couldn't see what he was doing, but from the concerned look in the physician's eyes, he knew that an abrupt change had taken place. He turned to Cindy. "Here . . . hold this down hard again. I'll be right back." He walked to the little group of people two rows away.

"Doctor . . . ?" Mike said it quietly.

Mannheim looked up, then straightened, standing in the aisle, resentment still in evidence. "Yes?"

"We've got two more people back here—they need your help badly."

The two men stood looking at each other for a long moment. Recognition and apology passed between them, flowing both ways—a telepathy that neither understood.

Terry brought a steaming cup of coffee to Mannheim as they walked to the rear, the doctor hesitating as they walked past the seat where Cindy was holding the pressure pack on Susan's shoulder. Mike took the doctor's arm, almost spilling the coffee as he gulped it down, and pulled him away from the two passengers that were nearby. "Doctor, the captain's back there on the floor—his leg's shattered—we need to check him first."

Mannheim looked into the second officer's eyes. "Jesus, that's all we need."

"Don't worry—the airplane's flying, and the copilot and I are both qualified pilots." The doctor looked relieved. They walked to the rear of the cabin.

As they passed the two bodies in the last row of seats, Mannheim stopped. "Who are they?"

"A prisoner and a federal marshal—we were taking them to Chicago."

The doctor quickly lifted Riese's eyelid and put a hand to his throat, checking for a sign of life. There was none. He looked at Greco, and instinctively knew that checking him would be a waste of time. He had seen enough death stares at Cook County General. The two men knelt next to the captain.

"Pete, this is Doctor Mannheim"—he looked at the doctor—"it *is* Mannheim, isn't it?"

"Yes. Now, Captain, if you'll just——"

Pete cut him off with a wave of his hand. "Mike? Does Stan know anything?"

Mike didn't hesitate. "Not yet—just about the hydraulic failure. I haven't had time to tell him anything else. He's going over the procedures for getting this thing on the ground." Mannheim's eyes widened perceptibly. He

Protect

YOUR PROPERTY with the **CIS**

Please send details without obligation.
Tick plan(s), tear out card and post today.
Postage is paid.

MORTGAGE PROTECTION PLAN ☐
FIRE AND DOMESTIC COMBINED ☐
MOTOR INSURANCE ☐
LIFE ASSURANCE PLANS ☐

NAME ....
....
ADDRESS ....
....
....
....
....

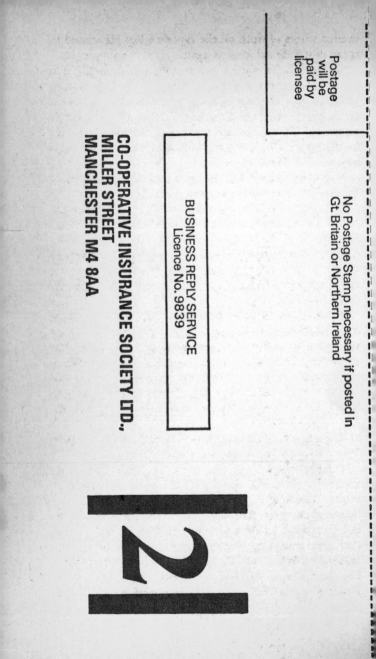

wanted to get to work on the captain's leg. He started to speak, but Pete cut him off again.

"Doctor, this is *my* job—when it's finished, we'll get to yours." He turned to the flight engineer. "Mike. Get up to the cockpit. Stan needs all the help he can get. The doctor and I will take care of things here, then I'll get up there somehow." The big pilot's moustache flattened in a grin as Mike got to his feet. Pete looked at him. "Good boy—now go on."

Mannheim stayed Mike's departure momentarily with his hand. "Do you carry any plasma on the airplane?"

Mike and Pete looked at each other. Mike finally said, "No." He stood a moment longer, then turned and walked forward.

Mannheim began to remove the tourniquet to inspect the wound. As he did so, he had a rush of admiration for the man he was working on. His head rang with the words "You have no choice!"

Mike walked the full length of the Coach cabin, pausing only briefly next to Susan. Christ, she looks terrible, he thought. He saw that Cindy was putting a third pad on the girl's shoulder. He squeezed her arm, his eyes giving Cindy the reassurance she needed, then continued toward the cockpit, ignoring the inquiring glances of the passengers he passed. He stopped once more as he went through the First-Class section.

A small boy stood in the aisle, blocking Mike's progress. "Sir?" His voice was small, frightened. "Can I help?"

The flight engineer was annoyed at the interruption. He wanted to get to the cockpit, yet the boy's expression, almost a pleading for acceptance, prevented Mike from brushing past him. He knew intuitively that this was the boy Terry had mentioned when she had brought coffee. Perhaps it was Mike's own shattered home as a child that made him hesitate. "Look," he said as he gently moved the boy aside, "we're going to be pretty busy for a while—I can't stop to talk now, but if there's anything you can do for us, anything at all, we'll let you know. The biggest help you could be right now is to sit down and stay there, OK?"

The boy nodded, disappointed. "OK."

Mike started for the cockpit, then turned. "What's your name?"

"Kevin."

Mike grinned and quickly left. He took a deep breath before he opened the cockpit door.

> *"The First Officer is second-in-command. Should the Captain become incapacitated, he will assume the duties and responsibilities of the Captain. He will therefore be familiar with those duties and responsibilities."*
>
> Page 4, Para. 3
> Transcon Flight Operations Manual

11

Stan Burkhart turned in the copilot's seat as the door closed. "Where the hell have you been? And where's Pete? We've got problems here. Jesus H. Christ! And Terry! She wouldn't tell me anything, that old bat—what the hell is going on?" His tension was obvious—the strain of being alone, unknowing, was starting to show.

Mike sat down before he answered and studied the copilot for a moment, formulating his thoughts. "Stan, we've got big problems back there, too." Mike nodded toward the cabin. Stan's brow knitted in a frown. "The first noises we heard were shots. Apparently, that prisoner got the marshal's gun. He wanted to get a hostage for an escape—sort of went bananas."

"What do you mean?"

Mike took a deep breath. "Well, he shot a bunch of people after he got the gun. The marshal—he's dead—and——"

"What happened? I heard more shots later," Stan interrupted before Mike could finish. They were quiet for a moment, then Stan said, "Go on."

Mike told Stan what he had seen, briefly sketching in details of the confrontation with Greco, ending by saying, "Pete got the gun from the floor and shot the prisoner." He paused, pacing the information, waiting for a reaction from the copilot. There was none. "Stan—Pete's been shot. In the leg. It's pretty bad, his leg's at a funny angle—I think the bone was shattered—and he's bled a lot. We put a tourniquet on it."

The copilot slumped back in his seat, his eyes instinctively scanning the instrument panel. They fixed on the yellow warning lights still burning brightly in front of him. The instrument vibrator's steady ticking was the only sound that could be heard above the wind noise as they sped eastward. He seemed to gather himself, then turned back to Mike. "What else?"

"Well, Cathy got hit—just a scratch, really. She's OK. And the girl with the baby, Jerry's sister, I think, was cut pretty badly by some glass that shattered." He paused. He and Stan had flown together often, but they weren't close friends. Mike was unsure what to say to him—how much to tell him about Susan. Mike was perhaps the only person on board flight 602 who realized how important the copilot was now. He feared that the news of Susan's serious wound would throw Stan's normally cool thought processes into a jumble.

Stan said, "Any more? What about the prisoner?"

Mike was glad for another moment before he had to tell him about Susan. "He's dead."

Stan had a vision of the scene. He fought a momentary wave of nausea. "Anything else?"

"Yes." Mike paused for breath. "Susan's been shot."

The constant sound of the altimeter vibrator seemed to fill the cockpit. Stan put his hand to his forehead, his right arm resting on the sill of the big side window. He watched the clouds, brilliant white in the intense sunlight of thirty-seven thousand feet. "How bad?"

Mike decided to play it down. "She was hit in the shoulder. We've been using pressure packs. There was a lot of blood, but I don't think it'll be too bad. There's a doctor on board. He's attending Pete right now, then he'll take care of her. He seems like a fairly competent guy."

Stan was beating his right fist slowly on the window's edge, all his silent rage centered there—slowly pounding the unyielding metal. The 727 shuddered and recovered sluggishly as they entered an area of light turbulence. The motion brought Stan back to the very real problem of flying the airplane and taking care of nineteen passengers, six crew members, and two bodies.

Transcon selected its pilots very carefully. For the past ten years, applicants had been subjected to a battery of tests that staggered the imagination and left the applicant in a state of mild lunacy—tests to determine personality, visual-motor coordination, ability to work in confined spaces, IQ, general knowledge, and on and on. The testing took two full days, the physical exam another half-day. The Transcon Personnel Department accepted one in thirty applicants to fill the pilots' seats of their aircraft.

In the cockpit of flight 602, those selection procedures were proving their value. Stan's mind had run the gamut of emotion—fear, anger, and guilt about Susan—in a matter of seconds before hauling itself out of an emotional snake pit back into the real world.

The airplane shuddered again as they passed through another area of turbulence. With the autopilot trying to cope with a decreased control ability, the 727 stayed in a five-degree bank for a few seconds before returning to a level attitude. Stan lifted the heavy book from his lap and handed it to the flight engineer: "I've checked through the hydraulics, and we've done just about everything there is to do. See if I've missed anything. I want you to do a couple of things, too. First, tell one of the girls to come up here when things are under control back there, and give me a full report. How long before Pete gets up here, any idea?"

Mike spread his hands. "It'll be a while, Stan—I don't really know."

"OK, we're going to have to assume that he's out of action for now, and start making some decisions until he gets back here to take charge."

Mike remembered the pain he had seen on the captain's face and thought to himself it would be on another flight that Pete Douglass would be making decisions—he wouldn't be much help to flight 602.

Stan kept talking. "Then, get Dispatch on the radio, and get the weather for all the closest airports. Tell them that we're"—he looked at the DME dial, a digital readout of distance to the radio station that they were navigating on— "a hundred miles from Omaha VOR. Check Omaha, Des Moines, maybe Offut, anything that's close by—I want field conditions as well as weather. Tell them we're descending to twenty-five thousand because of the hydraulics, and ask them to check with maintenance to see if they have any ideas that might help." Stan paused for a moment. Pete Douglass' team concept wasn't wasted. "Anything I've forgotten?"

Mike shook his head. "Not that I can think of. Do you want me to say something to the people?"

"No, I'll talk to them in a minute. I'm going to use emergency authority."

Mike nodded. "Emergency Authority" is a term used when the captain of an airplane takes control away from all agencies on the ground. Normally, the captain is in command, but responsible for following procedures and regulations set up by the FAA and other authorities to expedite handling of all air traffic. When a captain declares that he is using emergency authority, their role becomes one of assistance and aid rather than control.

Stan leaned across the cockpit and dialed in the "Mayday" code on the transponder—an instrument that is used to identify the aircraft on the traffic controller's radarscope on the ground. It gives the controller the ability to separate the many targets that he sees, and to identify them.

In the darkened room of the Minneapolis Air Route Traffic Control Center Hank Gorsky, a trainee with three months' experience, was working high altitude sector number four. He sat hunched over the scope, munching a sandwich between gulps of coffee. There had been no time for lunch, which wasn't unusual because the Center was undermanned. The storm had cut the traffic load in half in Hank's sector, which made his job rather easy this afternoon. He was working only three airplanes: Transcon 602, eastbound for O'Hare, United 28, eastbound for New York, and Continental 25, westbound for San Francisco. He was opening his mouth to take another bite from the roast beef sandwich—he never took it. The scope before him brightened as the center blip on J-60 blossomed into a large green blob. He dropped his sandwich and swung around to the supervisor, who was walking up and down behind the row of controllers. "Hey, Frank! We've got an emergency code!" He quickly swung back to the scope as the supervisor hurried to stand behind the young trainee. Hank Gorsky pressed the foot pedal that activated his microphone: "Transcon six oh two—verify emergency transponder code!"

The pilot's voice was tense, Hank thought, as he replied. "Roger, Transcon six oh two squawking Mayday. We're descending to two five oh on the airway. If there's anyone under us, get them out of the way!"

The controller could tell by the tone of the pilot's voice that he didn't have to ask him if he was declaring an emergency. "Minneapolis Center, Roger." He scanned the scope quickly. Thank God it's a light day, he thought. The only problem was the Continental trip, at thirty-one thousand, forty miles east of 602. "Continental twenty-five, turn right to three two zero, vectors off the airway for descending traffic!"

The Continental captain had heard the exchange, and replied, "Continental twenty-five, Roger, right to three two zero."

Hank was watching the green blob on the scope, mesmerized. "Twenty-five, Roger." He said it automatically. At the same time, the supervisor had gone to the controller working the sector adjacent to Hank's on the east side.

"Clear J-60 at all altitudes above twenty-four—we've got an emergency in sector four." The controller nodded and began vectoring the four planes that he was working off the airway. The supervisor returned to stand behind the trainee. He was pleased with the way Hank was handling it so far and felt that to relieve him would be unnecessary.

Hank stepped on the pedal to key his mike again. "Transcon six oh two, what is the nature of the emergency, and what are your intentions?"

The controller supervisor shook his head. The kid is cool, he thought; he'll make a good controller in a couple of years.

The Transcon pilot's reply was coming over the speaker. "Uh, we're just going to descend now. We've had a hydraulic failure of both systems, and we've had a shooting on board."

"Jesus!" The supervisor whispered under his breath, "That poor bastard, he's got real trouble."

The pilot continued. "We're checking with the company now for current weather at the nearest available airport with long runways. You could help on that score—see what you can come up with—something with decent weather that's close by."

"OK, six oh two, we'll see what we can do."

"And, Center? We'll want a vector straight for the airport that we decide on—as few turns as possible, with a gradual descent throughout, OK?"

"Minneapolis Center, Roger, Transcon." Hank Gorsky noticed that the Continental trip was nearing the edge of his sector and had already passed the descending Transcon flight. "Continental twenty-five, Center, turn left to two four zero and rejoin the airway, on course. Contact Center on one three two point five five!"

"Continental twenty-five, left to two four oh, Center on thirty-two fifty-five." There was a pause. "Good luck, Transcon—so long."

Stan keyed the mike: "Thanks." He felt a surge of emotion tighten his stomach muscles, realizing how much he loved the people he worked with, knowing that only other pilots could know the turmoil he was going through. He turned to Mike, seated at the flight engineer's table. He was listening on the other radio, writing furiously as the Transcon dispatcher relayed information about weather and field conditions. Mike's face was creased in a deep frown.

Stan flipped the altitude hold switch to *Off* and tilted the control knob down. The 727 reluctantly started to descend. He pulled the power back to keep the speed down. In the rarified atmosphere at thirty-seven thousand feet, Stan didn't want to incur any mach buffet—a condition caused when air passing over the curve of the wing in certain spots exceeds the speed of sound. Stan's mind was repeating his first instructor's favorite words, "slowly and gently," as he eased the crippled aircraft toward the thicker air at twenty-five thousand. When he was satisfied that the autopilot was doing its job, he reached for the handset and turned on the P.A. system. Again, Pete Douglass was in the cockpit in spirit if not in body, because he had always let his crew do much of the P.A. work, so Stan wasn't uncomfortable speaking, even with the added pressures of their situation.

He took a deep breath. "Ladies and gentlemen, may I have your attention, please! This is the flight deck, and I'm the first officer." He decided to keep it on the light side, for the moment—he had to calm everyone down before he could tell them what the problems were. "It seems that we've got a few problems." That's an understatement if there ever was one, he thought. He pressed the button again. "I'll go into detail about our situation later, but right now, I would like every passenger to take a seat and remain there. We have a doctor on board to care for the people that were . . ." He had a fleeting vision of Susan—the heather-green suit, the blood, and hesitated before resuming—". . . were wounded, and anyone in the aisle will only hamper our efforts at caring for them. So please, sit down." A thought came into his head. "I am going to leave the cockpit door open to facilitate communication between myself and the cabin crew and the doctor. I ask that all of you remain seated and not enter the cockpit under any circumstances." He paused again, trying to think what else he should say now. "Could Dr. . . ." Stan released the button and turned to Mike. "What's the doctor's name?"

"Mannheim."

". . . could Dr. Mannheim come to the cockpit when he's able and give us a report on the condition of the passengers?" He paused again, constructing the phrases he wanted to use. "Now . . . we also have another problem. The aircraft's hydraulic systems have been damaged, apparently by the shooting, so that compounds the trouble. As some of you experienced travelers may know, we have backup systems, and they are functioning normally. But because of the hydraulic problem, we will be landing at the nearest suitable airport. We're getting weather information now, to find out what the choices are, and I'll be back with you soon to explain further the situation. I ask that you all remain calm—the airplane is flying well, and there is no immediate danger. Thank you." He hung up the handset and turned to Mike.

As the doctor hovered over the captain's leg trying to establish the extent of the injury, Pete Douglass' mind was a maelstrom of confusion. First, there was the pain—an immense amount of pain. He thought he was hallucinating for a moment as he imagined that Mannheim was a surgeon and he was Kitty. He wanted to tell the surgeon that the lump was not on his leg, but in his breast. The airplane rocked slightly, and he thought that was odd, because an operating room is supposed to be motionless. The rush of air from the holes in the lavatory wall sounded like the hissing of anesthetic, and he wondered why it was a steady hiss, instead of a rhythmic one, like his breathing. Another assault of pain washed through him, bringing him back to reality—to the airplane, to the doctor bending over his leg.

The pain did not erase the memory of his wife, and as he sat half-erect, he missed her. He needed her. He wanted her. His mind went into another whirlwind, of self-pity this time—*why* Kitty, why not someone who deserved to get the big C? He hadn't told her, but he was sure that he would get home and find her without a breast.

He looked through a red curtain of pain and saw one of the stewardesses leaning close to the doctor—was it Terry? He heard the doctor speak to her: "Get me something small, round, and hard. I need it to press against the artery—otherwise your captain will bleed to death." Pete saw the girl's look of fright—a brief expression on her face—then the fear changed to determination, and she left. He realized then that he had to do something that he didn't want to do. Thinking about Kitty was comforting, but with a supreme effort, he shoved the thought of her to the far reaches of his consciousness. The mental effort helped ease the pain. He heard his copilot's voice on the P.A. system—he relaxed a little. He realized that he had to get to the cockpit. He began running through the options open to him as captain—what airports were close at hand, what the hydraulic loss involved. Intuitively, he was aware that if he were to abandon his responsibility to the aircraft and the people aboard it, he might never see Kitty again. Making his brain work for him had all but removed the pain in the lower half of his body.

Joseph Mannheim was puzzled. As he finished putting the tourniquet back on the captain's leg, he noticed that the man was smiling. One of the other pilots had just finished speaking on the P.A. system. "I don't see any humor in the situation, Captain," he said abruptly.

Pete looked at Mannheim. "I'm not amused, Doctor." He nodded in the direction of the cockpit. "I'm pleased at how Stan's taken over."

"Stan?"

"The copilot. That was him talking. We're descending, in case you hadn't noticed." He grabbed the doctor's arm and gripped it tightly—Mannheim was surprised at his remaining strength. "Doctor. Do whatever that young man says—the problems we have aren't going to get any better, they're going to get worse!" Pete briefly explained the hydraulic problem.

The doctor's eyes widened as Pete finished. "You mean that we're going to crash?"

"No, we're *not* going to crash . . . but the landing is going to be a bitch, and Stan's going to need all the help he can get. That's why you're going to help me up to the cockpit."

"I can't. You shouldn't be moved." He pointed to Pete's leg. He had used the seat belt extension for a tourniquet again, but he had inserted a small can of tomato juice beneath it to press against the femoral artery at mid-thigh, blocking the artery to prevent a recurrence of the heavy bleeding.

"Doctor, I've got to be up there!"

"Medically, I can't allow it!"

"Doctor! I'm still the captain of this airplane, and you have nothing to say about it. Now there are other people hurt, and they need you—so stop arguing and get me up there!" The grip on the doctor's arm tightened.

Joseph Mannheim looked at him for a long time, then rose slowly and walked toward the front of the cabin. He signaled to the head stewardess to come back. When she reached him, he started speaking quietly. "Find two passengers who can help the captain up to the cockpit. Tell them to be very careful, and not let the belt on his leg slip, OK?"

Terry nodded and left. Mannheim was impressed with the professional way the girl was taking care of things. Like most other airline passengers, he had assumed that the stewardesses were no more than waitresses, not realizing that the majority of the six weeks' training that they must have is devoted to evacuation, cabin safety and related emergency procedures. He went to where Susan MacKenzie lay back, pale and unmoving. He gently moved the stewardess who was standing next to her, holding a blood-soaked pad to the girl's shoulder, positioning himself in front of her to get a clearer view of the wound. As he pushed his glasses up on his nose, he realized that his headache had vanished. His mouth hurt from the hot coffee that he had gulped down to steady himself. The coffee and the activity had sobered him.

Mannheim looked up at the young stewardess. She was obviously shaky, her hand trembled as she held the pad in place on Susan's shoulder. He gently moved her hand away from the wound, his eyes switching from her face to the wounded girl's shoulder. "What's your name?" He sensed her need for reassurance.

"Cindy . . . Cindy Weston."

He looked at her briefly, then back to the wounded girl. "Well, Cindy, I'm Joe Mannheim. I'm a doctor, and I'm going to need your help. Would you go to the rear and bring the first-aid kit up here?"

The girl hesitated, then said, "OK."

"Good girl."

Cindy left, thankful for having something else to do. She had to wait momentarily while the two men that Terry had recruited supported Pete between them. They moved slowly up the aisle, having to turn sideways along the narrow path. When they had passed, she picked up the first-aid kit and followed them slowly.

Joseph Mannheim was hunched over the redheaded girl, looking closely at her face. He didn't like what he saw. Her face was an ashen gray, her eyelids fluttered occasionally—she was obviously in shock. There was a large volume of blood. Bright-red blood that indicated arterial bleeding. He knew that the front was an exit wound—he had noticed the bits of blood and flesh on the seat in front of her. He felt for a pulse in her right wrist—it was almost nonexistent. He moved his hand to her throat—the pulse was stronger there. He was sure that the bullet had nicked the subclavian artery—a nasty wound under any conditions, possibly fatal in the present surroundings. His mind quickly catalogued the other possibilities for a wound of this kind—pneumothorax, possibly cracked or chipped first rib, there could be a dozen more problems.

The captain moved slowly past, motioning his human crutches to stop. "What do you think, Doctor? How is she?"

Mannheim looked up and shook his head. "Bad . . . she's lost a lot of blood, and it's in a tough place to stop the bleeding—I don't know."

The captain nodded and indicated to the two men that he wanted to keep going. As they slowly left, Cindy arrived with the first-aid kit.

Mannheim said, "If there are any scissors in there, get

them out." Cindy produced a small pair with rounded points. "Now—hold this pad down against her shoulder." He switched hands with the stewardess, took the scissors, and carefully began cutting away the soggy woolen material around the wound. As he was cutting, Terry came over to them.

"Doctor—Cathy, the other stewardess, says she feels all right, and wants to help."

He looked around, momentarily annoyed at the interruption. The blond girl's forehead had stopped bleeding, and there was a large gauze bandage on it. "All right. If she feels up to it, I'll need a lot of fresh clean cloths—towels, napkins, anything—see if she can get them. Then come back here."

"I should go to the cockpit and tell them what's going on."

"No—you stay here, I may need you. I'll go up when I'm finished."

He turned back to what he had been doing. As he lifted the material away, he noticed that the wound was no longer surging, as it had been. The blood was oozing out in small, measured amounts. He figured that the artery had gone into spasm, but there was no guarantee that it would stay that way. The only thing he could do was to put continuous pressure on the wound and hope that the girl's constitution could sustain the blood loss.

Cathy arrived, carrying a large stack of lime-green napkins. They were freshly laundered, and the doctor realized that they were probably the most sterile thing on the airplane. He looked up at the blond stewardess as he took two of the napkins. "I'm sorry about the way I spoke to you, Miss." It was the closest he could come to a sincere apology.

Cathy smiled, then grimaced as the smile stabbed pain through her forehead. "That's all right, Doctor, we always need one bastard on the airplane—it keeps us on our toes."

He was about to reply sharply again, when he saw the smile and realized that she was only half serious. "Yes," he said, "I guess you do. Do you feel up to helping Cindy here, with holding the packs on this girl? It's the only way we can keep the bleeding to a minimum."

Cathy looked at Cindy, then replied quickly, "Sure . . . I'm fine."

"Good. I'll buy you all a steak dinner if we get out of this." He started to leave.

"Doctor?"

"Yes?"

Cathy smiled at him. "*When* we get out of this."

He nodded, embarrassed, and left. He stopped where Terry stood, next to the young mother. "I'm going to the cockpit—just make sure that she doesn't try to rub her face. I'll be back to look at her after I've talked to the captain."

The two men who had been helping Pete slid him through the door, depositing him on the rear observer's seat. He sat sideways, facing the engineer's panel across the cockpit. His wounded leg dangled at a crazy angle, his foot at a right angle to his body. Pete didn't feel it; his whole leg had gone numb.

Stan turned in his seat, having leveled off smoothly at twenty-five thousand feet. He had to shout because of the increased air noise at the lower altitude. "Jesus, am I glad to see you! Can you make it up to the seat OK?"

Pete shook his head. "No way, Stan—you'll have to do it from there. I'd be more in the way in my seat than I am back here. Tell me what's going on."

Stan turned back to the front as a call came from the controller. Mike began to tell the captain what they had found out before he got back to the cockpit. "Pete . . . everything close by is either below minimums or closed— the closest airports are O'Hare or St. Louis. O'Hare's about ten minutes further, but Stan and I feel it's the best choice —longer runways and better crash equipment."

"Sounds reasonable . . . go on."

"We're at twenty-five thousand because one of the yaw dampers is out—still on J-60, but Stan's told them he expects a vector straight to the outer marker once we decide where we're going."

"OK. Tell Stan to get a vector for O'Hare." The flight engineer swung his seat around and spoke to Stan, who in turn spoke to the controller. Five seconds later, the aircraft was in a slight bank, changing heading by ten degrees. Pete grimaced as a new wave of pain swept up his thigh, landing with a force in his lower back. The pain gone, he continued, "What have you decided about the landing?"

"Well, we were just starting to talk about it when you got here. Stan thinks we should prepare for an evacuation."

"He's right. How long to get to O'Hare?"

Mike looked at his watch. "We figure about two forty-five, Chicago time—an hour and five minutes. The company's running a new flight plan now, figuring on twenty-five thousand for both St. Louis and Chicago—we should get it any minute. When I called for the weather, I only told them there had been a shooting, I didn't say anything about injuries—I thought I'd wait until the doctor had a chance to look at everyone involved."

"Good thinking." He chuckled softly, the effort bringing back the stabbing pain in his hip and thigh. "You guys really don't need me here—maybe I should go back to First Class and sit down and relax." His face contorted with another wave of pain.

The flight engineer leaned closer. "Pete? Are you all right? I can get the doctor up here."

The captain waved him off with his hand. Using all of his willpower, he forced himself to think about their impending landing. Again, he was surprised to find that mental effort blanked out the pain. "Tell Stan that when things are settled down back there, he'll have to make an announcement about the evacuation preparations. We'll get Terry in the cockpit first, and give her a full picture so that she can answer questions from the passengers." His leg was numbing again—it felt as if there was nothing below the tourniquet. Nothing but cold.

Mike had swung his chair back to the engineer's panel, adjusting the cockpit temperature control. It had gotten very warm. Pete Douglass looked at the second officer's broad shoulders—the only part of him that he could see above the seat back. He thought it was funny that he had never noticed what a big man Mike was—he was built like a tight end on a football team. Tall, but not thin. The captain's eyes wandered around the cockpit. He wondered why cockpits were always painted gray—a bluish metal-gray color that hadn't changed in the twenty-seven years he had been working for Transcon.

God, he thought, have I spent a lot of years in the cockpits of airplanes! If he had analyzed it, he would have been startled. Pete Douglass's logbook had over twenty thousand hours in it—that was only flight time. If you considered the time spent sitting in the cockpit, waiting for delays, sitting during through trips, and waiting for passengers to deplane, the total time would have almost doubled. Figuring twenty-four hours a day, seven days a week, Pete Douglass had been in the cockpits of airplanes for over four years.

His gaze traveled to Stan, busily talking on the radio. He remembered his copilot days—he had begun his career with the airline in the right seat of a DC-3. The standard equipment then had been a rubber apron and a putty knife. The apron was to keep your pants dry flying through heavy rainstorms, because the front of the cockpit leaked like a sieve. In spite of the apron, you always got drenched. The putty knife was to scrape ice from the front of the windshield during winter—that didn't work too well either.

He had met Kitty on a DC-3. He smiled at the thought. She had been a brand-new hostess, on her first trip with Transcon. He had been instantly smitten, and within three months had proposed to her. Most of his fellow pilots after the war were single, and they all mourned his loss, but all managed to drink a great deal of liquor at the reception. Four of those friends were dead now, victims of a struggling airline industry's fight to attain larger and faster means of transportation through the air while neglecting some of the limitations of their environment. His thoughts were abruptly halted by Joseph Mannheim's arrival at the cockpit door.

"We've got to get this airplane on the ground. That girl with the shoulder wound will be dead in a half hour!"

Mike had tried to stop him from saying it, but he was too late. Stan spun around in his seat, his face white, features sharpened in startled anguish.

"What do you mean?"

The doctor was not used to having a statement questioned, and his reply was sharp. "Just what I said—that girl is bleeding to death, and I have no way of stopping it. She needs plasma or blood, and there isn't any on this airplane."

Mind racing, Stan looked at Mike. The flight engineer met his gaze for a moment, then looked away. Neither of them wanted to say it, but they both knew they were locked into a time frame that couldn't be altered.

"What about a direct transfusion?" Stan was looking at the doctor hopefully.

As insensitive as Mannheim was, even he could sense that the girl with lovely copper hair was more than just a passenger. He shook his head. "You've been watching too much television medicine. We don't have the equipment. No tubing, no needles, no cross-match kit—it's impossible . . . I'm sorry."

"Are you sure about the time?" It was Mike. "The half hour, I mean?"

"No one could be sure, exactly. A half hour is a guess. It could be more, it could be less. She's lost a great deal of blood already. We've slowed the bleeding, but I suspect that an artery was nicked by the bullet, and there's no way to put pressure directly on it." Mannheim bent down to look at Pete's tourniquet. He fiddled with it, tightening it slightly, then straightened up.

Pete looked up at him from the observer's seat. "We're going to call the company and tell them what we need when we get to Chicago. Can you give us a list?"

"*Chicago?*" The doctor looked at Pete incredulously.

"It's the closest airport that's open and has adequate equipment—crash equipment as well as medical."

"Oh." He had been so engrossed with treating the people in the cabin that he had almost forgotten about the airplane's crippled hydraulic system. He recoiled at the words "crash equipment."

"What will you want, Doctor?" Pete asked.

He readjusted his horn-rimmed glasses, thinking. "Plasma—lots of plasma. Other than that, just tell them to be prepared for gunshot wounds. The hospitals will know what to bring. I can't think of anything beyond that, except that we'll need provision for getting three people into ambulances—make sure they're aware of that." He looked at the copilot, seeing that he was still looking anxiously at him. "About the girl—a lot will depend on her constitution, how strong she is, her will to live. Do you know her well?" The doctor squeezed past Pete, getting closer to the copilot. He was surprised how small the cockpit was.

Stan was saying, "I used to. I haven't seen her for a long time."

"Do you know anything about her health? Has she been sick or anything?"

The copilot shook his head. "She didn't say anything last night." He thought of her warm strong body beneath him in the hotel room. "As far as I know, she's strong and healthy. She's a nurse—she used to work at St. Francis."

"I wish to hell it had been someone else—I could have used her."

Stan turned to look out the window. The undercast was higher now; he saw that they would be entering some cloud layers ahead. "So do I," he murmured, "*so do I*."

Mannheim turned to the captain. " I don't want you to move—you shouldn't even be here. Just sit and relax—but for God's sake, don't try to move around!" The captain nodded his assent.

The doctor was about to leave. "I'm going back to see what else I can do—there isn't much. Is there any way I can communicate with you up here without running up and down the aisle?"

Mike said, "There's a phone in the galley, over the door. Just press the button marked *Cockpit* and talk. Don't forget to push the button on the handset." He noticed that the man's expensive suit was smeared with blood-stains.

Mannheim shook his head. "Too unwieldy. I may not be able to leave the girl."

Pete said, "Tell one of the stewardesses to relay messages."

Mike interrupted. "Pete, I have an idea." He got out of his seat and edged past the doctor. He stood at the entrance to the cockpit, looking down the aisle. Kevin Stryon was seated about halfway back in the First Class section. Mike raised his hand and motioned to him. "Kevin! Come up here!" The little boy rose from his seat, hesitated briefly—unsure—then strode to the open cockpit door ignoring the inquiring glances of the other passengers. His left arm bumped against his chest as he walked.

"Did you want me?" His eyes blinked rapidly from behind the too-large glasses. He seemed bewildered, but excited at the idea of being the center of attention.

"Kevin, this is Captain Douglass." Mike motioned toward Pete, sitting close to the cockpit door.

The boy held out his hand. "How do you do."

Pete shook Kevin's hand, then gritted his teeth and turned away as a wave of pain passed through his thigh.

When it had passed, he looked at Mike, then back to the boy. Mike spoke quickly. "Pete, the girls are going to be busy with preparations for evacuation. Maybe Kevin here can run any messages back and forth." He put his hand on the small shoulder. "Do you think you could do that?"

The boy looked at Mike. "I . . . I can do it."

"Are you sure?"

Kevin stood up a little straighter. "I'm sure."

The captain hesitated. His assessment of Kevin had been the same as Mike's—the boy would be accurate. "Good idea, Mike." He looked at the boy again. "Go with the doctor, Kevin, and run up here if he wants anything." As they left the cockpit door, Pete said to Mannheim, "Send Terry up here, will you?"

A thousand miles south of flight 602, another struggle had been going on, unseen by humanity. It was a struggle for power in a way. The swiftly moving leading edge of the storm, depicted on a weather map as a line with a series of pointed symbols along it, had met a high-pressure warm air system centered over New Mexico, depicted as a line with rounded edges. The round edges and the pointed edges engaged in a little dance of sorts, dipping and bowing, giving here, then moving there. The warm front acted like a balloon that one had stuck a finger into, its perimeter being indented for a while. Then, when the pressure against it became too great, it shoved back. The storm reacted like the finger in the balloon, rebounding in the only direction that was open—eastward. The battle had had taken some of the fight out of the storm, but it would be another hour before meteorologists on the ground would find out through observations of pressure and temperature that its course had altered. Instead of heading for the Ozark Mountains, it was heading more easterly—toward St. Louis.

12

Three men were standing behind Connie Barstow: Lars Gunter, whom Connie had relieved as Chief Dispatcher several hours ago, Lars not wanting to leave now because of the crisis on board flight 602; Glen Meyer, the Chief Pilot for Transcon in Chicago, who at the time was biting an elusive hangnail; and Ralph Dorcek, who had just come from the press room. Connie was unruffled by the horsepower gathered at his shoulder. He was busy talking to the copilot on flight 602 through a direct hookup arranged by Arinc, the private communications network maintained cooperatively by all the airlines. The speaker on top of Connie's computer console was turned to full volume, and in addition to the three men standing behind him, several other people had stopped working to listen to the dialogue.

Stan Burkhart's voice sounded calm and unwavering. ". . . the doctor has requested that ambulances be available for three people. Also, we'll need a lot of plasma. We're to tell the hospital to be prepared to treat gunshot wounds. Uh . . . " The voice wavered briefly, then continued strong and precise. Only Meyer and Dorcek knew that the calm was a forced control, and that the copilot's insides would be in knots. "The only other thing is the crash equipment for our arrival."

Connie picked up the mike on his desk. "Roger, six oh two—we have all of that. We'll get to work on it right away. Anything else?"

The speaker crackled to life again. "Yes—give us the current O'Hare weather."

"Roger. Stand by." The dispatcher picked up the weather sheet and started reading. "The thirteen hundred Central was fifteen hundred broken, twenty-five hundred overcast and four miles in light snow . . . "

"Give me that!" Glen Meyer had taken the microphone from the dispatcher's hand. He started speaking as he looked out the big windows along the back wall. "Stan? This is Glen Meyer. The visibility is down to about three miles now—it looks like it might be around a mile or so for your arrival, but we don't expect it to get any worse than that." He hadn't wanted to step into the conversation, but he knew, far better than the dispatcher, what was going through the pilot's mind and wanted to give him the best information possible. He continued. "The weather people say that the wind will be southeast for the next two hours or so, around twenty to thirty knots. Set up for runway one-four right—it should be blowing right down the runway. If it isn't, you might consider going to Detroit." The Chief Pilot was thinking about the crosswind limitations that Stan would have to face because of the hydraulic failure, something the dispatcher might not be thinking of.

There was a pause, then Stan's voice came through the speaker. "No go, Glen. The people that are wounded are bleeding badly, and we've got to get on the ground. I just hope to hell the weatherman is right."

"So do I. If there's anything else you need, let us know. You've got all the help there is."

"OK." There was another pause. Unseen to those on the ground, Mike had handed a sheet of paper to the co-pilot giving their new arrival time for O'Hare, using the computer data that had been relayed to them. "We're going to, uh . . . revise our arrival time. Now estimating over the outer marker at two thirty-four, local. We won't call again unless we need something. We're pretty busy up here."

Glen Meyer still had the mike. "OK, Stan. Give a call if we can help." He paused, searching for some reassuring words. Not finding them, he simply said, "Good luck." After a few seconds, Connie Barstow reached up and turned down the volume on the speaker. The people who had been standing motionless started back to whatever they had been doing, without speaking—a silence hung over the Dispatch Office.

Meyer and Dorcek stood looking at each other—both pilots, both sharing thoughts, unspoken, of what the atmosphere on the flight deck of flight 602 must be like. Glen Meyer broke the silence. "I've got to call Bob Quinlan in New York—he doesn't know yet. Want to come along?" The former captain, now vice-president, nodded and they walked the twenty yards to the Chief Pilot's office.

It was a small room, the walls covered with the inevitable pictures of aircraft. Glen sat heavily in the chair behind his desk, reached for a pipe with one hand and picked up the phone with the other. Ralph Dorcek sat in a small chair in the corner of the office. He was about to speak when Glen motioned with his hand and started talking into the phone.

At a dozen locations around the airport, machinery was being put into motion—the machinery that would, directly or indirectly, be a part of the arrival of flight 602. Calls had been made by Transcon Passenger Service to three local hospitals to obtain the necessary medical equipment that would be standing by. Dispatch had called the O'Hare fire department and the Air Force fire department at the edge of the field and informed them of the impending landing some forty-five minutes away, detailing the nature of the emergency so that they could know what to expect. Transcon's Gate Control had set up a special area for the people who were even now arriving at the airport to meet passengers from the flight. Aircraft Planning was busily hunting down another aircraft to use for the continuation of 602 from O'Hare to St. Louis and New York. The Chicago crew schedulers were busy calling reserve pilots and stewardesses to the field to cover the trip. At the airport post office, a truck was readied to drive onto the field and remove the mail from 602's belly should the airplane be disabled and unmovable. Transcon's medical staff, along with several other airlines that maintained medical departments at the airport, checked supplies and equipment that might become necessary. In all, more than three hundred people were involved in trying to provide the best and safest conditions for the crippled airplane's arrival.

In New York, at La Guardia Airport, Bob Quinlan was in his office having a talk with one of his captains. It was not a formal hearing, by any means. The captain's aircraft had struck a food truck with the left wing tip the day before while being guided into the gate by a mechanic.

Bob Quinlan was in the middle of asking the captain why he hadn't requested guide men to help him maneuver the aircraft in the congested area when his phone rang. He picked it up. "Bob Quinlan."

"Bob, it's Glen Meyer. We've got an emergency going on here—it's one of your crews."

"Hold on a second, Glen." The Chief Pilot covered the phone with his hand. He looked at the captain seated across the desk. "Dan—this may be a long call, and it's important. I'll call you at home later, OK?"

The captain got to his feet and nodded. "Sure, Bob." He started to leave, and the Chief Pilot smiled, deepening the wrinkles at the corner of his eyes.

"No sweat, Dan—I'll talk to you." The pilot left the office and Quinlan swung his chair around to face the windows and said into the phone, "Go ahead, Glen. I had someone in the office."

"Flight six oh two had a shoot-out aboard between Salt Lake and O'Hare. The crew is New York-based, captain's name is Douglass—we got it from your crew scheduler. He's been shot, we don't know how badly."

"Oh, Christ, that poor bastard!"

"What do you mean?"

"Nothing, really." He had remembered Kitty's being in the hospital, but decided not to mention it. "Give me everything you know."

Glen Meyer relayed all the events, as they were known, to the New York Chief Pilot, being as brief and to the point as possible without leaving out pertinent details. Quinlan wrote on a pad in front of him, occasionally injecting a question when something was unclear. The conversation took only five minutes.

Bob Quinlan gazed across the airport at Flushing Bay as Glen wrapped up the details of the preparations being made at O'Hare. He was thinking about the three pilots in the cockpit of an airplane a thousand miles away. He had been the Chief Pilot for three years and during those three years had made a constant effort to know the men who worked for him as well as he could. He created an image of Pete Douglass in his mind. They had known each other for at least fifteen years, and even flown together on occasion.

Stan Burkhart was an easy man to know. He and Stan had had a head-on battle at an Air Line Pilots Association meeting the year before over positioning ground equipment on the ramp—Stan was working as Safety Chairman for the Association, and Bob had been invited as a guest speaker at the meeting. He ruefully thought of the heated discussion that had taken place. Stan had been right, but he had been unable to convince ramp service to change their policy. Bob Quinlan knew that Stan was a competent copilot, and for the most part professionally unemotional.

Mike Fuller was another side of the coin. Bob didn't know him well at all. Mike had been in New York for only a few years, and all the Chief Pilot could remember was that he had longer than usual hair.

Glen Meyer was finishing his description of the preparations being made. He said, "So that's about it. I plan to hold a meeting with the copilot and engineer, along with the stews, after they land. We'll have another crew take the flight on to St. Louis and La Guardia." The one unspoken word that both of the men were thinking was *successfully*, tacked on after *land*. Each knew the grim possibilities that existed, yet didn't want to acknowledge them by using that word. "Tell me a little about Stan—I've only met him once or twice, and it sounds like he's running the show now."

Bob Quinlan paused before replying, visualizing Stan Burkhart as he had seen him last—occupying the right seat of a 727. It had been two months ago, when the Chief Pilot had displaced the captain on a line trip. The captain had stayed at home and gotten paid for the trip, while Bob flew to keep his proficiency up. As Chief Pilot, he was able to get away from his desk only once a month—sometimes less—to do this, and on this trip sequence Stan had been the copilot. It had been a four-leg sequence, what the pilots call a turnaround, leaving New York, going to Buffalo, then Chicago, south to St. Louis, and back to New York, returning the same day.

During their trip, Stan had tactfully not said anything about their confrontation at the ALPA meeting, and they had discussed Transcon's marketing philosophy for most of the trip. Because Bob hadn't flown for a while, he flew three of the four legs, rather than alternating them with his copilot, and Stan had flown the final portion of the trip—St. Louis to La Guardia. He was impressed with the young copilot's flying ability—he was smooth, unhurried, seemingly having an easy time controlling the seventy tons of machinery. The approach into La Guardia was what impressed the Chief Pilot most. It was a tricky approach, to say the least, flying up the East River past New York Harbor, then breaking off and flying out over Long Island to the vicinity of Shea Stadium, then making a left turn back to the airport. Bob remembered that he had come in high, the engines throttled back somewhat, and had slowed the aircraft through judicious use of flaps and landing gear so that throughout the twisting turns over noise-sensitive areas around the airport, there was a minimum amount of noise on the ground. Stan had planned it so that when he rolled out on the final approach to the runway, he was exactly on the proper glide path and, as they passed the stadium at a thousand feet, had smoothly restored the power necessary for the landing. He had dealt easily with the capricious wind currents caused by the dike at the end of the runway and touched down almost unnoticeably, gently slowing the airplane. The performance had been superb, really, and several passengers had stopped at the cockpit door with favorable comments which Stan had countered with claims of being just lucky. Bob Quinlan would have expected as much from most of his captains, but the copilot had shown a skill normally acquired only after many years of experience.

The remembrance vanished and he spoke into the phone. "Well, Stan's a good pilot—one of the best copilots I've got here." He paused, searching for a phrase. "If I had to have a copilot on six oh two running things, I guess I would want it to be Stan Burkhart. Does that answer your question, Glen?"

"Yes, it does—I'll remember what you said. Let's see, I have to get some things done. Is there anything else that I've forgotten?"

Quinlan thought for a moment. "Does the press know yet?"

"Yes, I'm afraid they do—though God knows how they found out. Ralph Dorcek's here, he just came up from the press room."

"OK, Glen—call me after they land. So long."

"Good-bye, Bob."

In actuality, the press had found out by a rather devious means, though not devious on the part of the news media. An amateur radio operator had by chance heard the initial exchange between Minneapolis Center and the copilot of flight 602. He had called a local television station, which in turn had called the network headquarters in Chicago because they were an affiliate, and they had phoned their reporter at O'Hare. Normally, there are no television crews at the airport; but on this day Mayor Daley was returning from Washington after having testified at a Senate subcommittee hearing dealing with crime in the nation's large cities. In Chicago, Mayor Daley is news, so the major networks, newspapers, and local stations all had sent their best reporters to meet the arrival.

It had taken only fifteen minutes from the time the amateur radio operator had made his phone call until the network reached its reporter at O'Hare. When he heard the story, he led a parade away from the gate where Mayor Daley was to arrive over to the press room at Transcon Airlines. Within twenty minutes, there was a crush of some thirty-eight reporters, along with camera crews and radio crews, demanding that Transcon confirm the story.

Each airline maintains a room somewhere near its gate area known colloquially as the "press room." It is also used as a conference room, a place for celebrities to hide from the public, a sometime crew-briefing room, and a place for off-duty passenger agents to have coffee. It was now being used as a press room in the fullest sense of the word. At one end of the oblong space was a raised platform on which sat a lectern. Chairs were lined up facing the platform, as in a miniature auditorium. Today, the chairs were full and reporters were standing along the wall.

Herman Glaston, the Public Relations director for Transcon, was now standing behind the lectern trying unsuccessfully to obtain some semblance of order. Ralph Dorcek was standing behind him to his right. On the lectern was a prepared statement that he had hurriedly typed only moments before, using the information that Dorcek had given him. The group of newsmen finally quieted, waiting for Glaston to begin.

"Gentlemen"—he looked around the room and hastily added—"and ladies, I am going to read from a statement that we have prepared, and then take some questions. I realize that all of you want a lot of detail, but you must realize that our information is somewhat limited at this point, so please bear with me." He picked up the sheet of paper and began reading:

"At approximately one o'clock, Central Standard Time, a shooting took place aboard Transcon flight 602—a Boeing 727 enroute from Salt Lake City to O'Hare. Two passengers are dead . . ." A murmur went through the crowded room. Herman Glaston waited for the noise to die down. ". . . a federal marshal, and a prisoner he was transporting. Apparently, and let me emphasize the word *apparently*, the prisoner is the individual who did the shooting. Two other passengers and one crew member have been wounded—the extent of the wounds is not known. We expect flight 602 to arrive at O'Hare at approximately two forty-five." He looked up at the group. "That is the end of the statement—I'll take questions now." A dozen people raised their hands vigorously. Glaston searched for a friendly face and found it—one of the network newsmen whom he had known for some time. He pointed. "Mr. Crane?"

The newsman rose. "Why is the flight coming to O'Hare? Why not land at a closer airport?"

The PR director smiled for the first time since entering the room. "Now, Paul, you know there's a storm in the Great Plains—you've been covering it for almost twenty-four hours. O'Hare is the closest field that's not closed by the storm." He pointed to a network man with a rather florid face—the one who had received the story initially.

"Mr. Glaston, our original information mentioned that the airplane was damaged. Would you comment?"

Glaston mulled the question over in his mind. The airline industry does not intentionally withhold information —they may shade it slightly on occasion to avoid some of the wild speculations that can erupt from a story and be damaging to the airline or the crews. In all air tragedies, there is always an eyewitness—a farmer, a housewife, someone totally unqualified—who is placed in front of a camera or microphone and, in his or her moment of glory, becomes dramatic—and inaccurate.

It was this kind of sensationalism, then, that Herman Glaston was weighing in his mind. He finally spoke. "Yes . . . there is some damage—the aircraft's hydraulic system has been impaired." He quickly added, "As most of you know, all aircraft have backup systems, and that is what the aircraft is using now."

"Could the airplane crash?" He hadn't seen who asked the question, but it had been a woman's voice.

"Yes . . . there's al——" A buzz filled the room, and he waited for it to die out. "As I was going to say, there's always a slight possibility of an accident whenever something isn't normal. We have the airport emergency equipment standing by. But, let me reiterate, the aircraft's backup hydraulic system is functioning normally!"

"Mr. Glaston? Which one of the crew members was injured?" He saw her now, the woman who had asked the previous question—an attractive brunette standing along one wall.

He hesitated. "We don't know." It was the first time he had ever lied to the press, and he felt badly, but the mood in the room was one of ugly speculation—there hadn't been any good hard news in weeks, and they thirsted for something sensational to report. He picked up his papers and said, "Ladies and gentlemen, that's all I have time for now —I'll hold a press briefing at three o'clock, after the aircraft in question has landed. Thank you."

The reporters were asking more questions, but Herman Glaston ignored them as he left the room with Dorcek. The media people scrambled out of the press room to reach the phones in the terminal lobby.

The executive vice-president put his hand on Glaston's shoulder. "You did a good job, Herman—I know you didn't like to say that last bit, but you had no choice." The PR man just nodded glumly as they walked back to the Operations Office.

It took less than ten minutes from the time Herman Glaston left the Transcon press room for the news of flight 602 to be broadcast on radio and television. It was too late for the afternoon papers to cover the story fully; however, a few of the late editions were able to insert a short description into front-page space that would otherwise have been used for pictures of the first Santa Claus to appear on the streets of Chicago. Santa would have to wait for Saturday's editions.

Ellen Kasvakis was momentarily annoyed. She was sitting in front of the television set (the "Abominable Eye," Stan called it), watching the second of her favorite series of soap operas. Harriet was about to tell Jonathan that she was going to break off the affair when the screen suddenly went blank. It annoyed Ellen because she had been searching her relationship with Stan, much as Harriet had been doing, and her thought train was now rudely interrupted.

She looked around the living room. It was warm and rich —much like Stan's personality. The room had a comfortable, slightly used look to it because Stan felt that people didn't visit for a person's furniture or carpeting, but to be with friends—so the Irish coffee stain on the carpet had stayed for months, despite her pleading with him to have the rug cleaned. Ellen had tried to add touches of her own feminine neatness to the place, but Stan had been resisting for the year that she had been living with him.

In fact, she thought, that had been the subject of their serious discussion two nights ago, before Stan left on his trip. They had finished their lovemaking and he had gone into the bathroom. She had been lying on the bed, curiously frustrated because, as she saw it, Stan had become more mechanical lately. Oh, he still satisfied her desires physically, yet there was a strange lack of involvement on his part, and she was wondering whether it had always been so, or whether it was a new attitude that had recently formed. Ellen had been formulating her question when he came back into the bedroom.

"What the hell is this?" He was holding a small china basket with several soap buds in it. She had bought it that day to brighten up the bathroom.

His vehemence startled her, and she forgot what she

had been going to say. "It's . . . it's a little thing I bought for the bathroom, Stan—I thought we needed something a little nicer for guests."

He had sat down on the bed with a strange look on his face—sort of a cross between exasperation and anger. He spoke softly, as he always did. "Ellen, please. I asked you not to get this kind of crap yet. When my house is our home, then I'll want you to get all the lovely little things you desire, but until then—please, leave it the way it is, OK?" For a moment, Ellen was afraid that he was going to throw the delicate china against the wall. He held it for a while, then slowly got up and walked to the dresser that he had bought used and refinished when she moved in, and put it in a drawer. He came back to the bed and got in, lying next to her quietly. Ellen had been so surprised that when she finally directed her thoughts to the subject of their lovemaking, and decided what to say, Stan was gently snoring. She decided to wait until morning and quickly went to sleep herself.

The morning had been rushed, as usual, and there had been no chance to discuss what was troubling her. Now, she had decided to bring it up when Stan got home from San Francisco tonight. She was once again marshaling her arguments when the screen brightened, and an over voice announced:

"Ladies and gentlemen, please stand by—we bring you Jackson Herder with a special news bulletin, just received in our newsroom."

The man on the screen looked up into the camera as he laid down the papers he had been studying. His face was expressionless as he read from the teleprompter placed slightly to the left of the camera: "Good afternoon. There has been another in the latest series of dramatic incidents aboard jetliners today, this one apparently not a hijacking attempt. A fusillade of bullets rained through the cabin of Transcon Airlines' flight 602 in the skies over northern Nebraska at about one P.M. Chicago time. Two are known dead, two passengers and a crew member were wounded. The extent of those wounds is not known. A spokesman for Transcon stated that the airplane's hydraulic system is damaged, and that the possibility of a crash exists. Flight 602 is expected to land at Chicago's O'Hare Airport in about thirty minutes, and the airport has ordered crash equipment to stand by.

"In other news today, the giant snowstorm that has crippled most of the western part of the country continues to move eastward. Travelers' warnings and stockmen's warnings have now been issued as far as . . ."

Ellen sat straight up, clutching the white terry cloth robe tightly to her breasts. She stood up quickly and ran into the kitchen where they kept a large calendar by the phone. What she feared was confirmed in Stan's small, neat handwriting: *Flt. 602—2100 arr. LGA.*

She walked slowly back to the living room. Jackson Herder was finishing the news bulletin: "Stay tuned for continuing reports. This is Jackson Herder in Chicago." The screen went blank, then Jonathan's face returned, but Ellen didn't notice. She was reacting to the news as all airline people react—stunned, then realistic. She knew intuitively that the news would be overplayed, because air disasters are still big stories—but knowing that Stan was on that flight and that one of the crew members was injured caused her mind to spin in a whirlpool of speculation. She deduced that the crew member was a stewardess, because the shooting had been in the cabin. The news had said hydraulics, and even though she wasn't good at mechanical things, she knew that the aircraft had many systems, and that the landing should go all right. The thoughts eased her tension somewhat. She thought about calling the stew office at La Guardia to see if they knew anything, but dismissed the idea because, looking at her watch, she realized that the shooting had happened only forty-five minutes ago, and they wouldn't know any more than she did.

She went back into the narrow kitchen and poured herself a cup of coffee, gazing blankly at the trees that lined their block on Nineteenth Street. The leaves were all gone —the barren limbs crisscrossed in forlorn patterns against the gaily painted brownstones across the street. She took a sip of her coffee and stared, deciding to wait for Stan's call—she knew he would call soon.

In the living room, Jonathan and Harriet were speaking angrily, their voices unheard and unimportant.

Jerry Guccione cursed as a blue Cadillac cut into his lane on the freeway. He had stopped at a little restaurant to have another lunch on his way home from the airport and made a date with a wild-bodied blond waitress whom he had noticed the week before. She was big and buxom, and a little crude—which Jerry liked. He was thinking of the coming evening when his favorite rock song came on the car radio—one about a braless girl with a see-through blouse. He reached over and turned up the volume, beating his hands on the wheel in perfect time with the blaring guitars. He was a truly happy man today. Julia had gotten off all right for Chicago, and he had called his parents from the airport to tell them what time she and little Jennifer would be arriving. They had sounded excited at the prospect of seeing their new granddaughter for the first time.

The radio, volume still turned up full blast, jarred him back to the present: " . . . shoot-out on Transcon's flight 602 at about eleven o'clock Pacific time. Two are known dead . . ." Jerry listened intently to the remainder of the broadcast and decided instantly that he would return to the airport. He swung his car through a police turn-around in the center island of the freeway and sped back toward the Golden Gate Bridge. He figured he

could make the airport in thirty minutes if he hurried—
he made it in twenty-eight, breaking every speed limit
along the way. Fortunately, none of the California Highway Patrol saw him, and he breathed a little easier when
he pulled through the gates of the Transcon employees'
parking lot.

He left the car and ran to the maintenance section. A
new supervisor was on duty, one that Jerry didn't know
very well. Jerry ignored him and picked up the phone,
dialing the maintenance center at O'Hare. A voice at the
other end answered. "Transcon Maintenance, O'Gorman."

"Hey, O'Gorman—this is Guccione in San Fran."

"Oh, hi, Jer—what's up?"

"What do you know about flight 602?" His voice was
tense, and he was breathing hard from his run through
the parking lot. The Maintenance Supervisor was standing, staring at him questioningly. Jerry waved him off with
his hand and listened attentively to what the Chicago
maintenance foreman was saying.

"I don't know too much, Jerry—she's got a complete A
and B system failure, that's all we know. It's going to be
a bitch to fix once they get on the ground."

Jerry's mind raced. "What about the shootings?"

O'Gorman covered the phone for a minute while he
spoke to a line maintenance supervisor, then returned to
the phone. "We don't know anything about that, Jer.
Sorry." He paused. "Is it important?"

"You're damn good and right it is—my sister and god-
child are on that airplane!" Jerry almost shouted it into
the phone. The supervisor standing next to him looked
away, embarrassed.

O'Gorman's tone turned serious. "Jesus, Jerry—I'm
sorry. Is there anything we can do here?"

The mechanic turned over several possibilities in his
mind, then came up with an answer. He knew that Transcon, like every other airline, had an incredible channel of
communication among maintenance people, one that could

bypass channels easily—a sort of unspoken grapevine that could accomplish things that vice-presidents could not. He spoke into the phone. "I know the copilot on the plane—his name's Stan Burkhart. Can you get one of your people to him when they get on the ground and explain that I've called, and to call me when he can? I'll be at the airport here. The extension's"—he looked at the battered black phone—"three fourteen. I'll wait here."

"OK, Jer. I'll get someone to find out. We'll get to him, don't worry."

"Thanks, O'Gorman." The barrel-chested mechanic placed the phone down on the cradle slowly, then walked across the room to a chair and sat down. He picked up a copy of *Playboy* and began to leaf through it. The center-fold pictured a melon-breasted girl stepping from a shower, the water droplets still clinging to her honey-pink body. For the first time in his life, Jerry Guccione didn't care. He replaced the magazine on the low table and looked at the clock. It was almost noon.

She looked for the fifth time in as many minutes at the small travel clock on the nightstand next to her bed. The small hands said that it was almost three o'clock. It was light outside, so it must be afternoon, she decided. Her throat was dry, and her left side hurt—it was a dull, constant pain, centered in the area of her left armpit. She forced herself to touch herself one more time, to reassure herself, to know that it wasn't imagination—her breast was still there.

Kitty Douglass had been repeating the ritual for three hours, alternately dozing and waking as the anesthetic wore off. Each time, she would move her hand and feel the swell of her breast. It was sore, but it was there. She was more awake this time, awake enough to whisper "*Thank God*," then to look around the room sheepishly to see if anyone had heard her. She was in a private room, and there was no one there. She was terribly thirsty, and was about to press the little button pinned to her pillow when a young nurse walked in. She smiled at Kitty.

"I see you're awake." Her voice was warm.

"Yes." Kitty's throat hurt—a result of the airway tube used during surgery. "Would it be all right if I had some water?"

The nurse moved silently to the nightstand and poured water from a pitcher into a glass and handed it to Kitty. The water was the sweetest thing she had ever tasted, its coolness bathing her throat.

The girl was standing next to Kitty's bed and poured another glass when she had finished drinking the first. As she handed the glass back to Kitty she said, "Has Dr. Sangford been in yet?"

"No . . . at least not that I know. I've been a bit dopey. How long have I been back in this room?"

The young girl shook her head. "I'm not sure. I came on duty at ten this morning, and you were already out of the recovery room then. It must have been a short operation."

Kitty looked at the girl hopefully. "Does that mean . . . I mean, do you know what they found?"

The nurse shook her head. "I really don't know, Mrs. Douglass. Dr. Sangford said he would look in on you soon. I saw him in the corridor just a while ago." The nurse paused. She actually did know that the tumor was benign, and she was happy about it. She had grown to like Kitty—she exuded a strength that was unusual. Most patients were always fawning and weeping, but Mrs. Douglass was different. She hadn't told her, however, because she knew that Dr. Sangford wanted to tell Kitty the good news, and she had learned in her short career that stealing the surgeon's thunder, especially when the news was good, was bad form. She smiled again. "Would you like a light lunch? I can get you something if you feel up to it."

Kitty realized that she was ravenously hungry, she hadn't

eaten since the night before. "That sounds wonderful. It's not too much trouble?"

The nurse smiled again. "It's no trouble, Mrs. Douglass. I'll be right back." As she reached the door she turned and said, "Would you like the television on?"

Kitty was allowing herself to become hopeful about the results of the operation—the diversion would be helpful. "Yes, please." The nurse turned the set on. The screen jumped to life, Gregory Peck's worried face filling the screen. Kitty said, "Thank you," and the nurse left, the big door closing quietly.

She was just becoming interested in the movie when another face appeared on the screen, this one in color:

"Good afternoon. Repeating an earlier news bulletin, there has been a serious shooting aboard a Transcon Airlines' flight. Two passengers are known dead, others and one crew member have been injured. The flight is Transcon's flight 602, enroute from Salt Lake City to Chicago . . ."

602! That's Pete's trip! Kitty sat upright in bed, ignoring the pain in her left side. She began to chew on the cuticle of her right thumb, a habit that she indulged in only when she was worried. Pete had always kidded her about it, saying that she was still in the oral stage of development. Her face slowly drained itself of color as she listened to the news report.

" . . . The flight is expected to land at Chicago's O'Hare Airport in about a half hour, and emergency equipment is standing by because of damage to the aircraft. Stay tuned to this channel for further developments."

Kitty was still sitting up when the nurse returned with a tray containing some soup and a small plate of sandwiches. She quickly set the tray down on a table near the door and went to the bed. "What's wrong, Mrs. Douglass?"

After the initial shock, Kitty was regaining the control that was so characteristic of her. She turned to the nurse.

"Have you heard about the shooting on one of Transcon's airplanes?"

"No, not really. I haven't been near a radio or television. Is that why you look so upset?"

"You don't know anything about it?"

"No, Mrs. Douglass, I haven't heard anything. What's the matter?"

"My husband is the captain of the flight! I've got to find out what's happened!" Her voice was controlled, but the nurse could tell that she was becoming agitated by the way her face was drawn tightly across her lovely high cheekbones. The young girl moved to the bed, gently putting her hands to Kitty's shoulders and easing her back to the bed.

"Now, Mrs. Douglas, you lie back and try to relax—I'll go out and see if I can find out anything about it. But you mustn't move around." She knew that the operative procedure had been simple, and there was little danger for her patient, yet she wanted to find Dr. Sangford and get him in to look at her. She also knew that there was a television set in the lounge at the end of the corridor, and the usual contingent of patients that were ambulatory would be clustered around it. One of them might have heard something about the airliner. She looked at Kitty, seeing that she would stay horizontal, and after patting her shoulder comfortingly, walked quickly to the door. As she left, she said, "I'll be back as soon as I can find out something."

Kitty nodded, reassured just enough to give her the necessary strength to remain in bed. "Thank you," she whispered as the nurse left. Her mind spun with the possibilities, running over and over again the words that the newscaster had said. She reasoned, much like Ellen Kasvakis a few miles away, that the crew member who was injured must have been a stewardess, because the pilots rarely went into the cabin. That eased her mind a bit. She wished that the television had been more specific about the damage to the airplane. Yet she knew that Pete had had problems before—between her training as a stewardess years ago and living with Pete, she had a tremendous respect for the structural and mechanical integrity of the planes that her husband flew.

She wondered whether this had been a hijacking attempt. The newscaster hadn't said whether it was. Her mind wandered to the day almost a year ago when she had been glued to the television set for seven hours, knowing that Pete had been hijacked, praying that the young man wouldn't use the gun.

When Pete came home, the long hours of terror over, he was a changed man. Kitty remembered how he had gone into the den that night and sat at his desk, writing letters to the President, to senators and congressmen, demanding that the United States get off its collective ass (his words) and do something—the only way to stop aerial piracy, he wrote, was an international treaty, similar to the one that was being worked on with Cuba, agreeing to the return of hijackers to the country of origin. Barring that, suspension of air service by all other nations of the world to those countries that harbored the criminals.

The letters had been answered, mostly with bland excuses, and Pete had been just another statistic added to the list of flight crews and passengers who had faced terror in the air, then been quickly forgotten until the next time. Pete had not given up, however, and a report was sitting at home on his desk that he was preparing to present at the next Air Line Pilots Association convention in Las Vegas. It proposed new ways in which the international association of the airline pilots of the world could bring pressure to bear on their governments to stop, once and for all, the threat of air piracy.

Kitty realized as she stared unseeing at the television set that Pete, with his renewed determination, hadn't mentioned their son nearly as often as he used to. The new project had given him a renewed direction for the tremendous drive that he had, and diverted his attention from Petey's death. As her mind played with the recollections, she began to minimize the present crisis and it made her relax. She looked at the clock—it was a little after three. She was confident that Pete would call soon, that she could tell him just how proud she was to be married to him— and, most of all, how she loved him.

In the cockpit of flight 602, Pete Douglass was dozing fitfully, his head nodding with the awkward motion of the aircraft. The feeling in his leg was all but gone, and he was cold . . . terribly cold.

"During takeoff and landing, flight attendants required by this section shall be located as near as practicable to required floor level exits . . . in order to provide the most effective egress of passengers in the event of an emergency evacuation."

Federal Air Regulations
Part 121.391 (d)

13

Terry Dunlap strode quickly back to the galley area from the cockpit. The few passengers in the First Class section followed her movements unrelentingly. She ignored their questioning eyes and entered the comparative safety of the galley area. Cathy was efficiently packing up the buffet units, storing the glasses, trays, coffeepots—all the paraphernalia of cuisine aloft. She worked quickly, piling everything into the storage units and closing the doors, checking to make sure that each latch was tightly secure in its slot. She was fitting the last door in place when Terry came into the tiny work area.

Terry hesitated, then spoke with a measured steadiness.

"Pete and Stan want us to get ready for an evacuation."

The two girls looked at each other, only a foot apart in the confined space. Cathy's hand was still holding the latch on the last storage cover. They looked into each other's eyes—steadily—a path of understanding and determination bridging the distance. They could have passed for starlets. They were attractive, intelligent, and personable. But now the years of working in the rarified atmosphere of thirty-five thousand feet melted away—the thousands of trays run out, the millions of smiles, the miles of walking up and down the aisles with a second round of drinks or coffee—all this fell away, replaced by a sense of purpose that an average passenger does not even think about, the real reason that stewardesses are on an airplane, the idea that lurks just below a flight attendant's conscious mind during every landing and takeoff— *getting the passengers out fast.*

They had been trained to think in seconds, literally. Every year, they would see in evacuation training the graphs showing that after ninety seconds, in a crash-fire situation, the death rate soars to a near vertical line— ninety seconds before everyone left aboard the airplane begins to die instantly. They were trained to open doors, to inflate escape slides, to find their way to any exit on any airplane in Transcon's fleet without being able to see. The training was started in stewardess school, using mock-ups of the aircraft type. The lights were turned out, and occasionally smoke was introduced into the cabin. Using other stewardess trainees as passengers, each girl had to find her way to an exit and open it, then direct her classmates out. The emergency training was where Transcon lost most of its aspiring flight attendants—they either quit or were washed out of the school because they could not pass the course.

The two women looked at each other for another moment, both minds racing. Cathy finally broke the silence. "I figured we'd be evacuating, that's why I got all this stuff cleared up." She gestured to the storage units. It wasn't a desire to be neat that had prompted her to clean up the buffet area—she knew that, as well as being a serving area, the galley door was one of the primary evacuation routes. Having loose trays or linens strewn about would have been dangerous. "What did they tell you?" She nodded toward the cockpit.

Terry took a deep breath. "There's a chance we'll run off the runway when we land. Pete said the hydraulic system controls the nosewheel steering. Without it we won't be able to steer once we get on the ground—at least not after we slow down." She looked at her watch. "We've got thirty minutes, maybe less, to prepare the cabin. How sharp are you on emergencies?"

Cathy twisted her attractive face into a grim half-smile. "I had recurrent evac just three weeks ago. I'll take a quick look at the book again, though." She paused, thinking, "What about Cindy? You want to tell her? I think she's rattled already."

Terry nodded. "I'll tell her. Why don't you go back and relieve her with the doctor—you can tell him what we have to do. Send her into the galley and I'll tell her about the evacuation."

"OK." Cathy started to leave the galley. Terry stopped her, putting a hand on the other girl's arm.

"Thank God we've only got nineteen people to worry about!" They looked at each other again, Cathy not replying, the bond between them appearing as it always did with flight crews when they were faced with difficult situations. It was an awareness that all people who fly, pilots and stewardesses alike, have—that in the environment in which they work, the possibility of swift tragedy exists. They live with it daily, not thinking about it because they have an inherent faith in their own abilities and in their training, but the knowledge is always there.

Cathy left the galley and walked back to where Joseph Mannheim was hunched over Susan. Cindy was standing behind him holding the stack of green linen. Her face was drained of color, and fear and insecurity were written across her eyes. She looked up as Cathy approached.

"Here—I'll take over for a while. Terry wants you in the galley."

Cindy handed the linens to Cathy and nodded, thankful for a chance to leave the grisly surroundings. The pile of blood-stained napkins on the seat next to Susan was growing alarmingly.

The doctor acknowledged the change of helpers with a nod, busily concentrating on the work in front of him. The girl's shoulder was completely exposed now, the soft moss-green wool having been pulled away from the wound. Cathy was amazed at the whiteness of Susan's skin, accentuated by the contrast with her copper-colored hair. She was struck again with how beautiful the girl was. Mannheim looked up, momentarily satisfied with the new pressure pad on Susan's shoulder. He said to Cathy, "She was conscious for a moment—said something about Stan. It was a little incoherent, but I guess it's her husband or something."

Cathy shook her head. "It's the copilot—they're close friends."

"Jesus!" He looked at Cathy's forehead, probing with his free hand. "How's your head?"

She had almost forgotten about the bandage covering the left side of her brow. She reached up and pressed gently. "It's all right—it only hurts when I laugh."

Mannheim gave a short grunt. "Still won't forgive me for being a little touchy, huh?"

They looked at each other, smiling.

"You're going to be even touchier when I tell you what we have to do now," Cathy said.

He looked backed at Susan, readjusting the linen napkin. "What's that?"

"We've got to get all the people on this airplane ready to evacuate after we land."

"Oh?" he said, dividing his attention between the stewardess and the wounded girl. "What does that mean?"

"We're going to have to move everyone closer to exits, instruct people how to use them. I don't have time to explain it all right now, you'll hear about it in a few minutes. There is one thing, though. We'll have to move Susan for landing. She's got to be on the floor, against a forward bulkhead. We'll put her across from the galley."

Mannheim frowned. "I don't like it. It won't be good for her injury—I've almost got the bleeding stopped and moving her may open it up again."

"It'll be worse for her if we go off the runway—she'd never survive sitting in that seat the way she is!" Cathy turned to Kevin, sitting across the aisle. He had been listening intently to their conversation. "Go and get that young man up there, sitting next to his wife." She pointed to the couple sitting four rows away. "We'll need help in moving Susan up to the front of the cabin." The boy left quickly.

The full impact of their situation was finally reaching Joseph Mannheim. He said quietly to Cathy, "What about her? If we crash, I mean."

The blond stewardess quickly resolved the turmoil in her mind. "If there's no fire, there won't be a problem. If there is a fire, we'll probably have to leave her." Her lip trembled slightly as she finished the last sentence.

"You can't do that!"

"Doctor Mannheim, there are eighteen other people on this airplane, plus the crew. I must think of them first. Susan is immobile, and has to leave last, because I can't block an exit trying to get a bundle out of it. We may not have the time." Her eyes pleaded with him. "Don't you see? *We have no choice!*" She looked away quickly.

Mannheim was startled, his mind spinning. Those words again, he thought. He shook his head, trying to clear his thoughts. Busying himself with Susan's shoulder, he resolved that he would get this lovely girl out of the airplane—by himself if he had to. The young bridegroom arrived, and together, with Cathy holding the pressure pad in place, they gently eased Susan out of the seat and toward the front of the Coach cabin.

Cindy Weston couldn't read the printing in her stewardess manual—it was blurred through the tears. She had set it on the serving counter and begun to reread the evacuation procedures when her fear took hold. The words were frightening, the airplane was frightening, the blood was frightening. This wasn't why she had become a stewardess! She wanted the travel, the glamour, the excitement of jetting across the world, carefree and easygoing. But this! This wasn't the way she had pictured it at all. She remembered how she had almost dropped out of stewardess school after emergency training, but changed her mind when the instructor told the class that the chances of ever having to use the knowledge were very slim, that most girls go through a ten-year career without once ever having to evacuate an aircraft—all of which was quite true. But now Cindy, after only two weeks, was faced with the imminent prospect of having to deal with all the terror that had been shown her and the other thirty-one girls of her class. With an effort that surprised her, she managed to regain control enough to be aware that Terry was just hanging up the telephone to the cockpit.

Terry touched her arm, noticing that the younger girl was having trouble maintaining control. Once again, she was thankful for having such a light passenger load, because she could sense that Cindy would not be a great deal of help. She said softly, "The cockpit's going to make an announcement, then we'll have to go to work—stay here for a minute and study the book. Cathy and I'll start things in the cabin." She left, hoping that Cindy would be able to come to grips with the problem. As

Terry started toward the cockpit, she was vaguely aware of Mike's voice on the P.A. system.

Mike had been chosen to make all of the announcements from now on, because they had begun a long, slow descent into the Chicago area, and Stan had kicked off the autopilot, trying to get used to the airplane without hydraulic power to the flight controls. The big airplane responded heavily to his attempts, the ailerons and elevators taking an inordinate amount of physical strength to move. It was much like having the power steering go dead in a big, heavy truck, only the problem was three-dimensional. Pete could not reach the P.A. system from his seat in the rear of the cockpit and, if he could have, would have been ineffective because he was now in a gauzy twilight on the border of consciousness. So Mike Fuller was elected to talk to the people.

Somewhat nervous, he used a full minute to compose his thoughts before he pressed the button marked *Passenger Address*.

"Ladies and gentlemen, if I may have your attention for a moment." All in the cabin looked instinctively to the cabin ceiling, as if seeing the recessed speakers would improve their hearing. Mike took a long breath and continued: "As you know, we have quite a problem on our hands. One of the larger ones is that our hydraulic systems have been damaged, and this impairs our landing control capacity." He chose his words carefully, trying not to be too technical, yet trying to get the right feeling into what he was saying. "In a moment, our stewardesses will be instructing you in preparation for an evacuation of the aircraft." He paused, and a murmur went up in both cabins, the passengers looking around, trying to see the others' reaction. "Let me emphasize that this does *not* mean that we will have any sort of crash—we have backup systems on the aircraft that were designed for just this instance, and they are working normally. But because the hydraulic condition does exist, we want to be prepared in the event that our landing does not go normally. Also, you should know that everything that is humanly possible is being done on the ground to prepare for our arrival." Mike wanted to allay any fears they had, and yet, at the same time, impress upon the passengers the seriousness of the situation. He felt that he was doing badly and looked around the tiny cockpit, trying to find reassurance, but Stan was talking to the traffic controller on the radio, and Pete's eyes were closed. He pressed the button on the handset and continued: "I'm going to ask that you pay close attention to the stewardesses—they are thoroughly trained for this procedure, even better than we are in the cockpit, so please pay strict attention and follow their instructions. The purpose of all this is to get you all out quietly and quickly, should we have to evacuate. We will be pretty busy in the cockpit from now on, so any directions will come from the first stewardess." As an afterthought, he added, "Thank you."

Terry waited until Mike had finished, then picked up the handset at the front of the First Class cabin and began instructing the passengers about what they would be doing. Her first action was to move all of the passengers to the First Class section, where they would be easier to control and instruct. When they had all seated themselves she began to describe the position that they would assume for landing—seat belts tightly fastened, their hands hugging their knees, their bodies bent forward as far as possible.

After they were familiar with the position, Cathy and Terry began to take all the things from them that could possibly cause injury during the evacuation: pens, pencils, and sharp objects, even high-heeled shoes. These were placed in individual pillow cases and locked in the forward lavatory. When the roundup of personal possessions was finished, each girl began to recruit helpers from among the younger men on the flight, telling them how to stand at the bottom of the evacuation slides and help expedite the flow of people as they came out of the airplane.

Most of the passengers were busily studying the small green cards that were in the back of every seat—they diagramed the emergency exits on the airplane and how to open them in case the stewardess was not able to do it. Terry was momentarily amused because the same people had, only two hours before, completely ignored the cards when she mentioned them before taking off from Salt Lake. Now they devoured the contents, not only because their lives might depend on the information they learned from them, but because they were all frightened, and any excuse to keep busy was a welcome substitute for fear.

Terry had been purposely graphic when she explained the operation of the doors and exit slides. The reasoning behind moving all the passengers to the First Class section was excellent. It put all the people between the two most efficient exits on the plane: the front main cabin door and the galley door, also a big wide door. Terry had described how to open the door in the event that the stewardesses were unable to: pull up and fully rotate the handle, then push out. When the door opened, a slide pack would be lying outside the fuselage of the aircraft, attached to the sill of the big door. On the right side of the sill, there would be a red handle which, when pulled, would inflate the escape chute. She explained that they were all in the front because of the time involved—the big doors could handle two passengers a second, which would enable them realistically to evacuate the entire passenger load in less than fifteen seconds once the doors were open.

While Terry was busy demonstrating the door operation to the men she had selected to help, Cathy was doing the same thing with Joseph Mannheim. They had moved Susan to the floor, just aft of the bulkhead separating the Coach and First Class cabins. She was lying across the cabin, parallel to the front row of seats. Cathy had taken pillows from the overhead rack and sandwiched them between the girl's left side and the bulkhead to cushion her body from any impact. Her head was at the side wall of the cabin, her feet almost opposite the galley door, across the aisle from it. Joseph Mannheim was seated in the center seat in the group of three, listening intently to the stewardess. As he listened, he noted her change from a pleasant, attractive girl to a very businesslike woman, completely in control of herself and her situation.

Cathy was saying, ". . . so I'll be right across the aisle in the center jumpseat"—she turned and pointed to the small seat on the other side of the aisle—"and I'll get this door open. Cindy and Terry will be in the front, working on that door. When we get the signal to brace, you do it too, only holding Susan firmly against the bulkhead, OK?"

Mannhein nodded. "I understand. I'll need some more napkins, though. This hole in her shoulder has opened up again."

Cathy looked at her lying on the cabin floor—pale, weak-looking, yet somehow peaceful. "Doctor? Is she dead?"

He lifted her eyelid and saw the pupil contract, then felt at the base of her neck. The pulse was there, but very faint. He looked up at Cathy. "No. She's still alive—barely. There's no way of knowing how long we have—she's lost such a tremendous amount of blood. Moving her didn't help." He gestured to the increasing dark stain on the fresh napkin.

Cathy turned to the galley. Cindy was standing rigid, her hands on the work counter bracketing the stewardess manual open in front of her. Cathy saw that the mascara around her eyes had blurred and smudged. "Cindy. Give me another pile of napkins. They're in the compartment over the counter."

The dark-haired stewardess turned her head slowly,

staring at Cathy and the doctor as if she hadn't heard. The rest of her body hadn't moved.

"Goddammit, girl, get off your ass!" Cathy had hissed the words, loud, but not loud enough for the passengers up front to hear. Mannheim watched the two girls, confirming what he had already suspected. The younger stewardess was obviously not prepared to deal with the kind of problems that were facing her.

People react, when they are in mental shock, to different kinds of stimuli. Years before, a passenger had refused to evacuate an airplane that was on fire. The fire had not reached the cabin; only one wing was burning. All the passengers had been evacuated except one man who refused to leave his seat, sitting rigidly, staring straight ahead—something the airline psychologists call negative panic. The stewardess, the last person on the aircraft except for the captain, had pleaded with him to get up. When she realized he was not going to move, she said, "All right, you silly son of a bitch, sit there and burn!" With that, he got up, still in a daze, and followed the stewardess out the door. It was a classic story, one that was mentioned in all the airline evacuation courses, and unconsciously Cathy Armello had used the same tactic on her flying partner.

Cindy shook herself and opened the compartment to get the napkins.

Cathy said, "You help out here for a while, I'm going up front." When Cindy responded with a nod, Cathy left, walking toward the cockpit.

She studied the passengers as she walked forward. The older woman, the fat one who had been in the lavatory when Pete came out of the cockpit, was in one of the last rows. She was busily pumping on a rosary, her mouth moving in silent litany. The young newly married couple was seated in the first row on the right. Their hands were tightly entwined, their eyes locked in a look of love and fright. Across the aisle sat the businessman who had been so kind to Terry. He and the brand-new husband would be first out the front door if they evacuated, waiting at the bottom of the slide to help people rapidly away from the aircraft. It was a situation where women and children first could impede progress. Next to him sat Julia Pilero, her infant daughter on the floor against the partition in the same way Susan was protected. Her face had stopped bleeding, and she was busily worrying over her baby, not thinking about the little needles of pain that prickled her face and neck. In the second row, Kevin Stryon sat studying the emergency card, ignoring the older man who sat next to him. The man was staring blankly out of the window at the darkening gray cloud.

Cathy looked at the rest of the cabin, almost every seat filled, then at the empty Coach section beyond—the only sign of life was part of Cindy's uniform. At the very rear of the cabin, she could see the corner of a green blanket hanging from the last row of seats on the right, and Sam Riese's lifeless foot. The scene chilled her. She rubbed her arms with her hands, and went into the cockpit. All there was to do now was to wait.

Stan Burkhart cursed under his breath at the ungainly way he was controlling the aircraft. It was cumbersome and awkward to fly this way. Without the normal hydraulic power to the controls, he had to use a lot of elevator trim to keep the airplane in the attitude he wanted, more than he would have used normally, and he was having a hard time getting used to the exaggerated control inputs he had to make. He had found, through doing some gentle turns, that the rudder could help greatly while turning, even with its greatly reduced capacity, but he had to put almost full pressure on the rudder pedal to be effective. This caused him to have to readjust his seat closer to the control wheel, and it felt awkward. He checked the distance readout to the O'Hare VOR station. It was slowly unwinding past sixty-three miles. He was about to level the 727 at thirteen thousand feet when his earphone crackled to life.

"Transcon six oh two, turn right to zero five zero and descend to seven thousand."

Stan pressed the button on the control wheel and replied: "Roger, right to fifty degrees and descend to seven. We're leaving one three. And, Center? Did approach control get my request for a thirty-mile turn on to final?"

The controller's voice was calm. "Roger, six oh two, the zero five zero heading will put you onto the fourteen right localizer thirty from the marker."

"Thank you." Stan pulled back on the three throttles and began the descent. He could feel the airplane decelerate. They were between layers of cloud—light above, and a darker shade of gray below. It seemed dark, especially for two o'clock in the afternoon.

While Stan was concentrating on flying, Mike Fuller was rereading the procedures for lowering the flaps and landing gear. The flaps had a standby system to rely on, but it took much longer to get the flaps down by the alternate method. The landing gear would have to be cranked down, because it, too, was normally fed by one of the now useless hydraulic systems. The cranking receptacles were in the cockpit floor, and this also took a long time. The copilot had asked for the long, final approach so that he would be unhampered by having to make turns while Mike was extending flaps and landing gear.

The two pilots were thus engaged when Cathy arrived at the cockpit door, and neither of them noticed her arrival. She looked at Pete first. The captain was sitting slumped in the observer's seat, his head nodding with the gentle motion of the airplane. His eyes were closed, but she could tell that he would periodically try to get them open. She sensed the tension in the small space, and once again her intuitive sense of what to say proved right.

"I'm sorry, fellas—can't get you any more coffee. The galley's all closed up."

Mike looked up from the flight manual and smiled. Stan turned in his seat with a grin of relief on his face, but turned back quickly when his movement caused the right wing to dip sharply.

Cathy changed to a serious tone. "Things are as ready as they'll ever be back there. How long do we have?"

Mike looked at his watch, then at the distance to O'Hare on Stan's instrument panel. "About twelve minutes— maybe fifteen." Cathy nodded and started to leave. The flight engineer, reminded of something when reading the procedure for lowering the landing gear, stopped her. "Cathy? Send that kid up here, will you?" She looked puzzled, but went back and got Kevin Stryon.

"You sent for me?"

"Yes, I need your help." The boy's eyes brightened noticeably behind the glasses. "We're going to have to crank the landing gear down, and I want you to check the viewing ports and signal me that the indicators are in place." He drew a diagram on an old copy of a weather sheet, showing the boy what he would see, then told him where to lift the carpet in the First Class cabin to get to the viewing holes in the floor. Normally, Mike would have done this himself, but *normally* there would have been three pilots in the cockpit. There were other ways to check that the gear was locked, but Mike felt that the boy would be smart enough to know what to look for, and the knowledge that the gear indicators lined up on a visual check would be comforting.

The boy had been listening intently, and when Mike was finished explaining how the indicators would look, he said, "Do you think that you can do it?"

Kevin nodded emphatically. "Yes. When will you be lowering the landing gear?"

"In about five minutes. Cathy here will help you get the carpeting up. Be sure you put it back down securely after you're done—we don't want anyone to trip, OK?"

The boy grinned for the first time. "Roger!" He turned and left.

Mike looked at Cathy for a long time. He read the questioning in her eyes. She was biting her lower lip, unsure for the first time since she had seen Donald Greco struggle for the gun that had put them all in jeopardy. He took her small hand in both of his and squeezed—hard, not letting go. "Cathy, we're going to get through this like a breeze. Everything is going to be fine. We need you." He paused, searching her face. "And when it's all over, you're going to have a steak with me, and I'm going to make love to you like a madman!"

She looked into his eyes, big and brown and warm above the shaggy moustache. Cathy saw a warmth and feeling that she hadn't seen before. "Oh, Mike . . ." she exploded, laughing instead of crying, "you're impossible." She squeezed back with her hands. "And maybe what you said sounds like a good idea. *All of it*." She freed one hand and wiped her left eye, then smiled and said, "I've got to get back to the people." She left quickly, walking swiftly down the aisle.

Stan had leveled off at seven thousand feet and was starting to slow the aircraft to two hundred knots, getting ready to start putting the flaps down. They entered an area of patchy cloud—one of those quirks of the sky that contained confused air currents. The aircraft bucked and rocked, Stan working to keep them stable. Pete Douglass was awakened by the turbulence—he swung around in his seat, and moved to fasten his seat belt, a reflex action so ingrained that he would have done it in his sleep. As he fumbled with the heavy buckle, it scraped across the latch on the belt that compressed his right thigh. The tourniquet slipped about an inch, enough for the tomato juice can to fall silently to the seat. He did not feel it loosen—he did not feel anything below his waist on the right side. Within seconds, a new dark stain appeared on his pants leg, growing slowly larger.

The headsets crackled to life once more. "Transcon six oh two—contact O'Hare approach control now on one two seven point zero. So long, and good luck."

Stan was getting tired—his arms ached from fighting with the sluggish airplane. He answered without thought. "One twenty-seven zero—so long." He reached down to the knob at his left side and dialed in the new frequency.

> *"NOTHING IN THIS BOOK SHALL OVERRULE YOUR OWN GOOD JUDGMENT!"*
>
> Page 1, Para. 1
> Transcon Flight Operations Manual

> *"To err is human—to forgive is not Company Policy."*
>
> Graffiti on the men's room wall,
> Transcon Pilot's Lounge, La Guardia Airport

14

Bill Klavacs was sitting eight feet above the floor, his arms draped casually over the big steering wheel. He was smoking a cigarette, watching the smoke curl lazily toward the ceiling of the cab. He was sitting behind the wheel of a foam truck housed in a garagelike building known as Crash One.

There are three firehouses at the O'Hare International Airport: Crash One is located almost exactly at the center of the airport's eighteen square miles. Crash Two and Crash Three are located on opposite perimeters of the field, enabling equipment to respond to any location on the vast complex in under ninety seconds.

Bill Klavacs was surrounded by nozzles as he sat in the massive cab of the vehicle. There was a huge nozzle on the roof of the truck, fifteen feet in the air, that could be controlled from inside the cab. A smaller nozzle was nestled in the area of the front bumper, and there were several nozzles beneath the truck. Their function was to clear a path through, and protect the truck and its occupants from, pools of flaming fuel.

The foam truck is a marvel of the firefighter's science. Costing in excess of one hundred thousand dollars, its control cab resembles the cockpit of one of the jet aircraft it was designed to protect. It is ten feet wide, and thirty-three feet long, carrying two thousand, five hundred gallons of water and five hundred gallons of protein foam. The nozzle above Bill Klavacs' head could shoot a one-hundred-fifty-foot stream of the mixture at the rate of one thousand gallons per minute. The pumps develop two hundred twenty-five pounds of pressure. The truck is powered by two Ford industrial engines. Either one can be used for driving the all-wheel-powered vehicle or drive the big pumps, or both.

As he sat waiting, Klavacs wasn't thinking about the truck beneath him in terms of engineering accomplishment. He was thinking about the Transcon 727 that he would soon be waiting for in the snow at the intersection of the parallel taxiway for Runway fourteen right, and T-6, one of the exit taxiways.

He wasn't anything like a fireman in appearance—thin, wiry, his hair turning gray at the temples. He was soft-spoken, almost shy, except when he talked of his job— then he was full of enthusiasm. His brown eyes, reflected in the match as he lit another cigarette, were younger than the rest of his face dictated they should be. He took a long drag on the cigarette. The quick ones weren't so bad, he thought, but when you have to wait—to think about what's coming—that's when it gets hard.

This was the third alert today. Not unusual for O'Hare.

The first had been purely precautionary: a 707 landing with one of its four engines shut down. The second had been a quick one, and potentially more dangerous. A fully loaded DC-8 had suspected blown tires and returned immediately after takeoff. They had landed without incident.

Three hours later, Bill had been in the middle of a match-stick poker game when the tower called to tell them that Transcon's flight 602 would be landing with a complete hydraulic failure in forty-five minutes on fourteen right. Time! That was the problem. They had time to get to the trucks, time to get into their boots and coats, and worst of all, time to think.

The fireman, with fourteen years at O'Hare's battalion of the Chicago Fire Department, looked around the inside of the firehouse. To his right, the driver of the Dry Chemical Ansul Truck was reading a newspaper. He swept his gaze across the spotless floor. To the left, the Battalion Chief's car and an ambulance sat . . . poised, ready to go. He looked at the clock on the wall. Two twenty-five. His cigarette had gone out.

Bill Klavacs was reaching into his shirt pocket for matches when the speaker in the corner of the firehouse blared its message: "Crash One, Two, and Three. Transcon 727 with emergency is on Approach Control—take positions for Runway fourteen right."

The worry disappeared, replaced by position action. He slammed the foam truck into gear as the floor-to-ceiling glass doors swiftly rose into the roof.

"Flight 602's on approach control now, let's go!"

Glen Meyer sat behind the big glass windows in the Dispatch Office. The Chief Pilot had taken a chair from an empty desk nearby and pulled it close to the large pane, hoping to be able to see across the airport to the approach end of Runway fourteen right. The runway, almost a mile and a half away, was all but invisible through the falling snow. He sat hunched over, sitting forward on the chair, his elbows resting on his knees. He kept clasping and unclasping his hands as if he were kneading dough, his eyes never leaving the expanse of airport beyond the window.

One of the speakers in the Dispatch Office was turned up —it was tuned to the approach control frequency for landings on fourteen right, one of the two frequencies that are used at the world's busiest airport. He was monitoring the conversations, using the lower levels of his mind to sift through the talk between pilot and controller.

"O'Hare approach, this is United fifty-eight, heavy, descending to five."

"United fifty-eight, switch to approach control on one nineteen zero for Runway one four left."

A different voice answered, obviously the captain of the flight: "This is United fifty-eight, heavy, we're requesting one four right." The word *heavy* following a flight's number designated a large jet, usually a 747 or DC-10. The captain wanted a longer runway for landing.

Approach control answered: "United fifty-eight, heavy, the right one is not available—there is an emergency in progress at the airport."

Without hesitation, the pilot answered, "Roger, switching over to one nineteen zero. So long."

The speaker went dead. Glen inched his chair closer to the window, peering through the gray snow. With the sun above several layers of cloud, it seemed like six o'clock instead of two. The Chief Pilot stiffened as a new voice blasted over the speaker.

"O'Hare approach, Transcon six zero two here, level at seven."

The Chief Pilot listened to the voice carefully. It was calm, no hint of nervousness. Approach control answered: "Roger, six zero two, squawk ident."

Through the window, Glen could see the firehouse. The doors flew open, and a line of emergency vehicles streamed through the gaping opening, red lights flashing, casting eerie reflections across the snow. Two ambulances, called in addition to the airport's normal complement, followed the swiftly moving procession, their drivers unfamiliar with the airport and so forced to take a rear position through the flying snow. Glen Meyer was not by nature a religious man, but as he watched the crash trucks and rescue equipment disappear through the snow, he clenched his hands together, holding them still for the first time, and closed his eyes as he listened to the inanimate speaker —helplessly hoping that Stan Burkhart could pull it all off.

The approach controller's voice sounded far away: "Transcon six zero two in radar contact twenty-eight miles from the marker. Intercept the localizer and proceed inbound, speed at your discretion, you may descend on the glide path. Cleared for an ILS approach to Runway one four right, parallel approaches are in progress, localizer frequency is one zero nine seven. Emergency equipment is standing by."

"Transcon six oh two, Roger."

The noise in the Dispatch Office had stopped as pilots, dispatchers, and clerks stopped whatever they were doing to listen to the drama unfolding. The speaker continued: "Transcon six zero two, the O'Hare weather is sky partially obscured, measured six hundred overcast, visibility one mile in snow. The RVR on fourteen right is more than six thousand."

There was a pause; then the aircraft answered with a terse "Six oh two, Roger."

The pause in the conversation was a result of Mike's handing Stan the landing card, an eight-sided piece of white lucite with numbers on it that would be used for their landing. Stan put the card in the center of the control pedestal, covering the radar set, then answered the approach controller's last transmission about the weather. One worry was already gone—Stan thought that the weather would be worse than it really was. One-mile visibility with present-day lighting on the runways was quite adequate.

He reached forward to set the marker on his airspeed indicator at one hundred and twenty-eight knots—the speed at which he wanted to cross the runway threshold. The aircraft weighed one hundred and twenty thousand pounds, the card said, and engine power settings were listed also in the event of a missed approach. Stan didn't bother to set the engine pressure ratio numbers—he knew that there would *be* no missed approach. He turned to the flight engineer. "Mike. Let's start getting the flaps down—it'll slow us up some, and I want all the time I can get." Mike checked his flight manual, lying open to the page covering alternate flap extension, and reached up to the overhead panel just to the left of the copilot's head. He pressed down on two switches and the flaps started to move slowly . . . ever so slowly. The airplane yawed left and right as the leading edge devices lining the front of the swept wings extended in a random fashion, changing the clean, high-speed wing into a different shape, capable of slower flight.

"How much do you want?" Mike had to raise his voice above the noise as the 727 rumbled and vibrated with the increased wing area.

"Fifteen degrees!"

The flight engineer watched the indicators on the forward instrument panel creep past the markings on the dials. He noticed that Stan was working increasingly harder at the controls because of the slower speed. When the needles reached fifteen degrees, he released the switches and sat back in his seat, checking the book to see if there was anything in the procedure he had missed. There wasn't.

The airplane slowed to one hundred and seventy knots. Stan checked the distance readout on Pete's side of the cockpit—twenty-four miles to the airport. He yelled to Mike, "Start cranking the gear down!"

He didn't hear the flight engineer's reply because, as he looked over to the other side of the cockpit, he noticed really noticed for the first time, that *there was no one in the captain's seat!*

He hadn't thought about it—there had been no time to. But now all the decisions had been made, all the factors considered, and the only thing left was get the airplane on the ground. Simple enough under ordinary circumstances, he thought, yet there was nothing about the present circumstances that was ordinary. He looked again at the empty captain's seat. Stan was not a man who lacked self-confidence. He knew he could fly the 727 well —he had over three thousand hours as a copilot, almost half of that actually at the controls—yet in the back of his mind during that three thousand hours had been the knowledge that the captain was there—three feet away. If he had made an error, although he had never analyzed it in those terms before, the captain would extricate him. He hadn't actually flown solo, that is as pilot-in-command, for over eight years. And now it was on his shoulders— there wasn't anyone else.

Stan found himself feeling guilty for Susan—wondering if she were still alive, wondering if it was his fault that she lay in the back cabin, her life slowly oozing away in an aluminum tube a mile above the earth. If he hadn't talked her into coming back with them she would be in New York now, safe and secure. If the prisoner hadn't been on the flight, if Pete hadn't been in the cabin . . . if, if, *if!* His shoulders were starting to ache with the constant effort of controlling the big jet.

"Stan!"

Mike's yell brought him out of his trance. "Pete's passed out! There's blood on the floor!"

Stan quickly considered the new problem, his mind ticking off alternatives like a machine. He came to the only conclusion possible. "Leave him and get the gear down— we don't have time to do anything!"

Mike had got out of his seat when Stan called for the landing gear and gone to where the crank handle was strapped to the bulkhead behind the second observer's seat. As the airplane rocked in light turbulence, he had put his hand on the cockpit floor to steady himself. He felt something wet and sticky on the metal floor of the cockpit. That was when he had noticed that Pete's wound had started to bleed again. He had shaken the captain, getting no response, then yelled to the copilot.

Ignoring Stan's instructions, Mike Fuller took a precious twenty seconds to look at Pete's leg. It was obvious what had happened. He quickly slipped the tin can back under the makeshift tourniquet and pulled the seat belt extension as tight as he could make it, hoping it wasn't too late.

The flight engineer signaled to Kevin and the boy started peering into the floor through the viewing ports. Beginning with the nose gear, Mike opened a small door in the cockpit floor and started to turn the big red crank. He heard a loud noise as the nose gear fell into place and felt the 727 shudder and pitch as a new extremity was added to the aircraft's smooth exterior, creating more drag. The boy in the cabin smiled and raised his fist, clenched—their prearranged signal that the wheel was indicating down and locked. Mike moved on his knees to the left main gear slot. He yelled to Stan, "Left main next!" The copilot nodded and took a tighter grip on the control wheel, anticipating the reaction the airplane would have. Mike began to turn the crank.

Stan watched the instruments in front of him. They were intercepting the glide slope now, an electronic beam that would indicate the proper descent path to the runway. Just as he started easing the nose down, the left main gear extended, and he wasn't prepared for the yaw effect that one of the large wheels would have. He violently twisted the wheel to the right to counteract the new forces acting against the airplane. The wing slowly came up and he applied almost full rudder to stop the yaw. The big doors that opened for the landing gear, normally closed after the wheel was down, could not close now because they were hydraulically operated. Stan pushed forward on the throttles to overcome the tremendous drag that the doors created. He gave an inaudible sigh of relief as the right main gear came down to equalize the drag and he could let up on the right rudder pedal. His leg was becoming numb and he didn't know if he could have held the pressure much longer. They were descending at seven hundred feet per minute, perfectly aligned on the glide slope and localizer. The crossbars were centered.

Stan's earphones crackled. "Transcon six zero two, you're three miles from the outer marker. Contact the tower on one eighteen point one."

Stan didn't reply; he just changed the radio frequencies and spoke: "Tower, Transcon six oh two approaching the marker."

"Roger, six zero two, cleared to land on one four right. The wind is one five zero at twenty, occasionally gusting to twenty-eight. The equipment is standing by, the RVR is still six thousand plus."

"Six oh two, Roger." Stan was too tired to say more. He thanked someone, he wasn't sure who, that the wind had held and not created a crosswind problem. He yelled over his shoulder to Mike, "Put the rest of the flaps down —all the way to thirty degrees!" The engineer reached over Stan's head and held the switches, watching the needles inch slowly toward thirty degrees. *And tell the girls to get 'em braced!*

With his free hand, Mike pressed the stewardess call three times, telling Terry that the time had come.

Terry Dunlap was sitting on the jump seat near the front door, next to Cindy. The girl's cheek was bright red. She sat there trembling—an occasional jerk ran through her body as she tried to control her fear. Terry was sorry that she had slapped her, but there had been no alternative. When it became apparent that Cindy wasn't going to stop crying, Terry had slapped her hard, twice, then left the galley ignoring the doctor's uncomprehending stare. Well, she thought, at least it had worked. The girl has stopped crying and is able to sit next to me without going to pieces. She was thinking about what she would say to her once they got on the ground when she heard the three rapid chimes. She sensed Cindy stiffen next to her. Terry reached for the P.A. handset and picked it up. Her hand trembled—she couldn't stop the movement. She held the phone in front of her. "Ladies and gentlemen, please assume the brace position, and don't get out of your seats until the airplane has stopped!" She replaced the handset and watched as people's heads disappeared below the seat backs. Without thinking, she tightened the shoulder straps that were fastened to the large buckle at her waist. She saw Cindy doing the same. The young girl's face was expressionless, staring at nothing.

Cathy Armello had the same involuntary reaction as she watched from her seat in the center of the airplane. After Terry's announcement, the passengers disappeared, the backs of their heads sliding from view as if they were all kneeling in prayer. Without thinking, she tightened the seat belt and shoulder harness that pinioned her to the seat. She felt strangely calm—almost aloofly detached from her surroundings, an outside observer viewing the action. She looked to her left and thought, ludicrously, that all Joseph Mannheim needed was a prayer rug, and someone to face him to the east.

Joseph Mannheim was actually facing to the southeast. He was seated in the middle of three seats, his seat belt tightened around his lower body, with his hands outstretched toward the bulkhead in front of him. It *was* much like a position for prayer, except that his hands were gently but firmly bracing Susan MacKenzie tightly against the bulkhead. And he was praying.

The airplane wallowed sharply to the right, the motion causing Mannheim to look again at the girl's face. He saw a faint movement of her eyelids, barely discernible in the gray light, but he was sure he had seen it. Readjusting his hold on her shoulder, he whispered softly, "We're almost there!"

Kevin Stryon was frightened. He hugged his knees tightly—so tightly that the cast pressing against his shins hurt. As long as he had been busy, he hadn't had time to be afraid. Maybe it was because he didn't have his glasses on. The stewardess had made him promise to take them off after he had finished signaling that the landing gear was down, and now everything was a blur. It made him feel weak, defenseless. Kevin felt the hot sting of tears begin to develop behind his eyelids. He remembered his father saying that only sissies cried, so he squeezed his eyes tightly shut and gripped his legs even tighter. He wanted to be home for Christmas—either home, it didn't matter which one.

Stan's eyes flicked to the altimeter. One thousand feet to go. He risked a quick peek outside the cockpit, only to see an opaque whiteness. As he looked out, a strong gust of wind made the 727 yaw violently, dipping the right wing. He used all his strength to bring the wing up, but with the change, he saw that the localizer needle had moved a quarter-inch to the left of center. *Fuck the Windy City,* he thought as he hauled the control wheel to the left, straining to get the aircraft back onto the narrowing approach path. He had to use full throw on the rudders and ailerons to get any response. As they got closer to the ground, gusty winds capriciously tore at the airplane. Stan was sweating. He could feel the dampness under his arms and down his back.

He watched the altimeter unwind through the corner of his eyes. Six hundred feet. *Where the hell are the lights?*

Five hundred feet. *The bastards said the ceiling was at six hundred!*

The airspeed was at one forty-five. *Too fast!* Stan eased the throttles back an inch.

Four hundred feet! His arms were working furiously, his feet moving swiftly on the heavy rudder pedals.

"Lights in sight! Slightly left!" Mike's words washed

over him, bathing his brain in sweetness. He lifted his eyes from the instruments and saw them. They were beautiful —they were all that is good in the world. Stan wanted to laugh and cry. The brilliant strobe lights sped down the approach path, showing the way to the ground through the blinding snow.

"Runway—dead ahead!"

He saw the green threshold lights approaching rapidly as they descended. The visibility improved as they neared the earth. He was aware of a long string of vehicles on the taxiway as they thundered over the green lights, their red beacons rotating furiously, the snow catching the light and spreading it in a hundred different directions. His peripheral vision told him that they started to move as the airplane passed.

Over the runway, close to the ground. Still too fast. Stan jerked the throttles closed, felt his weight against the shoulder harness as the airplane decelerated.

They slammed down hard, sixty tons against concrete. The 727 started to bounce, then settled on the runway. Stan yanked the throttles into reverse with all his might, not caring whether he used too much power. More weight against his shoulder harness. He lifted his feet to the top of the rudder pedals and stood on the brakes. He knew that he'd have two or three good stabs at the brakes before the fluid ran out of the reservoir. He never let up on them, his feet pumping back and forth, trying to keep the big jet on the runway centerline. He saw the firehouse speed past on the left side, and knew intuitively that half the runway was behind him.

After what seemed an eternity, the brakes took hold and they decelerated rapidly. Stan could feel the vibrations against his feet as the antiskid system worked whenever the wheels passed over an icy patch.

The airplane began to yaw toward the left side of the runway—he saw the runway edge lights drawing closer. His right leg was straight out, trying by sheer willpower to swing them back down the runway. *Nothing happened!* Stan took a chance and let up slightly on the left brake, knowing that he was sacrificing what little hydraulic fluid was in the system. It worked. The nose slowly swung back parallel to the runway.

Slower now, the runway lights were no longer blurred as they went by. The aircraft veered to the left again. Almost stopped. The engines were still roaring as the reverse thrust created a mountainous plume of snow behind them.

Flight 602 stopped as the nosewheel sank into the soft mud at the side of the runway.

The two pilots worked swiftly, as they had planned. Stan pulled three red handles at the front of the cockpit, cutting all power and fuel. Mike's hands flew across the engineer's panel flicking switches and closing valves, minimizing fire danger.

In the cabin, the silence was overwhelming. They had heard the throbbing roar of the engines as the airplane careened and swerved down the runway, then . . . silence as the engines died. The lights went out. No one moved. Snow fell softly on the wings.

No sound. No whir, or whine, or hiss.

The muted wail of sirens, eerily distorted, pierced the stillness as the crash equipment neared the airplane.

Jennifer Pilero, wedged against the front lavatory wall, began to whimper softly, her tiny body wiggling beneath her mother's outstretched hands.

15

Mike was the first to recover. Stan sat slumped over the control wheel, all his energy drained. The deathly silence lasted for only a few seconds. Mike leapt from his seat and stood in the cockpit door, yelling.

"Everyone stay seated! There is no need to evacuate!" He had visions of their passengers running around aimlessly in the snow outside, and didn't want that to happen. As he rose, he saw Pete in the corner of the cockpit, his body angled in a frightening position. *"Mannheim! Get up here!"*

At the sound of Mike's voice, the tension broke in the cabin. The passengers were all looking around and laughing, talking excitedly, congratulating each other for being alive. There was a smattering of applause. Mike didn't understand why, then realized that they were clapping because it was one of the best ways to shake their collective fear. He saw that Terry was already on her feet, moving down the aisle to make sure that people remained seated. Cathy had also gotten up, and was standing where Mannheim sat, talking with him. Mannheim stood and stepped into the aisle, holding Cathy's arm and saying something, nodding his head, then left and walked swiftly toward the cockpit.

As Mike knelt next to the captain, he saw the rear door of the cabin open, and several men hurry inside.

Stan was out of the copilot's seat now, squeezing past the flight engineer's chair to join Mike at the entrance to the cockpit at the same time the doctor arrived. The two pilots made room for him in the crowded space. Mannheim lifted Pete's wrist. There was a pulse—weak but steady.

"Get some of that plasma up here fast!"

Stan watched as one of the men detached himself from the group clustered in the center of the cabin and walked toward them. He was carrying a wire basket full of bottles, much like a milkman's rack.

Mannheim looked up at Mike. "Help me get him on the floor."

Mike unfastened the captain's seat belt, and together they lifted Pete Douglass out of the observer's seat and stretched him lengthwise across the cabin floor just outside the cockpit. It wasn't until after they had gotten him positioned that Mike noticed Cindy, still sitting on the stewardess jump seat. She hadn't moved since the airplane had stopped. He gently reached over and grabbed her knee, shaking it. "Hey!" he said. "It's all over . . . why don't you help Terry look after the people?"

She sat for a moment, then nodded her head dumbly and rose. The seat slapped back against the bulkhead, out of the way. Mike thought she would lose her composure when she looked down at Pete, but she didn't. She walked gingerly around his horizontal form and moved toward the cabin, even managing a slight smile as she looked at Stan.

"Doctor?"

Mannheim looked up from where he knelt beside the captain, annoyed at the interruption. The plasma had arrived, and he was busy with the attendant getting the clear liquid into Pete's arm.

"What is it?" Then he saw the anxiety on Stan's face. "Oh . . . she's still alive—barely. Why don't you go back there?"

He shook his head. "I've got to take care of all these people first." He swept his arm across the front cabin. Just then, another figure arrived, joining the group at the front of the airplane. He had a business suit on, and from his breast pocket dangled a Transcon identification tag. Stan thought he had seen the man before, but wasn't sure.

"Can you get any power on this airplane?" He was looking at Stan, who was still blocking the door to the cockpit.

"Huh?" Stan realized then that it had quickly gotten cold in the airplane. The air conditioning had gone out when he killed the engines. The back of his shirt chilled his spine with its wetness. "Oh, yeah. Just a minute."

He reached inside the cockpit and flipped a switch that would start the APU. The chatter had died in the cabin, most of the passengers sitting silently, waiting. Stan could hear the whir of the APU's starter, then a subdued roar as it started. He reached for another switch and turned on all the electrical power. Lights came on, fans started whining, the airplane returned to life. He could hear air being forced through the ventilating ducts.

The man with the Transcon badge on his coat looked at Pete on the floor, then reached over him and picked up the P.A. handset. "Ladies and gentlemen, if I may have your attention for a moment." He paused, watching the passengers. "My name is George Kestler. I'm the Vice-

President of Passenger Services for Transcon. We have brought a bus to the airplane, and we will use it to transport you to the terminal building. It's parked next to the rear stairs, and I would like you all, once you have gotten all your personal belongings, to deplane through the rear stairs and onto the bus. Please be careful walking outside—the ground is very slippery. If you have friends meeting you, please don't worry—they have been told that you are safe, and are waiting in a special area for you." He paused, as if to say more, then said "Thank you" and replaced the handset.

Stan Burkhart was rankled by the man's air of indifference. He looked at Mike, still kneeling next to Pete's motionless form. Mike shrugged, then bent back to the captain. Stan was going to say something as Kestler left, but checked himself as the vice-president faced him.

"I don't know enough about airplanes to know how difficult your job was here, but"—he seemed to fumble with the words—"thanks. We expected a lot worse." He turned and walked away, leaving Stan with his mouth open.

The copilot stood in the door watching the passengers slowly leave. Each one would stop momentarily at the last row of seats, peering at the two bodies there. Stan realized that he hadn't seen any of it until this moment. He also realized just how tired he was. His arms and shoulders throbbed with a dull ache. He slumped against the doorframe as the last few passengers got out of their seats. An ambulance attendant was helping Julia Pilero into the aisle, holding her with one arm, and her baby with the other. Their eyes met briefly as she rose. There was a small, shy smile on her lips; then she turned and walked toward the rear, the white-jacketed attendant following slowly.

Kevin Stryon was the last to leave the cabin. Terry was standing next to him. He walked toward the cockpit, the two large volumes balanced in one arm against his hip. Mike Fuller looked up as he stopped a few feet away.

"Did I do all right, Mike?"

The shaggy moustache spread across Mike's wide face. "You did fine, Kevin, just fine."

The boy hesitated; then Terry gently turned him by the shoulder and walked him away. Mike called after them, "I'll see you later, Kevin!"

The boy peered back over his shoulder, his eyes blinking rapidly. "OK . . . Captain." He turned and straightened his shoulders as much as the heavy books would allow, then marched regally down the aisle.

Stan watched as he disappeared down the steps with the first stewardess. A man whom Stan didn't recognize was standing by the rear door. He waved out the door and two Chicago policemen, their blue and white checked hats plainly visible, entered the cabin. They were followed by two men in business suits. The foursome stopped at the rear seat, one of them lifting the blankets that covered Greco and Riese. They had a brief conversation, the men in civilian suits doing most of the talking. They stepped aside as four men in medical coats carried two stretchers up the stairs in single file.

One stopped where he knew Susan lay. Stan wanted to get back there. He could now—the passengers were off. He started toward the rear of the airplane, but the stretcher blocked the aisle in the front cabin. By the time he had let it pass, he saw the other one being carried out the rear door, followed by a third attendant holding a bottle of plasma in the air. He went back to the cockpit. Pete was on the stretcher, being lifted gently into the air. Mannheim held the bottle of plasma that was attached to his arm by a long plastic tube.

Stan stood there, his mind floundering, looking for something to latch on to.

Mike came to him and put a huge hand on the copilot's shoulder. "Stan?"

No response.

He shook gently. "Stan? It's all over—let's go."

A nod. "Yeah."

They got their coats and left the airplane, leaving their bags in the cockpit. They could get them later. As they walked through the cabin, Stan paused for a minute at the shattered seat on the left side. The upper part of the back was covered with a dark stain. He bent down slowly and pulled a small overnight bag from under the seat, held it a minute as if to weigh it, then continued toward the door, ignoring the two policemen standing at the rear seats.

The snow was cold and wet. A dozen vehicles were scattered around the 727, their red and white lights reflecting crazily off its polished sides. Stan looked around and saw Mannheim standing at the rear of an ambulance. By the time he reached it, the doctor was inside, sitting next to Susan, taking her pulse. He looked up as Stan approached. A plasma bottle was hanging from the top of the vehicle.

"Here." Stan lifted the small suitcase into the ambulance, placing it alongside the stretcher. "She may need this." Mannheim nodded.

A Transcon car pulled up next to the ambulance and Glen Meyer got out, pulling his coat tightly against the wind and snow. He walked toward the ambulance.

"Stan, I'm Glen Meyer." He had to yell to overcome the roar of jet engines at full thrust across the airport. "We need you for a debriefing—you can ride in my car and tell me about it on the way to the terminal!"

The copilot looked at Mannheim, then back to the Chief Pilot. "But . . ."

"We need you *now*, Stan!"

Joseph Mannheim interrupted: "She'll be all right, Stan —believe me!" There was something in his voice that was reassuring.

Stan looked at Glen Meyer and nodded. A pair of snowflakes had landed on her hair, stark white on warm cedar. Stan watched them melt, then smoothed the wet spot with his hand. He stepped back as an attendant closed the two rear doors and the ambulance slowly pulled away. DES PLAINES HOSPITAL was written across the white sides.

Stan Burkhart stuffed cold hands into the pockets of his overcoat and followed the Chief Pilot to his waiting car.

Mike found Cathy helping the last of the passengers get settled in the bus. "Come on," he said, "they want us over at the terminal. Terry and Cindy are already in the car."

He waited outside the bus door as she came down the steps, reaching for his outstretched hand to help her to the ground. They walked slowly to a green and gold car, Mike holding Cathy's arm with both of his.

"Are we still on for dinner?"

She looked up at him, unblinking. "Yes . . . dinner, and *maybe* the rest of it."

He laughed out loud and held the door for her. When they were inside the warmth of the car, Mike noticed that Terry was smoking a cigarette. "Hey! I thought you quit smoking!"

She looked at him. "I did—at least until today."

He turned to Cindy, wanting to say something to lighten her mood. She was sitting curled into the corner of the seat, her head against the window, staring at the snow. She made no effort to wipe off two glistening drops of tears on her cheeks. Mike turned to face forward as the car started to move, noticing that the crash trucks were returning to the firehouse in a parade of rotating red lights.

"Aviation in itself is not inherently dangerous. But to an even greater degree than the sea, it is terribly unforgiving of any carelessness, incapacity, or neglect."

Caption beneath a photograph of a 1920 biplane suspended in a tree. The picture hangs in the Transcon Pilot's Lounge, La Guardia Airport.

16

The ride to the terminal took ten minutes, longer than it should have because of the snow. They had to stop several times to let the snow-removal equipment pass, and once to let three fire trucks cross in front on their way back to Crash Two. The driver let them out at the end of the Transcon concourse. As they emerged into the brightly lit terminal they were met by Ralph Dorcek and Margaret Paulsen, head of Transcon Stewardess Service. She smiled as they came through the door.

"I'd like to see you girls in my office so that we can write a report on the evacuation preparations." The three stewardesses nodded in unison. Mrs. Paulsen saw that they were all a bit frazzled and added quickly, "Why don't you take ten minutes to freshen up? I'll meet you there."

Terry spoke for the group. "Fine, Mrs. Paulsen—we'll see you there."

As they started to leave, the "Great Stew in the Sky," as she was called on the line, held Cathy Armello aside. "Cathy? Is your head all right? You can go to medical if you like—I can talk to you later."

Cathy looked at Great Stew—an unfair name, because Margaret Paulsen was a stunning woman in her early forties and had a reputation of being the biggest soft-heart in the world. "I'm fine, Mrs. Paulsen—it's really just a scratch. I'd rather stay with the other girls."

"I understand. See you in ten minutes."

Cathy walked quickly to catch up to Terry and Cindy. Throughout the ride to the terminal, and up until now, Cindy hadn't said a word. Cathy joined them, putting Cindy between her and Terry as they walked to the office.

Ralph Dorcek was walking next to Mike. They saw Stan with the Chief Pilot fifty yards ahead, walking in the same direction. After Ralph had introduced himself to the flight engineer, both had been silent as they walked down the terminal finger.

The vice-president finally spoke: "The debriefing will be in Glen's office—there'll be a lot of horsepower there. Feel up to it?"

Mike nodded. "Sure." His face lit up as if he had just remembered something. "Mr. Dorcek? Do you think I can have five minutes? There's something I'd like to do."

"Sure, Mike, but don't take too long."

"Thanks. Do you know where the passengers from our flight would be right now?"

The older man thought for a minute, scratching the back of his head. "Passenger Service said they were going to put them in the VIP lounge until we could get their luggage off the airplane. Know where it is?"

"Yes. I'll see you in five minutes." Without waiting for a reply, Mike started off at a trot down the corridor.

He reached the VIP lounge slightly out of breath. He

stopped only long enough to adjust his tie and square his hat on his head, then opened the door. There were about forty people in the richly decorated room. As he looked around, some of the passengers said hello or came over to shake his hand. He finally saw them standing in the far corner.

Kevin Stryon was with his mother. At least, Mike assumed it to be his mother. She was kneeling down with one hand behind the boy's head, the other hand dabbing at her eyes with a handkerchief. He was talking to her excitedly, gesturing with his plaster arm. Mike unconsciously whisked his long hair back over his ears and walked toward them. "Hey! Kevin!"

He turned, his face lit up. He broke his mother's grasp and ran toward the big flight engineer. "Mike! I thought I wouldn't see you again!"

Mike laughed as he knelt down. "I told you I'd see you." He put his massive hands on the small boy's shoulders. Out of the corner of his eye, he saw the woman, a puzzled look on her face. Mike rose as she arrived.

Kevin said, "Oh," when he saw her. "This is my mother." He turned an eager face back to Mike.

As they shook hands, Mike said, "Mrs. Stryon, it's a pleasure to meet you."

The woman was tall, fortyish, expensively dressed. "My name is Mrs. Forest now," she said coolly. Her eyes were appraising him.

"Oh," Mike said. *I should have guessed,* he thought. "I was the flight engineer on your son's flight. I just wanted you to know what a help your son was to us." Her expression changed from bland to surprised. "You should be proud of him. He's quite a brave young man, but I'll let him tell you all about it." He avoided her questioning stare by kneeling down and talking to Kevin.

"Hey . . . I want you to have something." He took his hands from the boy's shoulders and reached to his own left breast, unfastening the gold and silver wings carefully. He pinned them onto the small pocket of Kevin's blue blazer, then straightened them. He stood up, but had to bend at the waist to stay at eye level. "I hope that whenever you see these, you'll remember how much we needed someone like you."

"Wow! I sure will!" He peered down at the wings, turning them up slightly with his hand to get a better view. "Thanks, Mike!" He turned to his mother. "Look, Mom! *Real* ones."

Mike looked at his watch. "I've got to go . . . Goodbye, Kevin. Maybe we'll see each other again." He couldn't resist adding one last comment. "I hope you'll write and tell your dad what a help you were." He looked at Kevin's mother. She stared for a moment, then turned away.

" 'Bye, Mike." Kevin was back studying the wings intently.

After one more glance at the two of them, Mike turned and left the lounge quickly. As he opened the door, he was almost knocked over by a small, squat woman wearing a dark dress and a mink coat. "Pardon me," he said quickly.

She was busily stroking the coat where he had run into her. She spoke with a thick, New York accent. "That's all right, I shouldn't hurry so much." She noticed Mike's uniform. "Say, maybe you can help me find my husband—I was supposed to meet his flight, but I was caught in the traffic. Ah! It was terrible!"

Mike sighed. It was an occupational hazard while in uniform. People expected anyone in an airline uniform to know everything. He was about to steer her discreetly to a passenger agent when something she said stopped him.

She was looking around the lounge as she spoke. "I asked someone about his flight, because I was late, you know, and the man said to come here, but"—she was taking another look around—"I don't see him. And why didn't the plane come to a gate like planes are supposed to?"

Mike tried to interrupt, but it was no use, she just continued on without pausing for breath. "His name is Dr. Mannheim, and I'm worried about him—he called me last night, very upset. I think he was drinking, and it's not like Joe to drink. He wouldn't tell me whether they won or lost his case, but since he was drinking, I think he lost. Oh, he never should have stopped to help that girl! I can't imagine where he is." She was looking around again, wringing her hands.

Mike finally stopped her by grabbing her two arms as she paused for breath. "Did you say Mannheim?"

"Yes, Joseph Mannheim. He's a doctor—a radiologist."

"And you don't know what happened on his flight?"

"No. What is there to know?"

Mike shook his head in wonder. The pieces were falling into place once again. "Mrs. Mannheim, your husband saved two lives today." She looked at him, startled but quiet. "We had a . . . an accident on board, and your husband helped us immensely. He's at the hospital now." He saw the fright in her eyes. "No, no . . . he wasn't hurt. He's there helping the people that were injured." He looked at his watch again and quickly told her what hospital, adding that one of the Transcon agents would arrange transportation.

Mrs. Mannheim looked bewildered as he steered her toward the reception desk in the VIP lounge, then left for the Flight Operations office and a meeting he didn't want to attend.

As he passed the corridor leading to the Stewardess Service offices, Cathy Armello came speeding around it on her way to Margaret Paulsen's office.

The flight engineer grabbed her arm. "Whoa there—what's the rush?"

She smiled, making the white gauze wiggle on her forehead. "I'm on my way to meet with Great Stew."

"Oh." He held her arm, preventing her from rushing off. "Are you all right, Cathy?"

Perfectly straight teeth flashed at him. "I'm fine, Mike."
She covered his hand with her own.

"Are you going to go home tonight?"

"I don't know. I really hadn't thought about it. Great
Stew said we'd have a couple of days off . . ."

"Why don't you stay here? We can have that dinner
downtown, I can get us a room . . ." He meant to say
rooms, but decided to let the slip go, waiting for a reaction.

Cathy stared up at him, searching his eyes, then apparently finding what she was looking for, smiled and
said, "Can I trust you to be good?" Her eyes sparkled with
mischief. "If I want you to?"

"Yes . . . if you want me to."

They parted, both feeling better.

Cathy straightened her hair before opening the door
to Margaret Paulsen's office. HEAD OF STEWARDESS SERVICE
was lettered in gold leaf on the door.

"Sorry I'm late." Terry and Cindy were already seated
across from Great Stew's desk. Cathy took the only remaining chair, smoothing her skirt as she sat down. There was
a man sitting in the far corner of the office. He was well
dressed, with a short haircut. He had a small leather notebook on his lap, a thin gold pencil poised above it.

"Cathy," Margaret Paulsen began, "this is Mr. Pel-
ligrini, from the Federal Marshal's office." The man
nodded to her. "He's here to find out what happened."
She turned her attention to all three stewardesses. "Terry,
you're the head stewardess, why don't you tell us what
you saw and did, then we'll hear from Cathy and Cindy."

Terry began to tell the story of flight 602, beginning
with their takeoff from Salt Lake. When she had finished,
Cathy added whatever she could. Then Cindy talked for a
short time. The hearing lasted only about twenty minutes.

Airlines want to meet with flight crews immediately after
an incident to record the facts while they are still fresh.

A formal meeting would be held a week to ten days later, attended by airline officials, the FAA, and any other people that might have an interest. In this case, the Federal Marshal's office would send a representative. Transcon's director of safety would be there, searching for ways to improve evacuation training, using the people that had actually gone through the experience.

When Cindy finished, the marshal thanked all of them and left. Margaret Paulsen sighed after he closed the door. "Now, girls—is there anything else that you'd like to talk about?"

None of them answered.

She smiled, softening her tone considerably. "I'll arrange for you to have the next four days off. Check with the crew desk for tickets back to New York. Call your domicile on Wednesday—they should know when the formal hearing will be held." She rose, signaling an end to the meeting. "I want to thank you . . . all of you for doing a fine job. I know it was rough." She smiled again. "See you all next week."

Cathy and Terry left the office. Cindy hadn't moved from where she stood. Her lower lip was raw from where she had been biting it.

The older woman looked up from where she had been stacking papers on her desk. "Yes, Cindy, what is it?"

The young girl hesitated, then blurted out in a half-sob, "Mrs. Paulsen, I want to resign." She sat back down and covered her face with her hands.

Margaret Paulsen walked silently to the door, closed it, then returned to her desk.

Stan Burkhart and Glen Meyer were stopped briefly on their way to the Flight Operations Office by a grimy-faced mechanic in Transcon overalls. "Are you Stan Burkhart?"

"Yes." Stan was a little surprised.

"Jerry Guccione called and asked me to have you call

him right away. He's at this number in San Fran." The mechanic handed Stan a piece of paper.

"Oh, Jesus. I forgot about Julia." Glen Meyer looked puzzled. "Jerry's one of our mechs in San Fran. His sister was on our trip." He turned to the mechanic. "I can't call him now. You call him, and tell him that Julia's fine. She's at the hospital. Tell him not to worry, that she wasn't hurt seriously. Tell him . . ." He paused. "Tell him that I'll take care of everything, and call him at home. Have you got that?"

The mechanic nodded as he retrieved the paper with grease-covered hands. The two men continued on their way down the brightly lit concourse.

"Was that the girl that got shot?" Meyer had waited until the man had left them.

"No—Julia's the one with the baby." Stan's mind was jolted with the thought of Susan. He wanted to find out what was happening at the hospital. He felt uncomfortable being with the Chief Pilot, and was trying to figure out a way to make a phone call to the hospital when they arrived at the conference room, just inside the operations area. He decided to wait when he saw the large group seated at the long table.

Mike Fuller entered the room behind the others. Ralph Dorcek introduced the two pilots around the table. "This is Gene Woodhouse, with the FBI." They shook hands with him. "Denny Johnson, Federal Marshal's office." Again, handshakes. There were seven people in the room that neither pilot knew.

After the introductions, Stan and Mike sat in two chairs next to each other on the opposite side of the room from the door, at the narrow end of the table. Glen Meyer spoke, rearranging some papers in front of him. "Mike, Stan, let me begin by saying that this is not a formal hearing on the incident—we'll have one next week. We'd just like to hear what you recall of the incident—any detail at all. I'm going to get Bob Quinlan in on this. We'll be using the speaker phone." He lifted a telephone onto the table from a nearby desk and placed a speaker alongside it. Pressing a button, he said, "Bob, are we hooked up?"

The speaker answered: "I can hear you fine, Glen." Stan recognized Quinlan's voice over the speaker.

"Stan? Why don't you begin?"

The copilot took a deep breath. "Well, we were about an hour out of Salt Lake. I was flying, and Pete said that he had to go to the lavatory. He left the cockpit . . ."

Stan briefly recounted the events, ending with his leaving the airplane. The men around the table listened intently, making occasional notes. When Stan finished, their attention turned to Mike, and he related the action in the cabin, leaving out only the details about Mannheim's initial reluctance to help. He felt that including that could have no bearing on the situation.

When Mike was finished, Glen Meyer turned to the speaker on the table. "Anything you want to add, Bob?"

Before he could reply, another phone rang on a desk behind Meyer. "Hold on just one minute, Bob." He reached behind him and picked it up. "Hello?" He was silent, listening to the caller. "Yes, Dr. Mannheim." A long pause as he listened. Stan gave an involuntary jump as he heard Mannheim's name. He watched Glen Meyer intently, trying to discern by his expression what was being said. Meyer was nodding his head and frowning; then his expression said that the conversation was almost over. "The copilot? Oh . . . yes, here. Just a minute." He pushed the phone over to Stan. "He wants to talk to you."

Stan took the receiver gingerly, almost afraid to touch it. "Yes, Doctor?" He listened for what seemed an eternity. Mike was watching him closely, saw his facial muscles relax, his eyes close in gratitude. "Thank you, Doctor. Yes, good-bye." He hung up the phone.

Mike looked at him anxiously. "Stan?"

"They're both going to be all right."

The big flight engineer put his hand on Stan's arm and squeezed—hard. They looked at each other, relief from the tension finally settling over them like a mantle.

Glen Meyer was talking into the speaker again. "Bob? That was the doctor at the hospital. Pete Douglass is in surgery. He'll be all right, they said, but it'll be a long time before he's able to work again, if at all."

The speaker was silent as Quinlan digested the information, then, "OK, Glen. I'll call his wife here. I'd like to talk to Stan for a minute."

"OK, Bob—I'll call you later." He turned off the speaker on the conference table and indicated a phone behind him. The copilot got up and walked to it, picking it up.

"Yes, Bob?"

"Stan, I'd like to meet with you and Mike in the office tomorrow morning."

Stan hesitated, then said, "I'd really like to stay here for a few days, Bob."

"Oh?" The word demanded an explanation.

"One of the injured passengers is a . . . a friend of mine. I'd like to make sure that she's all right."

"I see." There was another pause. "Well, I guess I can be there tomorrow morning. I'd like to look in on Pete anyhow. Can you meet me there at, say, ten-thirty?"

"I'll be here."

"All right, Stan. Good-bye . . . and thanks."

"Good-bye." Stan Burkhart hung up the phone carefully.

Bob Quinlan replaced the phone and swiveled his chair to gaze out of the window at a frenzy of activity on the airport below. Transcon's four o'clock bank of trips had left, and ground crews were positioning their equipment for the six arrivals that were scheduled to land at La Guardia in the next twenty-five minutes.

He thought of Stan Burkhart—and envied him. This train of thought emerged from time to time. Maybe he should give up the pressures of the desk and trade it for the familiar pressures of flying. He missed it, he knew that. He watched a Transcon 727 gracefully rise over the waters of Flushing Bay. There's so much to be done, though, and he knew, as always, that he wouldn't leave.

Bob Quinlan picked up the phone and buzzed his secretary. "Marie, would you get me Kitty Douglass' room at the Harkness Pavilion please? It's in the city."

Dr. John Sangford strode quickly into Kitty's room. He was tall, wiry, with quick movements. "I'm sorry that I couldn't get here sooner, Mrs. Douglass, but I was tied up with another patient." As he spread his hands, she noticed that they were slender, almost delicate—surgeon's hands. "I'm afraid that she isn't going to be as lucky as you are."

Kitty's face brightened, almost forgetting her preoccupation over Pete's trip. "Does that mean . . . ?"

"Yes. You have nothing to worry about. We found a small tumor, completely benign. The second lab report just confirmed it." He was smiling broadly, standing next to the bed now. The nurse who had been in before was standing behind him. A pleasant, gentle expression washed across her face like a painting. Sangford continued, "You'll be a little sore for a while—a few days, anyhow—but there's no reason why you can't go home first thing tomorrow morning."

She took his hand. "Thank you, Doctor. I . . . I don't know what to say."

"You don't have to say anything. I wish I could tell all my patients the same thing." Kitty noticed a fleeting sadness cross his face, then disappear. "There's something else. The nurse told me that you were concerned about the flight that was on the news?" She nodded, the fright returning. "I just heard in another room that they landed safely in Chicago." He patted her hand and started to leave.

Kitty physically relaxed, snuggling herself down into the soft pillows on the raised bed. Pete will be calling now, she thought. I can't wait to tell him.

Nurse and surgeon stopped at the door as the phone next to her bed rang, its sound acting like a switch, turning on a bright, excited expression on Kitty's face. She reached for the phone.

"Pete?"

There was a short silence, then, "Kitty, it's Bob Quinlan."

Sangford returned to the room as he saw her expression change. She was still his patient.

"Oh?" Cautious, timid now, she held her breath.

"How are you feeling?" His voice sounded stilted, as if he were forcing it into sounding light. Was this just a friendly call from Pete's boss?

"I'm fine, Bob—everything is fine." She waited, hearing a sigh on the other end of the phone.

"Kitty—Pete's been hurt." She gripped the receiver tightly, her knuckles turning white. Her iron will prevented her from crying out. She waited for him to continue. "He's in the hospital in Chicago. He was shot in the leg, but the doctors say he'll be all right."

All right how? Maimed? Disfigured? "How bad is it?"

"I don't really know, Kitty. I'm leaving for Chicago in about an hour. The message I got said that he'll be as good as new." He was taking a little license with what he had heard, but her silence made him want to gloss it over.

"When can I see him?"

"I don't know, Kitty. I'll call you when I get to the hospital. I've already made arrangements for you to go out there as soon as you can."

Somehow the tone of his voice made her relax.

"Can I give him a message or anything? He may even be able to call you himself."

The last sentence reassured her even more. She thought

for a long time, then said, "Tell him . . . tell him that Pudge is as pudgy as ever."

Stan sat in the stainless-steel cubicle quietly, surrounded by the antiseptic metal walls of the phone booth. He hesitated because he wasn't sure of the direction that he wanted the conversation to take. He wondered, not knowing how much to say. *Play it by ear*, he decided, it's no time for verbal gymnastics.

He inserted a coin, somehow comforted by the familiar chimes from the telephone. He dialed, then gave the operator his credit card number. The connection was made quickly.

Ellen Kasvakis answered after the first ring. "Hello?"

"Hi . . . it's me." His voice was flat.

"Oh, Stan! I've been so *worried*. Are you all right?"

"Yes, Ellen, I'm all right."

"Stan! What *happened*? You've got to tell me, the news reports have been so sketchy."

"Well . . . a lot has happened, Ellen." He fumbled with the words, not knowing how to continue.

"I *knew* you'd call, I just knew it." She sounded out of breath over the phone. "You can wait till you get home to tell me tonight—I'll cook a steak and we can just relax. I can't wait to hear about it. It must have been *horrible* . . ." He was finally able to break into her monologue.

"Ellen!"

"Oh." She stopped, jarred by the impatience in his voice. "I'm sorry, I'm talking too much. You must be exhausted."

"No, that's not it." Her words made him realize just how tired he was. He hesitated, sensing her tensions. "Ellen, I won't be home tonight, not for a few days."

"Oh?" Caution crept into her voice. "I could come out there tonight. I've got four days . . ."

"No, Ellen. I don't think so."

She was quiet. He could picture her biting her lower lip. "Stan? . . . is anything wrong?"

"Well, yes and no. I don't really know what to say. A lot has happened in the past few days. We have to talk. It's just that I don't know when I'll be home."

"Do you want to talk now?"

"No."

"All right, Stan." There was resignation in her voice, almost bitterness. "We'll talk later."

"Good-bye, Ellen."

There was no reply. She had hung up.

She had known it would happen. She had known for weeks, and tried to forestall it by playing a part that didn't suit her. Now she knew that there wouldn't be any *later* for them.

After she put down the phone, she got up without emotion and went to the hall closet. She got her suitcases and carried them into the bedroom and put them on the bed. She slipped out of Stan's white terry cloth robe and carefully hung it on the back of the bathroom door, then dressed quickly and began putting her clothes from the dresser neatly into the two suitcases. The first two drawers went quickly. In the third drawer, she found the delicate yellow and white china basket that Stan had placed there a few nights ago. It seemed to mock her as she carefully placed it in the smaller bag. Only then did Ellen Kasvakis allow herself the luxury of tears.

Stan Burkhart walked quickly from the phone booth to the front entrance of the terminal, ignoring the glances of travelers as he walked. He stepped out into the cold air. It was still snowing hard, but the visibility seemed a little better. He walked to the front taxi in the cab line, then paused with his hand on the rear door. A Lufthansa 747 was taking off, and as all pilots do, he watched it until it disappeared into the snow. When it was invisible, and the sound was gone, he got into the cab.

"Des Plaines Hospital, please."

The driver nodded and slowly pulled the taxi into traffic.

Lars Gunter looked at the wall clock. It was four-thirty. He had been in the dispatch office for twenty-two and a half hours, ten of those on duty, officially, because that was all that he was allowed, and twelve and a half unofficially. He was standing at the big windows along the back wall with Glen Meyer. They were watching a Transcon tug towing flight 602's airplane toward the hangar. A weather clerk came over to him and handed him two sheets of paper. He turned away from the window and read the top message.

SEVERE WEATHER BULLETIN #11 IS CANCELED. STORM WEAKENING IN INTENSITY AS IT APPROACHES MISSISSIPPI RIVER VALLEY. SNOW, MIXED WITH RAIN, CHANGING TO ALL RAIN BY 2000 CST AS WARM AIR MASS FROM GULF MERGES WITH LOW PRESSURE AREA. GRADUALLY LESSENING WINDS AS LOW MOVES EAST.

USWETHBUR

Lars smiled as he read. The weather clerk said, "I thought you might like to see these before you went home." He read the other piece of paper:

TO ALL TRANSCON OPERATIONS MANAGERS: EXPECT ROCKY MNTN STATIONS OPEN BY MIDNIGHT, LOCAL, WITH THE EXCEPTION OF N. DAK TERMINALS. ANTICIPATE NORMAL OPERATIONS BY NOON, LOCAL, TOMORROW. STATIONS MGRS CONTACT CENTRAL OPERATIONS IMMEDIATELY.

TRANSCON OPS. PLNG.

Lars Gunter handed the messages to the clerk. "Thanks. That's the best news we've had today." He turned to Glen

Meyer, who had been reading over his shoulder. "Wanna flip for a cup of coffee, Glen?"

"Sure."

The two men reached into their pockets for coins. Lars Gunter won.